Free Danner

LORETTA GIACOLETTO

www.lorettagiacoletto.com

Copyright 2011 Loretta Giacoletto
Cover design by Caren Schlossberg-Wood
Photograph by Graphics1976, Dreamstime
ISBN-13: 978-1477410912
ISBN-10: 1477410910
Library of Congress Control Number: 2012908246

This book is a work of fiction. Names, characters, places, and incidents are either products of the author's imagination or used fictitiously. Any resemblance to actual events, locales, or persons, living or dead, is entirely coincidental. All rights reserved. No part of this publication can be reproduced or transmitted in any form or by any means, electronic or mechanical, without permission in writing from Loretta Giacoletto.

Also by Loretta Giacoletto
In print or electronic format

THE FAMILY ANGEL

CHICAGO'S HEADMISTRESS

ITALY TO DIE FOR

FAMILY DECEPTIONS

LETHAL PLAY

A COLLECTION OF GIVERS AND TAKERS

YOUTHANASIA: A Short Story

THE BAKER'S WIFE: A Short Story

A Note from the Author

My thanks to Caren Schlossberg-Wood of Lost Marbles Design; to Jordan Giacoletto for the music selections; to Steve Giacoletto for his contributions to the Rat Pack and the Sunday Mass scene; to Mark Giacoletto for his input on Montana and its wildlife; to beta reader and marketing consultant Diane Giacoletto Lambert; and to Dominic Giacoletto for his continued patience and unwavering support.

Chapter 1

The first time I killed a man should've been my last, but what did I know then. This man, I didn't exactly hate him, leastways not at first, but due to a domino effect of weird circumstances, he'd been reduced to a festering boil on the butt of humanity, begging for a quick and painless removal. The man needed help doing what he couldn't do by himself. Okay, so I didn't exactly kill him with my own hands but I convinced him that dying was the right thing to do, the only thing. Damage control, it's what I did then and what I'm stuck with now. At twenty-two, jeez, give me a break, where did I go wrong.

Tonight I am driving on a two-lane highway east of Mobile, Alabama, with my current half-squeeze nodding off to the music of Dave Matthews while I discreetly follow a black Lincoln Town Car. Its chauffeur makes me no never mind but his boss in the backseat spells Bread and Butter with capital Bs, my one-way ticket to beaucoup bucks that so far have escaped me. I allow two cars between the Lincoln and my SUV, a gift from my former benefactor and didn'twannabe dad who cashed in his chips before I was ready to let him go. Not only did he introduce me to the Vegas scene, he wowed me with the great outdoors, unlike a certain Mr. Hollywood, another didn'twannabe who took my money and left me nothing but make-believe promises.

One of the cars up ahead turns onto a side road, leaving a Mustang convertible to separate my vehicle from the Lincoln and its passenger. A cigarette flies out of the back window, its tip left glowing on the roadside. The asshole who sucked on the filter has no regard for the landscape or those who maintain it. This I already know from a pricey character profile that didn't come out of my pocket. The convertible turns off at the next side road. Now there's just my SUV, one hundred feet separating it from a set of taillights and the contaminator of nature, even worse, mankind. This degenerate represents the lowest form of humanity, an abuser of animals and kids who has enough money and IOUs to continually avoid incarceration. I should be so lucky, having wasted the best years of my life in juvenile detention.

Headlights to my left, another car pulls onto the highway from behind, pushing me forward against my will. I close in on the Lincoln, unsure of my next move. But then nature takes over on my behalf, a night creature scurrying from the wooded area, its beady red eyes catching the Lincoln's headlights. The chauffeur swerves to the right, a simple act that makes me think he might have the heart his employer lacks. I brake hard and fast, as does the car behind me, judging from the squeal of tires assaulting my ears. My half-squeeze lifts her head in time to see the Lincoln hit a guard rail, bounce back and cross the highway, directly into the path of a truck speeding from the other direction. The Lincoln flips into the air, comes crashing down on the sunroof. Its horn sends out an eerie, soul-searching blast, the only sound escaping into an otherwise quiet night.

I pull over to the side of the road. The car dogging me does the same and from the driver's side a woman hops out. Cell phone plastered to her ear, she approaches my vehicle, leaving me no choice but to roll down the window.

"I've already called 911," she yells while passing by. "Do you have any blankets?"

No need for me to answer her question since I notice the truck driver partly responsible for this mess is now running toward the Lincoln's crumbled remains. He looks like he's carrying more than one army blanket, which relieves me from the first-aid gig I don't want any part of.

POW … POW, POW!

Without warning, the Lincoln explodes, hurling its junk into the sky, across the highway, and onto the hood of my SUV. A severed hand bounces off. My half-squeeze goes wide-eyed spastic, her delayed-reaction, gut-retching scream tangling my gut into one sorry knot. When it comes to blood and gore mixed with the emotional outburst of a high-maintenance female, I, John Earl Danner the Second, am not worth the price of a good shit.

Chapter 2

"But, Lark, I don't wanna go. Can't I please stay with you?" I fixed my eyes on hers, willing them to look at me, if only for a second or three. "I promise not to cause any more trouble."

"Sweet Jesus, you know I'd keep you if I could."

"I'm not sweet and I'm not Jesus. I'm eleven, big enough to take care of myself. And you, in a couple more years." She shifted on her stick-person frame, showed me the profile of her face—an older version of what I considered my own. "Look, this may be my last chance for a decent life," she said, using her country voice instead of the city one. "After things settle down between me and … and—"

"Greg, you said his name was Greg." Cripes, there'd been so many she lost track.

"Right, you know I can't think straight without my morning coffee." She leaned in, put her fingertips on my shoulders, and offered me her cheek. "Now give me some sugar before you get on the bus."

I hated when she did that in front of strangers, treating me like a little kid when I stood more than shoulder-high to her.

She pointed to the cheek. "Come on, Free. I don't have all day."

I glanced around the black and white checkered station, made sure no one was looking. Then I sunk my teeth into a blotch of her freckles and held on until I tasted blood. When she pulled away, tears streamed into the circle of my teeth marks, the only gift I could afford on such short notice.

"Why, you little shit," she said, brushing long strands of reddish-brown hair from her face. "What the F was that about?"

"As if you didn't know," was all I could manage before adjusting the strap of my canvas bag onto one shoulder.

I stepped onto the bus and handed the driver my ticket. Lark's voice followed me on board but I refused to turn around. She had her chance and blew it.

"Drop him off on the road to Dubois," she told the driver. "That's on Route 127 in the stretch before Murphysboro."

Moving down the aisle, I met the stares of nosey passengers, not one of them under the age of forty. I stopped at the tenth row, slid my bag against the window, and slumped down in the aisle seat, where Lark couldn't see me from outside, even if she tried, which I didn't think she would. I turned on my Game Boy to Super Mario, positioned my thumbs, and sent Mario's tiny figure to fight an army of bad guys. I didn't look up when the bus pulled away from Lark. For all I cared, she could go straight to hell—in a shopping cart, along with those sixty-three pairs of shoes she loved more than anything in the whole wide world.

People around me were talking so loud I finally upped the volume on Game Boy, a distraction that cost me one of Mario's five lives. No problem, I pulled up his brother Luigi to continue the battle. After making a couple of turns leading away from downtown St. Louis, the bus started across the bridge toward the crappy state of Illinois. I scooted over to the window seat, still managed to keep Luigi in the game but lost him over the river. Down below, this barge loaded with pipes was cutting through the dirty Mississippi, leaving behind churning water that reminded me of whipped cream sprayed from a can. And the whipped cream reminded me of real food.

After putting Game Boy on pause, I dug through my bag, found two packages of Twinkies and a bottle of soda. I unscrewed the cap, tore open both Twinkie wrappers, and sucked out all the creamy fillings. While chug-a-lugging my soda, I looked across the aisle to this round lady with shiny black skin. She wore church clothes and a hat loaded with fake flowers. Tacky, but what did I know. She pressed her full lips into a tight line and stared me down, as if I owed her an explanation.

Lark would've told her to bug off but not me because I had better sense. I pulled the bottle away from my mouth and told her the ugly truth. "My mom didn't have time to make breakfast."

"You still hungry, boy?" She rattled a shopping bag taking up the window seat beside her.

"Depends on what you've got."

She brought out a Ziploc filled with sandwiches. "Sliced bananas, peanut butter, and jam between thick slices of whole wheat bread, enough to feed the two of us and then some. Plus oatmeal raisin cookies, I made them myself."

"Never mind." Cripes, what did she take me for?

"Kids today, they got it so good they don't know what's good," Sandwich Lady said.

I lifted my shoulders, showed her my best hound dog face. "My mom don't want me anymore."

"Then you better off where you're going than where you been."

"Yes, ma'am. That's what she said too."

Enough with the sandwich social worker, her kind bothered me enough back home. I leaned my head against the window, resumed Game Boy, and played nonstop through every hick-dumb town in Southern Illinois, all the while ignoring the hole in my stomach growing bigger by the hour, or minute. I was thinking about asking Sandwich Lady for a handout when the bus stopped again.

"Dubois," the driver called out, his head tilted up to the rearview mirror. "This is where you get off, Game Boy."

Yeah, right. I put Super Mario on save, slipped him into my bag, and nodded to Sandwich Lady.

"Stay out of trouble, you hear," she said.

"Yes ma'am. I'm sure gonna try."

I shuffled up the aisle, my way of bugging the driver tapping his fingers on the wheel. He stopped tapping when I showed him my finger, the middle one. As soon as my feet hit the road gravel, he left me in a cloud of dust. I counted to ten before opening my eyes to a gray pick-um-up truck parked on the side of the road and two old people heading toward me. The man was John Wayne tall and walked like him too. He wore a Cardinals baseball cap, plaid shirt, and farmer's overalls—definitely not John Wayne. The woman's gray hair belonged on a French poodle, I'm not kidding. She weighed too much for her tight jeans, and should've been embarrassed but I guess at her age, size didn't much matter anymore. Behind her granny glasses were eyes the color of Lark's, but older and maybe wiser. Lark, how could she have done this to me, the best thing that ever happened to her.

Poodle Lady grabbed me, crushed me against boobs smelling like bacon and oranges. If I hadn't pulled away, she'd've smothered me with those fat pillows. Instead she poured on her Miss Piggy voice: "Oh, Johnny, it's so good seeing you after all these years."

After slobbering on my face, she passed me on to the farmer. He squeezed my hand with one rougher than sandpaper and pumped five times before letting go. "Ten years is nine and a half too long, Johnny. You were just a toddling tyke when Emily spirited you away from us."

Johnny? Cripes, I had to set them straight. "My name's Free and who's Emily?"

"Why that's your ma, son." Farmer guy leaned over and with a mouthful of stained, crooked teeth he said, "What's she calling herself nowadays?"

"Lark, Lark Danner."

The smile fell off his face quicker than Mario from the Game Boy screen. "Still a Danner, which tells me she never did hitch herself to a rich and powerful star."

So what, Lark had me, we had each other.

Poodle Lady poked her husband. "Hush, Jed. The boy can't answer for Emily's errant life style."

"Jed, is that your name?" I asked as we walked toward the truck.

"Actually, it's John Earl Danner, same as yours but without the Roman numeral two since I came first, as in: before you and always will. However, everybody who's anybody calls me Jed."

"Then I will too, and you can call me Free."

I smiled at the woman, not wanting to leave her out. "Same goes for you, ma'am."

By now we were standing alongside the truck. She pressed my face between her hands and smiled, showing me a set of teeth way better than Jed's. "It would please me to no end if you'd call me Grandma."

Get real. "No offense, ma'am, but you don't look like any grandma I ever saw in St. Louis. I'll stick with Mrs. Danner, if you don't mind."

I expected an argument from her. Instead she dropped her wrinkled eyelids and chewed on her lower lip before coming back with, "In that case Delores will do just fine."

Jed wasn't so easy. After clearing his throat, he spit out a wad of gook and rubbed it into the ground with the toe of his farmer's shoe, the kind that lace high on the ankle. One hand yanked the truck door open;

the other motioned me inside. "Let's go, Johnny. We still got some miles ahead of us."

"Please, sir, my name's Free."

"Not when you're with us. Around these parts, folks don't cotton to peculiar names or to peculiar behavior."

"Is that why my mom left?" I couldn't resist asking. Both faces soured, which served the old people right for getting into mine.

"Poor Emily, she just didn't fit in," Delores said. "But that's nothing against you. The three of us will perk along just fine, like coffee in the morning. Right, Jed?"

"As long as we're all on the same page and I'm doing the turning." He stuck his whiskered face in mine, and sprayed spit with his next words. "I seldom repeat myself, so for the last time get your butt in the truck."

"Jed! That's no way to talk to the boy, leastways not on his first day with us."

"It's okay, ma'am." I climbed into the cab. "I don't want any trouble." Just get me through the summer, that's all, nothing more.

The old people took their places on either side of me, two hunks of last week's bread sandwiching a thin slice of fresh baloney. We bounced like three soda bottles, the truck plowing over rolling green hills mixed with land as flat as an airplane runway, Jed's one hand on the wheel and the other holding up the frame of the open window. Delores clutched the frame on her side too, all the while playing field-trip teacher to my bobble head. While she pointed out the fields of wheat and corn and alfalfa, Jed pressed harder on the gas pedal, kicking up powdery gravel that soon dusted the three of us. But who'd the dust bother—me and only me, another reminder about not belonging. I rubbed my eyes until I sneezed into my hand.

"So, how is your Ma?" Delores asked, handing me a wrinkled tissue from her shirt pocket.

"She's okay."

"Still working nights at that fancy restaurant?"

"I guess."

"What about boyfriends."

I gave her the shoulder routine. They didn't need to know Lark's every move, but Delores couldn't leave it alone.

"Good lord, Johnny," she said. "Whatever do the two of you talk about?"

"The usual stuff."

After that nobody talked until Jed slowed down and pointed a grubby finger toward this two-story house, white with a lazy porch wrapped around two sides. "There she is, Johnny, the house your ma grew up in. And before her, me, and before me, my father and his father, that's four generations of Danners."

"And now you, Johnny," Delores said through a sniff. "We're so pleased to have you with us."

"I'm only here for the summer. My mom promised."

Chapter 3

Finding Lark took way longer than I expected but I finally managed to track her down in South St. Louis. After knocking around from one place to another, she'd landed in one of those narrow row houses with two stories and flat roofs that look more German than American. Tired red brick dating back to the turn of the twentieth century made up every building on the street. Old, really old houses, same old same I remembered from my years with Lark.

Since her ground floor apartment was located in the rear, I accessed the property by way of an alley lined with garbage cans waiting for the collector or the cats, whichever came first. Four cars were parked on a wide concrete slab in the backyard. I figured the best one belonged to her because she hated settling for anything less. A big tree shaded the remaining yard and accounted for the absence of grass while dirt turned to grit swirled through air on the verge of spring. I paused at the back porch, took a closer look at the building. Some of its bricks were cracked and broken; the mortar needed tuck pointing. A problem for the landlord, good luck with that, tenants. Next to the door a small air conditioner jutted from the window, making a racket that drowned out other racket from the nearby raised Interstate. All in all, the place could best be described as a third-rate dump.

I knocked; no answer. Ten-thirty on a Saturday morning, Lark should've finished sawing a ton of logs by now even if she'd crashed around three or so. I knocked again, still no answer so I turned the knob, still no luck. Next, the doormat, sure enough the key, right where I figured Lark would leave it. Old habits die hard, at least mine do. Hers too, I knew her better than she could ever imagine. Time can do that and I'd had more than my share. After jiggling the key into the hole, I made a connection and slipped into her living room.

Lark's attention to Housekeeping 101 hadn't changed one bit since the two of us were together. Newspapers scattered across the sofa and carpet, pizza leftovers doing a number on the coffee table, the sweet scent of weed lingering in a room lacking ventilation. A large plasma screen TV filled most of one wall. This I liked, but not the dingy curtains hanging limp from tall windows smeared with soot. As for the kitchen, if only Delores could've seen the mess—dirty dishes piled in the sink and on the countertop and table, crumbs dusting the linoleum floor. After checking out the fridge, I popped a Classic Coke and drained it without taking a single breath.

I heard a noise, sensed someone from behind, not Lark. Her I would've known by a change in the air.

"What the fuck's going on?" The voice belonged to a man, one in a foul mood, not that I should've expected otherwise.

I turned with half a smile on my face and gave him the onceover. Short, stocky, and growing enough fur on his body to weave a rug for the head going bald. His two-day growth of whiskers bordered a moon face with close-set eyes now glued to my face.

"Is Lark home?" My gaze trailed down to navy blue briefs he had no business wearing, what with his roll of belly fat overlapping the skimpy show of color.

"Who wants to know?" He spoke with a Mexican or something like that accent.

"Just tell her Free."

"You got a last name?"

"Trust me, there's only one Free."

He stared at me, all the while calling out her name, his voice growing louder and more irritated each time she didn't answer. On the fourth yell she showed herself, barefoot and wearing red boxer shorts with a black tank top. Standing beside him, she made a great Beauty to his Beast. Her long hair was redder than before; the freckles had faded into a muted tone. She'd added a few pounds but could've passed for a mean thirty-five, six years younger than her true age. This side of Cougarville, some guys would've said about her. Not me, I knew my place.

I played it cool, waited for her to make the first move, which took way too long considering the amount of time wasted since we last connected. After an edgy minute she stepped forward, wrapped her arms around me, and leaned her head to my shoulder. Her hair tickled my chin, sending out a fragrant combo of pineapple and coconut … pina colada, her favorite drink. An exchange of cheeky kisses were more bitter than sweet, reminding me of the day she sent me away, the day that changed my life forever. This time I knew better than to leave my teeth marks behind.

Lark pulled away first, arms outstretched as she took her time with me. A smile lit up her face, not that I needed it to know she was pleased with the new me.

"You're all grown up, Free." She leaned forward, touched her fingertips to the soul patch under my lower lip, moved on to the diamond stud in my left ear. "Nice touch, a one-two punch."

"Yeah, my in-your-face fashion statement."

"From my genes to yours," she whispered with smoke on her breath. The voice she then raised had grown huskier but still sounded country. "How long has it been?"

"Ten years." As if she didn't know; I wanted to say more but decided to wait for the right moment.

The boyfriend cleared his throat, one of those hey-don't-forget-about-me which I chose to ignore. Taking him serious was too much of a stretch, this barrel squeezed into tiny briefs. Lark, on the other hand, showed some mercy, motioning to him with the tips of her fingers.

"Hector, sweetie, get your ass over here. I want you to meet my brother Free."

His ass, her brother, give me a break. She hadn't changed one iota. Me either; I played along with her silly game. The man's face softened as he extended his hand to mine. I shook it, applying a firm grip to match his, neither of us meaning what little warmth we pretended to show.

"Yeah," the butthead said. "There is a certain likeness, the hair."

"His used to be as red as mine," Lark said. She lifted her hand to my hair, scrambled what I described as brown on my driver's license for the car I didn't have but planned to acquire someday soon. First things first, in this case: a job. And not just any job, one that paid big bucks to make up for those years I'd lost forever.

"Can you stay for lunch?" she asked, her way of being polite.

"I can stay longer, if you'll have me."

She puckered her lips into the familiar pout from my days as a kid. "Oh, Free, you know I would if I could. Unfortunately, my humble apartment has only one bedroom."

This time she tapped her hand to my cheek, poised to react in case I said what she didn't want to hear. Being no dummy, I stepped back, out of her reach.

"Tough break, kid," the man said, belching out his first laugh since our meeting. "Since part of the rent comes out of my pocket, I ain't about to settle for less."

"No problem and no inconveniencing either of you," I said. "This way, please." They followed me into the living room where I gathered the newspapers from the couch and folded them in a way that would've made Delores proud. "This here will do just fine. And don't you two worry about the TV. I'll keep it down low so as not to disturb a soul. Now about lunch ...."

Chapter 4

As we started up the long driveway, Delores made this big deal out of what she called the farm's greatest assets. One chicken coop the color of egg yolks and Jed's pukey green tractor that someday he might let me ride, other clunky equipment spelling nothing but work I wanted no part of, plus this barn painted bright red and looking way better than the house. Delores nudged me to make sure I paid attention. Hello, as if I had any choice.

"Over there to the left," she said. "Those cows standing up means the fish are a-biting."

"You've got a pond?" I was thinking a place to swim, me and the friends I hadn't made as yet.

"Pond, yes; fish, no," Jed said. "Farmers don't have time for such foolishness."

He stopped the truck and we slid out, sending a flurry of chickens across a yard already spoiled by the pecking and scratching and poop I made sure to avoid. Just then, this super-sized dog with red hair came galloping over, lifted its front paws onto my shoulders, and started licking my face. About the tongue, I didn't want to think where it had been before.

"Looks like you made your first friend," Jed said. "This is Rusty."

I ran my hand over the dog's hair. In a way it reminded me of Lark's, only not as silky. "What kind is he?"

"An Irish setter," Delores said, "a tad unpredictable but sweet as all get out." She patted Rusty's head and pushed him away from me even though I didn't mind him being there. "You must be starving, Johnny."

"I guess so." Rusty found my shoulders again but all his slobbering couldn't make me forget the gnawing in my stomach. "What day is it?"

"Thursday," Jed said.

My favorite, I needed to set them straight. "We—Lark and me—eat McDonald's every Thursday."

Delores threw her head back and laughed, showing me rows of tarnished fillings. "Lordy, lordy, Johnny, get your head screwed on straight. Can't you see, we're miles from the closest McDonald's. Besides, fast food has no business contaminating the stomach of a growing boy, not if you expect to whop Jed some day."

That I hadn't considered until she mentioned it.

"Don't even think about it, Johnny. I'll cut you down to size with a single digit." Jed showed me his gnarled thumb stained with ground-in dirt, the nail black from an old injury.

She shook her finger at him. "That'll be enough, Jed. You show Johnny around the house while I finish up the dinner fixings."

We went inside and I followed Jed through a bunch of dreary rooms filled with dark furniture, dark walls, dark window coverings, and dark floors. Old and worn-out, just like their owners.

Comfortable is what Jed called the place. On the plus side, their living room did have a TV, the old-fashioned kind in a wooden box. The dining room furniture was so old it had lost its shine. Not a speck of dust anywhere, except for those floating in a sunbeam that found a crack in the curtains.

Back in the sunny kitchen we found Delores slaving over the stove. She lifted the lid off one pot, waved steam in my direction.

"Chicken's almost done and it won't take but a minute for me to pop those light-as-air dumplings into the broth. My special coleslaw and pickled beets are chilling in the refrigerator."

"I like my chicken extra crispy, with a side order of the Colonel's biscuits."

"Not anymore." She wrapped my chin in her hand and squeezed harder than needed. "Wait until you taste chicken my way. There's no comparison. Right, Jed?"

"If you say so, Dee." He winked at her and gave me a little shove. "Come on, let's get you settled upstairs. You'll occupy the same room your ma once used, Johnny."

"She calls me Free."

"Trust my words, boy: no way in hell were you ever free. Not from the day you entered this world, and before. What's more, I saved the hospital and doctor invoices to prove it—all stamped *paid in full*." He set his foot on the first step of an enclosed staircase that could've used an overhead light bulb. "This way, Johnny, and don't forget your satchel."

Satchel? This old man must've grown up with the dinosaurs. The only good thing about climbing those stairs was not having enough light to see Jed's wide load swaying in my face. After the landing we walked to the end of a short hall where he opened this door and thumbed me inside. My eyes swept over a room not as girly as I'd expected, but it did smell like mothballs fresh from the microwave. And like the only attic I'd ever set foot in, this room felt as if every bit of air had been sucked out of it. There was a dressing table, not that I needed one. I pictured Lark sitting in front of the mirror, searching her face for any flaws that might've cropped up overnight, her daily routine in St. Louis even though I'd always told her how pretty she looked, mostly to keep her in a good mood. A lamp dangled from the headboard of the bed, and next to it, a nightstand matching the chest of drawers. Both needed painting, so what else was new. Two walls of shelves held books I couldn't imagine Lark ever sitting still long enough to read.

Jed folded his arms. "So, whadaya think, boy?"

"It's kind of hot up here." I wiped one hand across my forehead. "Maybe you could adjust the air conditioner."

Jed smiled without his teeth showing. He banged his hand against the window and raised it with a grunt. "Sure, how's this?"

A question that stupid didn't deserve an answer. So, I sat on the edge of the bed, opened Super Mario to where I'd saved it, and resumed my game while Jed picked his nose or whatever old guys do when they don't know enough to leave. He finally got my message and backed out the door. I kept working my fingers until Luigi fell off the screen for the third time. Time out, I paused my game, set it on my belly, and lay back on the pillow.

Fingers laced behind my head, I examined a dozen cracks in the ceiling while trying to figure out Jed and Delores. They hadn't given me much to work with. Dee, he'd called her. I couldn't imagine them ever being boyfriend and girlfriend. Or making Lark, ugh! They were old, probably as old now as when Lark skipped out after graduating from high school. Whatever was she thinking, sending me to a place like this, cripes. And over what—a simple misunderstanding I could've cleared up if only she'd given me the chance. But whose word did she take? Always the boyfriends'—never mind me, her only flesh and blood.

Oh well, what's a summer month or three, especially since I didn't have baseball anymore, having quit two seasons ago, after Lark made a scene with her then-boyfriend, a guy whose name neither of us could remember come Halloween. By this mid-August Lark would be begging for me to come back. Right now though, Delores was yelling for me to come and get it. She meant dinner.

And I meant to take control of my next game, a new one without Mario or Luigi or Lark's pond-scum boyfriends. I slipped my pals under the pillow and went into the hallway. Pausing at the top of the stairs, I took a deep breath, curled into a ball, and pitched forward into the sunny area below. Clunk, clunk, clunkity clunk ... ouch, ouch, and more ouches. I surprised myself, managing to hit every step before rolling onto the linoleum floor in the kitchen.

"Jesus, Mary, and Joseph! You too, Jed, get in here right now." Delores dropped to her knees and was all over me, cradling my head against those smelly boobs.

"You okay, Johnny?" the old man asked.

I rolled my eyes back in their sockets, giving me a blank picture and let out a groan—oh-h-h-h. Jed must've jerked me away from Delores. I didn't dare peek.

Pow! One smack to the back of my head nearly popped out both eyes. They opened to a bunch of stars and Jed leaning over me, holding up two fingers.

"How many do you see, Johnny?"

I squinted, let a few seconds pass before answering. "Four, I think."

"That's close enough," he said, pulling me up by one hand. "Now let's eat before those dumplings turn cold 'cause if they do, look out."

"Jed, quit your joshing." Delores rolled doggy-style onto her hands and knees and from there wobbled to her feet. "I can always re-heat the dumplings for a few minutes."

"No need, the boy's returned to a degree of normalcy." Jed stuck his face in mine. "What I mean is: you're as good as when you stepped off the bus. Right, Johnny?"

"Well, I do feel kind of dizzy." This was no lie. I did a Delores wobble, held onto her arm, and faked a sissy smile. "Any chance of me eating in the living room?"

"And scatter crumbs all over my good furniture—certainly not. What's more, if you were thinking about TV with your chicken, forget it. We don't get but three good channels and they run my soaps and game shows all afternoon."

"Dammit, you two, let's take this discussion to the table," Jed said. "I'm so hungry I could rip off a chicken's head and eat the rest of it raw."

Not me, I knew better.

Jed didn't believe in table talk, unless he asked for more food, usually with his mouth full and head bent over the plate. Delores talked non-stop and kept pushing bowls in my direction, insisting I take seconds. When it came to thirds, I begged off, which gave her an excuse to ask, "So how was everything, Johnny?"

"Okay. Can I go outside and play with the dog?"

"Why, yes, of course." She chewed on her lip again, before giving me a 'what for' in exchange for the compliment I should've given her. "You can play after we clean up this mess. You do help your ma, don't you?"

"Mostly we eat out, except on Sunday evening. Then we have pizza delivered."

"Such extravagance, it's so uncalled for." She clucked her tongue like one of those old hens in the yard. "As soon as things settle down, I'll teach you some basic cooking techniques."

No way, no how, not even Lark went that far. Cripes, already I missed her.

"Lark says my melted cheese over Tostitos is the best she's ever eaten. But she won't let me help in the kitchen." I showed Delores my hands, front and back. "Dishwater gives me bumps. They itch so bad I can't do my homework or sleep at night."

I didn't crack a smile when Delores clucked again. Or when Rooster Jed cranked himself out of the chair and strutted around the kitchen. They'd been on the farm too long, that's for sure. Jed puffed up his chest before he spoke.

"Since it's your first day with us, we'll give you a temporary reprieve. But starting tomorrow, I expect your help with the farm chores, same as your ma used to do. On the Danner farm everybody pulls his weight or takes a hike, understand?"

"Yes, sir. Can I go outside now?"

I took his grunt as a yes. Rusty was waiting at the back door, as if the two of us were already best friends. He jumped on me, knocked me down, and we rolled in a grassy area the chickens hadn't messed up. After our wrestling petered out, Rusty dropped a bone at my feet, and hopped around until I sailed it through the air. He galloped off like a wild pony, his red hair flying in the wind, just like Lark's hair did when the two of us goofed around in the park. She should've been there to see me, just a regular guy with his dog. My dog, that's how I already felt about Rusty.

***

The next morning Delores made me get up at seven, made me drink orange juice with pulp. Made me eat bacon and eggs, which weren't half bad after she showed me how to dip toast in the yolk. Sitting at this really old chrome and vinyl table, we looked through the picture window and watched Jed bust his wide butt.

"That's manure he's shoveling," Delores explained.

For an old man Jed moved pretty fast. His shoulders were as broad as Lark's last boyfriend, the one she claimed I scared off, as if I was a monster or worse.

"Lark says bacon puts fat on your hips." I dipped toast in the soft yolk of egg number three.

Delores eyed me from over the rim of her orange juice. "And what does she fix for you in the morning?"

"I do my own, usually Pop Tarts."

"I figured as much. I thought she didn't want you in the kitchen. You know, what with the possibility of a nasty rash."

I put down my fork, hung my head. "I do the best I can. She likes to sleep late and doesn't want me bothering her."

Unless it was our special time, I didn't go there with Delores.

Chapter 5

I guess Lark must've been okay with me figuring out the sleeping arrangements because she didn't open her mouth to object. Instead she blew the boyfriend a kiss from her fingertips, an excuse for him to backtrack into the kitchen like the cowardly jerk I'd already figured him to be. She sat down on this blue velvet chair that shouted second-hand and I took the sofa, its middle sagging worse than any swaybacked horse I'd ever seen. For a minute or so the only sound we heard came from the kitchen, a helter-skelter of rattling pots and pans, banging cabinet doors and a creaking fridge. Plus what I assumed was the boyfriend's Spanish tirade about me, Lark's *no bueno hermano*. If he only knew what we really meant to each other, all in good time.

"You'll have to excuse Hector," she said. "He's a professional chef."

Yeah, right. "One who works in his briefs?"

This made her laugh. "You caught us off guard and now he's acting out his frustrations. Poor guy, he's such a perfectionist." Without missing a beat she hit me with, "Why didn't you call first?"

"Why didn't you answer my letters, take my phone calls. All those years—"

"Let's not go there," she said, "at least for now."

"Whatever." It was all I could say.

"So, what've you been doing?" she asked.

"Let's not go there, at least for now." I flipped on the plasma and channel surfed until I landed on a Las Vegas poker tournament.

"Do you play?" she asked.

Not this game, others I'd played my entire life. "I'm not much on gambling."

"So why are we watching poker?"

"Just filling in some time before we eat."

Lark lifted her head and called out, "Hector, sweetie, how much longer?"

"Quit pushing," he yelled from the kitchen. "I ain't no damn magician."

Nor was he a professional chef; that I knew from the gitgo. "How long you two been together?" I asked.

She shrugged. "Hector's just passing through."

"He's legal?"

"I don't ask and neither should you."

"Hey, not my problem, just making conversation, that's all."

She crossed her legs, giving me a close up of this colorful snake winding upward from her slender ankle. "Nice." I said. "How long've you had the tatt?"

She looked down, slowly turning her ankle, as if she hadn't noticed the red, blue, green, and yellow before. "Four, maybe five years, a freebie from this guy I knew once upon a time. He had his own shop, a real moneymaker."

"Nothing comes for free." I must've hit a nerve; she sank deep into the velvet cushion, eyes fastened to the TV and its two-second flashes my clicking of the remote created.

After an embarrassing shortfall of meaningful conversation, she called out again, "Hec-tor, my stomach's giving me fits. How much longer are we talking?"

"Now, dammit." He took up most of the doorway, a chef's knife dangling from his chef's hand, a chef's apron tied around his chef's waist. "Get in here now, 'fore everything goes cold."

The guy meant business. He'd already cleared off the kitchen table, allowing us to sit down to a decent spread of beef tostados, tomato rice, and refried beans. He took his place at the head of the table. I figured, what the hell, why not, at least for now. Lark parked herself across from me, scrutinizing Hector's offering and probably thinking: oh brother, not this again.

He blessed the food his way—forefinger signing of the cross, and mumbled, "Dig in."

You bet. I shoveled food onto my plate, trying not to appear as hungry as my empty stomach, all the while trying to ignore the Cro Magnum's hairy exterior. As a courtesy and for no other reason, I said, "Lark tells me you cook for a living."

"The evening shift at this little Mexican place on Virginia Street," he said. "I get home around eleven-thirty and after a shot or two of tequila I expect absolute quiet for a good night's sleep."

As if I cared, Mister Only Passing Through. If only he knew the Lark I knew. Oh well, his time would come, same as every other jerk's. I leaned over my plate and started feeding my face. Forget about table talk. This scene could've fit a table of monks observing their vows of silence, the only sound coming from Hector smacking his lips.

After a while I said to no one in particular, "Not bad, I mean the food."

"What else would you mean?" Hector asked.

Lark shoved her half-empty plate aside. She twisted to the right, twisted one leg around the other, and lit up a cigarette. Smoke curled out the corner of her mouth, vulgar yet sexy. I didn't want to think of her in another twenty years when the smoking wouldn't look sexy anymore. Instead of expressing this concern to her I helped myself to thirds, leaving one portion of everything for Hector who quickly scooped it onto his plate, as if he didn't get enough beans and rice where he practiced his profession.

After lunch who cleaned up? Yours truly, because I offered and no one took the position about it not being right, what with me being a guest and Lark's pseudo brother. I took this to mean I was not considered a guest, but more like a member of the family, although my stay would likely be more temporary than permanent. While I scrapped dirty dishes, Lark and Hector disappeared into the bedroom and minutes later returned with him dressed in jeans and a white T, ready to make a public showing. They left, muttering something about picking up more groceries, which told me she was eating at home more often than in the restaurants or fast-food places she used to prefer. I watched from the window, curious as to which car they would pick. Shit, the worst of the four not-so-goods, an old Chevy with rusty fenders. Times must've been tougher than I'd imagined.

As for me, time to make myself comfortable. I brought in the bag I'd left on the porch, shoved it in one corner of the living room, and checked out the rest of the apartment. One queen-size bed, confirming Lark's earlier claim about there not being room for me, that is, until I convinced her otherwise. In her closet a shitload of shoes, sixty-eight pairs to be exact. Some things never change. Clothes with price tags still hanging from the sleeve, the kind she used to wear once before returning for a store credit or another outfit.

An hour later Lark and the boyfriend returned with long faces and plastic bags filled with groceries. I leaned against the doorframe, watching them put away stuff while they complained about the high cost of food. Figuring it my cue to belly up, I dug into my pocket, hauled out a wad of bills, and threw a twenty on the table. "This should cover me for a couple of days."

"You been to the store lately?" the boyfriend asked. He reached for the twenty but she beat him to it.

"Shut up, Hector. This is my place and Free is my … my brother."

"That's right," I chimed in. "And if you don't like my being here, Fat Boy, find another place to refry your beans."

"What? Nobody but nobody talks to me that way." His face turned this weird shade of purple. "You're nothing but a dumb-assed shit."

Way to go, I'd hit a nerve.

Hector lunged across the table and with both hands grabbed my shirt, giving me the opportunity to bust him in the mouth. He was spitting blood but came at me swinging, and managed to first clip my cheekbone and then my shoulder. Damn, the last jab hurt but I couldn't stop to rub it. Instead, I reached for the nearest appendage, his ear, and twisted until he squealed louder than a porker. I let go when he dropped to his knees, but should've held on because he punched me in the balls, causing a doubling over of shit-awful pain. At that point I heard a thud and was thinking metal on something just as hard—the guy's head. He slumped over and I looked up to see Lark, both hands gripping the pan he'd used for making tomato rice.

"Well, I hope you're satisfied," she said, pulling me to my feet. "You've been here, let's see …." She checked her watch. "All of four stinking hours and already managed to mess up my life, big time plus."

"You said he was passing through."

"Right, until something better came along. Your timing stinks."

Some things never change, Lark's attitude for one. A groan escaped from the boyfriend, relieving me from any guilt associated with the possibility of his sudden death. On the other hand, there was blood oozing from his head.

"What are we going to do with him?" I asked.

"Like this is my problem," Lark shot back. "I don't do stitches."

"I didn't figure you for beans and rice either."

"Jeez, do I have to think of everything."

She took hold of Hector's feet, leaving me the top end under his shoulders, and we half-carried, half-dragged him outside to the beat-up Chevy.

"The car's his?" I asked.

"Yeah, my only means of transportation, thanks for nothing."

We shoved Hector in the backseat and he groaned. He groaned again when she tossed me the car keys. "You do drive, don't you?"

"Well, yeah." I reached for the wallet in my back pocket.

"Forget the license. I believe you."

"You're sure?"

"Shut up, Free." She opened the driver's door. "Now get behind the wheel and make this happen."

"Okay, okay, but why don't you? Wait a minute; where's your license."

"Giving me fits. A temporary setback I expect to have straightened out next week."

Good, she needed me, if only for a while. I slid in, turned on the ignition while she held the door open.

"So, where am I taking him?"

She leaned into my face. "Just dump him off at the Emergency Room."

"And that would be where?"

"On Kingshighway, you know, across from the park. I thought you knew your way around."

"Sure I do, here and there but not everywhere."

"Shit." Lark slammed the door, went around to the passenger side, and got in. She exhaled a tired sigh along with directions to the hospital, directions she kept repeating with every turn and stoplight. The old clunker rattled and groaned along with its owner in the backseat but I didn't care. Any car was better than no car and I needed the practice driving.

"I'll get Hector's things later," Lark said. "Thanks to you, I don't expect he'll have the balls to come back."

"Wait a minute. You're saying this was my fault?"

"I'm saying it wouldn't have happened if you hadn't showed up." She rubbed her cheek. "Some things never change."

"Hey, you sent me away."

"I had to. What a little shit you were, biting me in public that day, at the bus station of all places as if we were no better than trailer trash. I could've smacked you right then and there."

"Yeah, except I wasn't a little shit any more, your main reason for sending me away."

By now we were heading north on Kingshighway with Forest Park to my left. Lark took me there once, a trip to the zoo cut short when she met a pair of irresistible biceps.

"Here, turn here." She pointed to the Emergency Entrance.

I'll give Lark this: she put on a good show, opening the car's back door while explaining to the hospital attendant how she found Hector in the alley, a neighbor she only knew by his first name. The attendant stuck Hector in a wheelchair and told Lark to follow him while I parked in the garage.

"No problem," she said. "I'm right behind you." As soon as he wheeled Hector through the sliding door, she slid into the passenger seat and told me to take off.

"Shouldn't you check him in or something?"

"Not my problem."

We drove a mile or so before Lark spoke again. "Fresh air, hard work, and proper discipline—that's what the case worker said you needed, and what better place to find that combination than at the farm of my youth."

"The hellhole you couldn't wait to leave."

"I loved you with all my heart, I really did. I was a damn good mother and gave you my unconditional love from Day One." She lit a cigarette and cracked the window. "But sometimes love creates a bunch of problems that turn into profound and everlasting hatred."

"I was only eleven. You sent me away."

"Shut up ... shut up."

She might've blinked away a tear; I couldn't say for sure.

"Not only did I give you life, I gave you the best years of mine—the twenties, as a model my most photogenic and profitable. Remember when you were five or so, the two of us climbing the ladder to the top of our game, a red-haired and freckle-faced team starring in those Sunday supplement department store ads, me passing for a teenager and you positively adorable as my kid brother."

"Until I outgrew the cute stage, that is."

"Was it my fault I didn't look old enough to be your mother, a curse or a blessing depending on the circumstances."

"Yeah, go figure. Was it my fault I looked too old to be your son?"

"If only you'd kept your mouth shut. But no-o, you always had to make yourself out to be more than what you really were."

Chapter 6

Lark worked two jobs, the steadiest, four nights a week as a waitress—she wouldn't tell me where—the other, off-and-on during the day as a nail specialist, again the location top secret. A professional she called herself, always flashing an impressive set of claws that were long and tapered, gleaming with red enamel never allowed to chip because she wanted to set a proper example for her clientele. Since banishing the loser boyfriend along with his car—a big mistake, since I could've used the wheels—she was now forced to travel by taxi. Not a day passed without her reminding me about the inconvenience my presence had brought upon her. I almost suggested she consider public transportation but didn't want to upset her any more than she already was, what with my crashing there and all.

To pacify her and because most of my cash went toward groceries, I spent part of each day job hunting, a serious effort to find work suitable to my capabilities, but got zero return for the efforts. Naturally, St. Louis fell short when it came to the backbreaking farm work I knew but didn't miss; but residential lawns were plentiful, which made manicuring them a possibility I planned to explore in due time. After all, I'd only been staying with Lark a short while, a sliver of what she owed me considering the years of parental neglect she managed to one-eighty into being my fault.

Being unemployed gave me a chance to reflect, to accept the misdeeds I could never change. Good for me, but not so good for Lark who didn't like revisiting the past. Every day brought more of the not-so-subtle hints about my leaving. Those I ignored by playing dumb. When she wasn't around, which accounted for most of the time, I kicked back and watched her DVDs and ancient videos dating back to when I depended on no one but her for my entertainment. Over the years she'd acquired a huge collection of movies, and our tastes tended to run on similar tracks. Oh yeah, we were cut from the same cloth, only I was smarter and had willed myself to succeed whereas she thrived on constant failure blamed on everyone except herself.

I'd come to St. Louis with a purpose, one near and dear to my heart and had been waiting for the right moment to approach Lark. It came one evening after we'd finished watching *Kramer vs. Kramer*, a topic near and dear to her heart, this tear-jerker that stuck up for a self-centered mom who walked out on her adorable kid.

I stretched my arms into a yawn and after the release, I hit her with this. "So, Lark, I guess you've been wondering why I looked you up."

"The thought did cross my mind."

She slid from her side of the sofa to mine, tapped my chin with her fist, and then leaned back to view the *Kramer* credits as they rolled up the screen. "More to the point: why you've stayed this long."

"This long, come on. It's only been a week or so."

"More like three." She kept her eyes on the screen, as if the assistant to Meryl Streep really mattered, or which catering company provided food on the movie set. "Look, Free, it's like this. I'm a creature of habit and—"

"Old habits and new, some you break and others deserve another chance."

"Enough already, you've made your point. Anyway, as I was about to say: times are tough, the economy stinks, and the few people eating out are getting even chintzier with their tips. I swear if one more table stiffs me, I will leave my so-called career in the restaurant industry for something more substantial. As things stand now, I'm barely in a position to support myself, let alone you."

"In other words, you're asking me to leave."

"ASAP if not sooner, and with no hard feelings on either side, okay?" Lark stretched her arms overhead, propped her bare feet on the coffee table, and wiggled her toes until they popped. Using the remote, she ejected the video and the TV returned to Channel 3. "Look, it's not that I don't care about your welfare because I most certainly do. You'll always be my son, warts and all."

"Those warts and all, I didn't acquire on my own."

"Did I insinuate to the contrary? No, I did not. Let's call a truce, at least for the short time we have left together. No more guilt trips, no more pity parties. Since I can't buy you a ticket to paradise, what would your leaving take?"

"The last ticket you bought me was a one-way to Southern Illinois."

"That was then and this is now. We've both come a long way, obviously you longer than me. So, what would it take?"

"Just one thing: his name."

"Damn, what's in a name? You make it sound so easy." She tapped out a cigarette, stuck it between her lips, and fired up the Bic lighter.

I moved to the velvet chair, making it easier to see her without turning my head. "Come on, Lark. I know you were a popular chick back then. God knows, you told me often enough, but give me a break."

"You want the name, just like that." She snapped one of those thin, manicured fingers against her thumb. Smoke accompanied the next words out of her mouth. "What is this: the Spanish Inquisition?"

"Life should be so easy. You owe me."

"Pu-lease, after what you did?"

"What about you? And don't change the subject, unless you're in no hurry for me to leave."

"Okay, the name, but you have to understand, I'm not for sure." She drew in, held smoke in her throat, and exhaled a ring lasting about as long as her many promises. "It was party time—I'm thinking Sammy. I do remember his face—nothing on the order of yours, by the way. You're a good-looking boy."

"I'm twenty-two and don't you forget it."

"Well, aren't you the streetwise smartass."

"I guess it's in my genes."

"Touché and all that jazz, sorry, I can't seem to shake the mom instinct deep within me."

I could've argued the point but wasn't about to make a mess of what I'd already started. "About this Sammy, he had a last name?"

"Of course, everybody has a last name."

"Not everybody. Not me."

"Get over it; you're a Danner, same as me."

"Not by a long shot. I'm a bone fide bastard. You never were."

"Don't get me started on that. For sure, it's not a road we want to travel down again. Not ever."

"Sorry." Not, we both knew I lied.

"And no, I don't recall his last name." Lark crushed out one cigarette and lit another. She got up, and yanked out the ejected video from its player. "Anything in particular you want to watch?"

Give me a break. We always wound up watching whatever Lark wanted. I shook my head so she flipped through the videos and selected a young Tom Cruise I'd already seen twice during those long hours while she worked. As soon as Tom's face hit the screen, she took her cue and started pacing the room, a caged cougar if ever there was. "Hell, the whole thing happened so long ago; what does it matter now. Look at you: all grown up and doing just fine without a daddy."

"I'd do much better if you'd let me stay, just a while longer 'til I get on my feet."

"How many times do we have to beat this dead horse? Our being together, living under the same roof, just won't work."

"We could make it work. I promise not to cause you any trouble."

"A promise you made before, more than once as I recall."

"Don't hold me to what happened years ago. I was a kid and didn't know any better."

"Sure you did. I didn't raise no fool for a son, anyway those first eleven years—the formative years and most important in my estimation. And in the estimation of experts, I might add." She stopped in front of me and leaned over, bringing with her the scent of tobacco when she kissed my forehead. "Come on, Free … Johnny. Do us both a favor."

"Since when did you ever call me Johnny?"

"When I still called myself Emily, now get a grip. You can stay until tomorrow morning, and then it's adios."

"I'm not leaving 'til you tell me how I got here."

"How should I know; you showed up one day, totally uninvited."

"That's not what I mean. I want my Jesus, Mary, and Joseph story."

"I know. Be careful what you ask for."

"How I got here, that much you owe me."

She popped a Coke and fired up another cigarette before plopping down on the sofa. It creaked, inviting her to blow another smoke ring. "I was just a kid too; not yet eighteen and already a party girl."

"And he was this handsome Prince Charming."

"More like a perpetual Joe College, nerdy with bad posture and granddaddy glasses—what was I thinking. Okay, maybe there was a mutual attraction. Sammy's few bucks helped pay the rent. He called me his Queen of Love and Beauty."

"You fell for that?" I couldn't imagine Lark ever being so naive.

"Duh … we hooked up but my heart was so generous he couldn't hang onto it forever. One night we were partying at this really cool dude's pad, enjoying a love fest of booze and drugs when Sammy caught me with some wannabe hotshot who later became a movie actor."

"No kidding, what's his name?"

"Nobody you would know. Anyway, without saying a word, Sammy yanked me to my feet and practically dragged me through the living room. I nearly died from humiliation."

I didn't say a word but let her ramble.

"When we got home, he held me tight and spoke through breath soured from one too many beers. He said I'd promised to love only him, which I did. Until he treated me like a special-occasion Barbie doll and introduced me to a slew of guys who wouldn't leave me alone. Was it my fault Sammy led me down the path of temptation, showing candy to a baby and then slapping her hand for eating it."

"So, how much candy did you eat?" I asked.

"Enough to make me want more, to know I could never be satisfied with just Sammy. I told him to take a seat or get off the bus. He got off all right but not before slapping me so hard I collapsed on the futon, that piece of junk he called our love nest. I came back at him with bared teeth and fingernails. I jumped him with the fury of those wildcats lurking around the farm at night."

Oh, yeah, I knew about the wildcats.

"Sammy retaliated, mostly to defend himself. He grabbed a handful of my hair and yanked it out. My hair, my pride, the roots detached from my skull. I screamed, sacrificing one nail as I raked five across his cheek and drew blood. I wrapped my legs around his waist, my fingers clawing through the back of his shirt as we dropped to the floor. Back and forth we rolled in the tiny space of my room until we wound up … well, you know."

"That's how I got here?"

She thought a minute. I waited.

"No … I think you were already on the way. Yeah, I started tossing my cookies soon after. Anyway, it was too late to undo the damage Sammy and I had inflicted on each other. Hours later and still on the floor, I awoke to find him gone, along with all his belongings but not our meager stash of money. That I kept hidden in my Cap'n Crunch box, the one place I knew he'd never check out."

"Serves him right, wailing on you, pregnant or not."

"Oh, I didn't tell Sammy about you. Maybe I should've. He'd have married me in a New York minute and our lives would've been different, his and mine and yours. The others too—damn, I can't bring myself to go there."

"His name, Lark, just give me his full name."

Chapter 7

Samuel Dean Lawford, what a mouthful. After making a few phone calls, I learned he resided in St. Louis, of all places at Bed and Bread, the city's premier homeless shelter, not as a guest but as B & B's guidance counselor. A double-whammy blessing for me since thanks to Lark, I now found myself among those having no place to lay their sorry heads at night. Not my first time, I might add and not in a prideful way.

At two in the afternoon I strolled into the public park located across from B & B, and took note of what must have been some of the shelter's more illustrious residents, pushed out for the day to soak up the sun or look for non-existent employment or find a place less demanding than the one currently providing them food and shelter. Both men and women, age-wise anywhere from twenty-so to sixty-plus and definitely dressed for failure, they were stretched out on the grass or leaning against a comfortable tree or sitting on wooden benches, feeding loaves of white bread to a gathering of demanding pigeons and ducks waddling over from the park's mini pond. This puddle of water was supposed to sooth the disenchanted, those pathetic bastards seeking oral gratification with long smokes in spite of the warnings about hazards to their health. Smoking, not my bag, never was. It plays shit with my allergies and clogs my sinuses. Maybe that's why I didn't put up more of a stink when Lark asked me to leave, although I would've stayed if only she hadn't been so pigheaded.

Having seen the St. Louis needy, I figured I'd be good for a brief B & B stay, one, maybe two days tops. And minus the burden of certain possessions requiring constant monitoring—my remaining money and top dude clothes. With that in mind I hopped a bus that took me further into the downtown area and checked my luggage into a locker at the bus station. Yeah, the same station where Lark dumped me eleven years before—same black and white checkered tile, same caliber of passengers waiting for their ride to Nowhere, USA. Damn, how could Lark have done such a thing to me—her own flesh and blood, her pride and joy, or so she used to tell me. If I'd been a vengeful person, which I don't consider myself, I'd've been thinking of ways to get even instead of wasting my time chasing down the guy whose sperm gave me life. This man, whoever he was, I could not think of as my father. The closest I'd ever come to a father was Jed.

Around suppertime I followed the hungry crowd to B & B. Of course, with every freebie comes a price—in this case, have-to-go-to church services before a delicious hardy meal, according to the man guarding B & B's door. His face reminded me of the fermenting bread dough Delores loved to punch, the rest of him a beefy wrestler with hair in dire need of shampoo. I didn't ask his name, having already ruled him out as the sperm giver. But, while everyone else pushed ahead of me, I did ask Beefsteak a pertinent question.

"Church services, you mean we have to sit through an entire Mass?"

"Nah, we're non-denominational Protestant."

"Yeah but—"

"It ain't negotiable," he told me and everyone else within earshot. "First you pray; then you eat."

"Where I come from we call that grace," a guy behind me said.

"Same as here," Beefsteak shot back. "Only our grace lasts longer than most places. Now are you staying or not?"

Since my hunger had to be fed before my mind could resist possible brainwashing, I agreed to participate. As did everyone else, including a few who claimed they were atheists and totally unredeemable. Inside the meeting room I didn't move fast enough for the regulars who grabbed every seat in the rear, and assumed the customary position of a captive audience slumped down with chins buried in their chests. I wound up front and center, the plastic bag containing my essential toiletries and one change of briefs slid under the folding chair and against my foot for safekeeping. Trust no one. That had been my mantra for some time, one of many depending on the situation I found myself.

A glance around the room told me what I already knew and what everyone else had already decided. Color me the out-of-place newbie— too clean, too well dressed, and way too young. And unlike some of these folks, I most definitely was playing with a full deck. Sure, I'd led a complicated life, one that continued to follow me wherever I went. But this should not have concerned the regulars, or as I now thought of them: a freebie batch of movie extras providing background support for the role I was currently playing.

I steeled myself for the evening's lecture … uh, sermon, which turned out not so bad because Preacher Dave's mission focused on the truly downtrodden, enabling me to focus on the comforting aroma of ham and beans drifting in from the kitchen. Ham and beans, one of the specialties Delores often forced on me. After a while, I'd learned to like them because it was easier than listening to her rants about the virtues of country cooking, as if those of fast-food were the temptations of Satan.

After a while Preacher Dave's words must've touched one person to the core because behind me came the sound of female sobbing. I was the only one who turned to see this woman standing up, hands clutching unspectacular boobs in need of a super lift. Her sobbing erupted into a wail, instilling in me a cringe that bottomed out in my sorry rear end. Crying, one of those emotions I have trouble dealing with, ever since those days on the farm.

"Don't go twisting your bowels into a pretzel," a voice whispered to my left. "Mandy pulls this every night."

I spoke without bothering to turn my head. "She must have a ton of problems."

"No more'n the rest of us. Anyways, she sure as hell knows how to shut off Dave, which makes her one sweet morsel on my plate." The movie extra wobbled to his feet and jerked his head toward the humanity jam forming at the doorway. "Come on, afore you miss out on the best part. It's chowtime."

After some pushing and shoving we finally made it to the dining room, bringing up the rear of a line moving faster than I'd expected. Something else was moving too—in the extra's hair. A closer look revealed lice at play. I stepped back. Big mistake because the guy whose foot I stepped on pushed me into Lice Man.

"Sorry," I told Lice Man and meant it in the most literal way. Lice can jump from head to head, this I know from personal experience.

"What's yours?" he asked, as if taking my food order.

"Huh?"

"Your problem, we all got a shitload or two."

Or three, his skin was casket-ready, eyes—ugh; breath, a shitload worse than vomit warmed over.

"Your problem," he repeated with an edge.

"Nothing I can't fix—a temporary setback."

"Sounds familiar, mine's going on nine years." He stepped forward with a noticeable limp and scrunched up his face.

Whatever his problem, I wanted no part of it. Having gone without food for over twelve hours, I arrived in front of the serving table with my stomach sending out SOS rumbles. Food, sawdust, whatever, I needed to fill the empty crater in my belly.

Lice Man nudged me with his elbow. "Name?"

"Huh?"

"Pay attention, kid. Your name, so's I can introduce you to the man."

Again, my foggy brain made me speak without first thinking. "Uh, Free."

"Amen, ain't we all." He grinned, showing me yellowed teeth before leaning into the table, his head jutting over the steaming pot as he inspected its contents. Satisfied, he pulled back, and addressed the server. "Fill 'er up. And for the love of God, do not skimp on those mouth-watering ham or beans. Same goes for my friend here. As you can see, he's still a-growing."

The server glanced up, eyes peering through pricey, wire-rimmed glasses that didn't belong in a place such as this. He must've thought the same about me. We eyed each other while he dished out the first bowl and handed it to Lice Man, along with two thick slices of bread. Lice Man jumped on the opportunity to introduce us. "Free, meet The Bishop."

A bishop, here? I genuflected with a slight bend of the knee. "Pleased, Your Excellency."

Laughter sputtered from Lice Man's mouth, along with a blessing of spit over his ham and beans. The Bishop reacted like he'd seen this before and moved the second bowl out of Lice Man's range before handing it to me.

"You can dispense with the misplaced reverence," he said. "The Bishop refers to a nickname I picked up some years ago. Maybe it's the same with you. A name like Free, I mean."

"It's a long story." One I had no intention of explaining to a bishop in name only. Besides, Lice Man was tugging at my shirtsleeve. Again with the infested head, he motioned for me to follow. I could've ditched him but instead tagged along like an obedient dog because B & B was no place to make enemies.

Rows of long tables filled the dining area. Although it was packed with eaters short on conversation, Lice Man managed to find us two ideal spaces. One across from the other, which resolved the issue of my having to rub shoulders with him and worry about the parasites jumping ship to search out new munchies in my hair. But our seating arrangement also brought me a better view of his rheumy eyes, which I figured unlikely to see another winter. Before digging in, he bowed his head in prayer, forcing me to make a hurried sign of the cross so as not to appear ungrateful for what I was about to receive. He looked up and I raised my brow, asking his permission to proceed. Not yet, he shot his hand in my direction.

"Nice to meet you, Free," he said. "In case you're wondering, I'm Jones Alexander the Fourth, but friends of which I now consider you among my chosen few, call me Jonesy."

His must've been some pedigreed, the Alexander lineage. After shaking his hand, I coughed into mine, an excuse to wipe it on my shirt. I lifted the tinny fork, and proceeded to shovel food into my mouth. The ham and beans didn't compare to Delores's but before these were half gone, I was already considering another run on the food. Before I could, the two guys on either side of Jonesy started talking about the caliber of B & B clientele, how the unwashed shouldn't be allowed to mix with the more refined. Cursing under their breath, they removed themselves to a pair of seats recently vacated.

Jonesy winked. "New people, I do believe they were referring to me. Now don't you get scared off too. After dinner I'm scheduled to undergo a thorough cleansing."

"You mean delicing?"

"No, I mean delousing. Don't they teach you kids anything about proper hygiene?" Time out, I changed the subject. "Are seconds allowed?"

"Sure, if you should be so lucky."

I pushed back my chair and stood up, only to sit back down again. Damn. The Bishop and another server were taking away the empty ham and bean pots. "That's it? Dinner's over?"

"Hell, no, there's always some excuse for dessert. If tonight's Wednesday, figure on rice pudding or bread pudding, take your pick, but don't wait too long or you won't get either. And don't worry 'bout bringing any back for me. Diabetes keeps me away from the sweets although in moments of weakness I find myself unable to resist certain no-can-haves. My condition is so discombobulated the docs wish to remove my grievous leg; but I told them no way, I'd rather sleep with the angels."

"Ain't that what you said when they took your toes?" asked a guy passing by.

"Only the first two."

"You tell 'em, Jonesy."

By now we were sitting alone so I used the time to my advantage. "So, Jonesy, how long've you been coming here?"

He lifted his eyes to the ceiling, as if pondering his toughest question of the day, or maybe the entire week. "Off and on about two years I guess, between this fine establishment and others in the general area. The cold don't agree with me so I usually winter in Florida."

"Ever heard of a guy by the name of Sam Lawford?"

He checked out the ceiling again. "Can't say for sure, I suggest you speak to The Bishop. Although he comes and goes almost as much as me, he knows just about everybody and everything."

I should've figured this on my own and decided to dump Jonesy at my first opportunity, as in that very moment since The Bishop was back at his station, spooning pudding from oblong baking pans blowing off steam from the oven. I held back until only a few people were waiting in line and then went to the end. When my turn came, I asked politely for the rice pudding and without hesitation The Bishop supersized my portion.

"You're new to St. Louis," he said.

"Not exactly, I've lived here and elsewhere." I did a one-hundred-eighty with my head. "But before today I never set foot in this place—no way, no how."

"Pride goeth before the fall, also when times are tough." He sucked in air through two rows of even teeth and gave me a second onceover, as if he might've missed something the first go-around. "You job hunting?"

Music to my ears, I hadn't expected this. "Absolutely, and I'll do just about anything so long as it doesn't break any laws." I exaggerated the legal stuff because I wasn't sure what to expect from him and besides he was moving me off track. "Anyway, what I'm wondering is could you point out Sam Lawford to me?"

"Perhaps we should talk first," he said.

"Suits me, I'm ready when you are."

The Bishop took off his apron. After asking the other server to cover for him, he drew two coffees from a large urn. I told him I take mine black.

"Is there any other way?" He jerked his chin toward a small table, away from the others. "Over there."

After we sat down, he leaned back in his chair, again checking out my face without speaking.

I made the first move. "About this Sam Lawford dude—"

"You're looking at him, kid."

Hel-lo, Samuel Dean Lawford, you mothereffer and I did mean it literally. As for the scrutiny from my end, I took plenty of time with his face, trying to find a similarity to the mirrored image I saw when looking at no one but yours truly. A face thinner than mine, with hollowed out cheeks and a shallow complexion in need of sunrays, his nose narrowed to a point whereas mine enjoyed a comfortable spread. Hairline moving north accounted for his high forehead—no thanks, most definitely not me and not what I had in mind for myself in another twenty-five years.

"Should I know you?" he asked just as I was ready to abandon any thoughts of kinship.

I hesitated but only for a moment. "Maybe, think back twenty-one years or so, to a party here in St. Louis."

He sipped from the mug, his hands what I would've expected from an artist—smooth and hairless with long, tapered fingers. When he spoke, the words came with a longing for what once was. "I partied day and night back then. What's more, I'm paying for it now, in ways you could never understand."

Please, not another sob story. I wanted nothing to detract from my own. "This would've been in a bachelor pad in the Central West End or one of those stately mansions on Lindell Boulevard. Think back to an attractive girl who wore her red hair long and straight."

His face went blank. I hate when guys do that; it's such a dead giveaway. You'd've thought I asked the Colonel's closest living relative for his crispy chicken recipe. My guy didn't look at me when he spoke; amateur liars usually don't.

"None of this rings a bell … Free, although back then I admit being partial to redheads, still am for that matter." He checked his watch. "Say, I don't want to be rude but where is this leading?"

"Her name was Lark."

"Lark … Lark, hmm."

He scratched one ear shaped an awful lot like mine, close to the head and just the right size. "If not Lark, maybe you knew her by Emily … Emily Danner."

"Yes and no, if you're referring to Desiree Danner who used to be Charity, a name that brought certain expectations she couldn't live up to—her words not mine. Some people are givers; others such as Desiree or Charity are takers. That's just the way they are."

"Yeah, tell me about it."

"As I recall, we partied together on more than one occasion. How is the ol' girl, well, I guess she's not that old, considering how young she was then—still in her teens as I recall. Wait a minute—I hope you're not the bearer of bad news."

"That depends. She's my mom and thinks you might be my dad."

My comment caught him in the middle of another sip which stuck in his mouth before he had a chance to swallow it. A spray of coffee flew across the table, sending brown splatters over the front of the only tee I'd brought with me.

"No, no, no, kid … I mean … what is your name again?"

"Free Danner, actually John Danner the Second, but I prefer Free, which is what Lark always called me. She never married."

"And obviously put you at a huge disadvantage."

"That's why I'm here." I was about to say more when somebody started yelling, "Fight, fight!"

Samuel Lawford pushed his chair back. "Don't go away," he said. "I'll return as soon as I resolve this conflict."

Yeah, right. End of conversation and the last I saw of him that evening.

Chapter 8

Home sweet home at B & B, just me and the cot I chose because it hugged the wall, the closest thing to privacy in this poor man's Motel 6. My situation went from bad to worse when Jonesy plopped down on the cot next to mine. Fortunately, a turban of plastic wrap covered his head to contain any survivors of the delousing, a precaution that in my book elevated B & B to a five-star facility.

"Thanks for saving me a spot, and not to worry," he said, latching his hands under the plasticized head. "As of this moment I am cleaner'n a referee's whistle."

"I believe you."

"And why not, you're all heart, a kid like you, I can tell." He rolled to his side and propped himself up on one elbow to get a better look at me thinking I'd rather be anywhere than next to him. Sure, I could've left the hellhole, walked a ton of streets until I found my own private shelter closer to the Mississippi or under a viaduct or an overpass, but I wasn't about to let The Bishop off that easy.

"Man, what I wouldn't give for a sweet rub," Jonesy said.

"Well, don't set your sights on me," came a voice from Jonesy's other side. "Serves you right for blowing off Miss Priss."

"That'll do, Grumbler. Don't you be disrespecting our number one gal," Jonesy said, his eyes still on me. "Mandy'll get over it. She always does. Right, Free?"

"If you say so."

"About that rub?"

"Don't look at me. I'm so tired I couldn't screw up a wet dream and that's saying a lot."

"The boy comes with a sense of humor," Grumbler said.

"A must if you're ever going to survive this shit," Jonesy said. "And don't be putting the young man down. His name's Free."

"Free as a bird, just like the rest of us."

"You're whining again."

"Which is why they call me Grumbler. Now if you don't mind, I'm gonna shut my mouth and close my eyes."

"Before lights out? I guess it's all that sunshine and fresh air what done you in," Jonesy said, winking at me. "Looks like it's just the two of us, Free."

"Make that one. I wasn't kidding about being tired."

Did he take the hint? No way, he started with a rundown of the best shelters between here and Florida, in case I decided to try my luck elsewhere what with jobs not that plentiful in St. Louis, not that I could expect much improvement down south what with the present state of the economy and conditions not about to improve in the near future. On and on he went with me grunting every so often when all I wanted was a long string of Zs.

"Your family's in this vicinity?" he asked without taking a breath.

"Would I be staying here if they were?"

"Don't be asking me to answer for you. Most of my family's gone, anyway those what count. Them what's left don't want much to do with me. When I was younger and had money, well it was a whole different story. Did I ever tell you about the time I ...?"

Enough, I'd heard all I could stand to hear. I opened my mouth into a wide yawn and then leaned over to remove my shoes—big mistake.

He jerked upright, kicked my leg, and lowered his voice to a whisper. "Are you out of your flea-picking mind? Unless you plan on walking barefoot tomorrow, I suggest you keep those better'n-anybody-else's shoes where they belong. On your feet, the socks too, especially if the heels are intact, I mean without holes or the slightest hint of holes."

My shitty worn-out Nikes, he had to be kidding. Now the good ones were a different story. Them I'd left locked up at the bus station.

The ones on my feet were minutes away from the nearest trash can but I didn't want to open more dialogue with Jonesy so I came back with, "Gotcha. Thanks for the warning."

"Don't mention it." He hacked a few times before assuming his elbow recline, again prepared for more bonding with me, like some junior high basketball coach trying to mold the player he sees as his next superstar. On and on Jonesy blabbered until the lights went out. I eased back on the bed and followed his lead of lacing my fingers behind my head, creating a position I hoped would serve as a buffer between said head and the questionable pillow below, and soon closed my eyes. Our corner of the dorm went quiet as a city morgue until Jonesy decided he couldn't sleep.

"Free, you still awake? Come on, nobody nods off that fast on bean night. Free? Free?"

"What is it, Jonesy?"

"I just wanted to say thanks, you know, for putting up with me."

"You're welcome, now good night and sleep tight."

"I always do, even when the bed bugs bite." He snorted through a laugh I couldn't share. "Just kidding, no I'm not. Sometimes they bite and sometimes they don't, those nasty creepy critters. But for you, I don't think so. Even the bed bugs aren't that stupid. Free, are you awake? Free?"

Yes and no. I snorted like a sleeping pig until he shut up. Minutes later with him snoring for real, I started counting sheep, five hundred of them, forward then backward. When the animals started screwing each other, I turned off my brain and gave them some privacy.

Chapter 9

Any morning that I wake up remembering only half of my nightmares allows me to face another day. It worked my first B & B morning and with no bites from vermin fighting for their fair share of the bed. Maybe Jonesy knew more than I thought he did. We hadn't left the dorm yet and already he was talking about how the two of us would spend our day, on the park bench because of his diabetic feet. Grumbler chimed in, offering instead a personal sightseeing tour, as if I haven't seen the zoo and the Arch and the entire riverfront. In both cases, I remained polite but uncommitted since I'd half-planned on checking out Lark, without her knowing, of course.

    Breakfast lineup for the sheltered masses brought no surprises—steaming oatmeal, stacks of toast, and so-so scrambled eggs from super-sized cartons which reminded me of those breakfast yawns I endured after my time on the farm. Nowhere did I see The Bish, as I'd renamed him last night after Jonesy had stopped his yapping. Maybe The Bish had slept in, maybe he realized I was his kid. Maybe he decided to skip out before giving me a chance. What a crappy way to start my day. "Pass the ketchup, Jonesy. I'm starving."

After breakfast Beefsteak opened the side door and ordered everyone out into the fresh air of traffic fumes and other urban pollutants. I should've moved faster, should've jaywalked instead of waiting for the light. I should've given Jonesy the 'up-yours,' stomped on his cripple foot, told him to bug off. Instead I let him latch on to me like *Midnight Cowboy's* Dustin Hoffman one of Lark's favorite movies. Except I was no boy toy prostitute and considered myself better looking than Jon Voight in his prime and I still had years to reach mine, what with the natural talent God saw fit to give me. That combined with a few acting lesson … I figured, look out Hollywood.

That St. Louis morning was a perfect example, with Jonesy as Hoffman's Ratso limping alongside my version of Voight's Joe Buck, and talking non-stop while I—minus the Stetson and leather tooled boots—was engaged in a two-way pretense. To him, I acted interested. To everyone else, I acted kind-hearted to the pathetic loser. I walked ramrod straight but wasn't sure if I fooled anyone except myself. Worst case scenario, I didn't want anyone thinking we were related. Yeah, color me the day's biggest fool.

After skirting the downtown area for over an hour, we circled back to the park near B & B, not my choice; Jonesy's feet wouldn't carry him one more block. Neither would his lungs after all the one-sided conversation before his sentences turned into one or two words. The man was teetering on the edge and I being who I am did not want him saddling his-side-kick me, with an emergency situation.

"You gonna be okay?" I asked after we landed on the nearest bench.

Unlike the night before, he struggled to speak, taking a breath after each word. "Sure, Free. And thanks for asking."

"Quit thanking me, will you."

"Can't help myself … you got so much going for you."

Damn, just what I didn't need. Every time I stood up to leave, Jonesy did too. So I spent the rest of the day with him holding court on the bench because I didn't want him dragging behind me. When I said something about needing a soda, he directed me to the nearest vending machine and asked me to bring him one too. Him having no money made me his prime banker.

"There's a diner down the street, 'bout two blocks east," he said. "Check out the alley behind it. Sometimes they put out a pretty good spread."

"No way, I'm not that hungry."

"But I am. Fact is, I feel kinda woozy." His head teetered on its turkey neck. Water seeped from eyes on the verge of closing forever.

Shit, I hadn't signed up for this: new best friend, banker, and nursemaid. What next? I left, unsure about returning, but I did, along with the soda, two donuts and three bagels.

Jonesy circled his tongue over lips cracked with dried blood. "What, no cream cheese,"

"The rats beat me to it."

"You jesting me?"

"No, I'm not."

"How old?"

I shrugged. "How should I know? Take a bite and decide for yourself."

"Not the bagels, dimwit. How old are you?"

"You first."

He opened the palms of both hands, spread his fingers, and did a mental count. "Sixty-one and not counting on sixty-two, it ain't in the cards." He could've passed for seventy-five and gave me time to absorb this before he asked, "And you?"

"Old enough to drink."

"Which tells me nothing."

Exactly. I slumped into the bench, hoping to chill his prying.

No such luck, he knuckled-punched my forearm. "Hey, no fair, we agreed and now you're reneging. Just wait 'til the gang hears about this."

"Twenty-two, and don't ask me anything else."

"Twenty-two, you gotta be kidding. You're a baby with the soul of an old fart."

"It's a genetic problem."

Jonesy shook his head. "The worst of the worst and not easily resolved. You know, inheriting the sins of our fathers."

And what about the mothers, I didn't mention mine.

Throughout the day B & B residents stopped by with their take on treating Jonesy's bum foot, without giving it up to what they all referred to as *the butchers*. Meanwhile, Mandy the boob-thumping wailer had given herself to an aerobic workout, circling the block in purple canvas high-tops, belongings stuffed in a hobo bag slung across her back. This mishmash of plaids and prints draped her body, as in a skirt down to the ankles and sweater too hot for any summer day in St. Louis. She waited until the last of Jonesy's advisers wandered off before cutting across the grass to his throne. My first close-up of her revealed an ageless face marked with sunspots, creases, and endless wrinkles gravitating toward her scrawny neck. A knit shirt wrapped into a scarf covered her hair, except for the few strands of wiry gray stuck on her forehead. She didn't speak but slid the sack from her shoulder and knelt at Jonesy's feet. From there, she rolled onto what I figured a skinny ass and crossed her legs yoga style.

"Hello, good-looking," Jonesy said with a grin that took some years off his face.

"Shut up, you pathetic cocksucker excuse for a human being."

Me the invisible grunt, she ignored, humbling but nothing new.

"Ain't this a gasser," Jonesy said to her, "worshipping at the feet of me, your one and only."

"You wish."

"Then rise, bitch. I don't want you slobberin' all over my shoes."

"Shut up. I know a thing or two 'bout sugar diabetes."

"Mandy thinks she knows everything," Jonesy explained to me.

She poked her fingernail into his ankle. "That hurt?"

He hesitated before answering. "Didn't feel a thing."

She pulled a sturdy twig from under the bench and poked him again. "How 'bout now?"

"Maybe a twinge or two."

After that she did nothing but asked, "This?"

He twitched. "Ouch, a real doozey if ever there was."

She lifted her head, observed him through suspicious eyes. "Liar, liar, pants on fire."

"Bitch, bitch, you're worse'n a witch."

Her voice softened. "Take off that shoe. Come on, lemme have a look see."

"Scram. You make me sick."

She undid the yoga position, rolled to her knees, and stood up. "Don't go blaming me for what ain't my fault."

I wasn't sorry to see her leave but couldn't resist asking Jonesy, "How well do you two know each other?"

"We used to be lovers afore we legalized our sinful pleasures, thus becoming man and wife. From then on it went downhill faster'n a runaway caboose."

***

Another Preacher David sermon, another Mandy performance—this one with more wailing than the night before because she started sooner and he wasn't ready to give her the floor yet. It became their version of

American Idol, him shouting over her wailing until he said grace and released the hungry to Beefsteak. Instead of waiting for Jonesy, I avoided him, casually pushing myself to the head of the line, a good idea turned sour. Thanks to Jonesy's cohorts working even harder at sending me back to him.

When I got there, he spoke through a pained wince. "Hungry?"

"That depends on the menu."

"Stew, with plenty of potatoes, fewer carrots, and pieces of meat this big." He bent his forefinger to the web of his thumb and made a tiny circle.

"Okay, I'll make do."

"Me too. It's as if we're soul mates, you and me, don'tcha think?" He wobbled, grabbed my arm to keep from falling.

"You okay?" I asked, surprised by my concern.

"Sure am, with you by my side."

I moved forward with the line, leaving his hand behind to flounder in midair.

He closed the gap between us. "Wait up, will you. About the stew, I almost forgot the best part—biscuit dumplings. They ain't feather light but they don't sink either."

My evening started looking better, but not because of the biscuits. I noticed The Bish spooning out more grub, and played it cool, pretending not to give a shit if he didn't give a shit.

"I oughta be fronting you," Jonesy said as we neared the stew. "It's a seniority issue, should they be scraping the bottom and there's only enough for one."

Whatever, I stepped behind him. "Sure, don't bother waiting for me."

"Good idea, I'll find us two spots, same as last night."

Jonesy and The Bish exchanged greetings, while I stood back and let a few stragglers ahead of me. By the time my turn came, The Bish really was scraping up the last of the vegetables, along with a few slivers of meat floating in a weak excuse for juice.

"I guess you ran out of dumplings," I told him.

"For you, kid." He scraped around some more, pulled out the fattest dumpling I'd ever seen.

"Thanks. Oh, and by the way, my name's Free. Free Danner, in case you forgot."

"No chance of my forgetting. About the conversation we didn't finish last night, you want to go another round?"

"Wouldn't be here if I didn't."

"No, I didn't think so. I'll catch up with you later."

I turned to find a seat, anywhere but next to Jonesy, when someone let out a yell.

"Man down, man down!"

The Bish came from behind the serving table and hurried in the direction of more yelling, with me at his heels, the food tray shaking in my hands. Four tables into the dining area a gathering of eaters parted like the Red Sea to make way for The Bish. That's when I saw Mandy kneeling on the floor with the head of Jones Alexander the Fourth cradled in her lap. He was totally out of it, his face drained of life and turning an unhealthy shade of blue.

"Do something afore he expires," Mandy wailed. "Do something, all you God-fearing sinners and the lesser servants of Beelzebub!"

Neither of those applied to me so I did nothing.

The Bish, however, did take charge, which only seemed right given his lofty position at B & B. "Stand back, give the poor man some air," he said. While the sheep obeyed, he whipped out his cell phone, punched in 9-1-1, and started talking.

Meanwhile the guy next to me yelled, "Anybody know CPR?"

Damn, I didn't need this. "Yeah, me," I said, handing my food tray to a pair of waiting hands, one of which was already digging into the stew before my knees hit the floor. Mandy didn't look up so I nudged her and said, "Excuse me, ma'm."

It took two more nudges and encouragement from the gang before she gave up Jonesy's head, carefully setting it to rest on the floor beside me, and scooting herself off to one side. I leaned over Jonesy, tilted his chin and head back. Using my thumb and forefinger, I pinched his nostrils to cut off the air and covered his mouth with mine.

"Do whatever you have to," Mandy said with a sob. "But if he don't make it, tonight I'll cut your eyeballs out after you hit the snooze button. As God is my witness, I will."

She continued her rag on me, an out-of-tune symphony to my unspectacular show of breathing life or death into a man unwilling to cooperate on either level. By now The Bish had knelt down, ripped opened Jonesy's shirt, and was pumping his chest each time I lifted my mouth away from Jonesy's. We kept up this routine for another two minutes before Jonesy coughed up a wad of dumpling dough and started breathing on his own. Mandy jumped to her feet with as much grace as an alley cat. She started dancing up and down the aisles while our audience clapped in appreciation.

As for me, I was worn out and not sorry to see the emergency techs wheel Jonesy out on a stretcher. But learning The Bish had climbed into the ambulance with him really pissed me off because there went another day of meaningful dialogue down the toilet. Later, Beefsteak spread the word about Jonesy's condition being up for grabs, which put a damper on extending my stay at B & B due to Mandy's latest hysteria over a man who supposedly despised her as much as she did him. I avoided her for the rest of the evening, not out of my fear of her, but the other way around. Although the woman lived in la-la land, she should've been afraid of me, very afraid. If she hadn't made such an obvious stink over Jonesy, I would've given him a free pass into the next world, a world far better than the one currently hosting his flea-bitten existence.

Chapter 10

Two months of summer, two months of hell, with me working every morning and half the afternoon alongside Jed the Slave Driver, I mean anything from milking cows and Delores's hybrid goats to mending fences and cleaning a hot chicken coop that stank worse than St. Louis garbage during the collectors' strike. I don't think the old man had learned one thing about me in all that time since he couldn't stop talking about himself or the good old days of his youth. Or, the dangers of living in a too-liberal society. Or, water moccasins waiting for an unsuspecting boy to come swimming by. Or, the nearby sightings of wild animals—coyotes, foxes, and cougars. What next, Indians? I nodded with a smiley face and never talked back because nothing I ever said mattered. Nor did I talk much about Lark anymore although she never left my thoughts. If only she could've seen me, she'd have taken me back in a flash. My skin was tanned, not freckled like hers. I'd put on weight and grown so tall that one Saturday Jed and Delores decided to pop for some new clothes.

They took me shopping in Carbondale, my first time at the local mall, and let me pick out a ton of school clothes, the kind St. Louis kids were wearing before I left. And what they'd better be wearing when I got back but you never know about city kids, even those who, according to Lark, didn't have a pot to pee in. Carbondale was okay until we walked past the food court and the smell of fresh pizza grabbed me and wouldn't let go. Jed's antenna went up, sensed my craving. He dug his finger in my back, prodding me forward.

"Don't even think about it," Old Money Bags said. "We've already spent a bundle on you."

Okay, how many times did he have to remind me: no fast food for the mere sake of oral entertainment. What about me, starving didn't count for nothing. To get my mind off food, I mentioned something to Delores about buying a DVD player, not just for me but for the whole family.

She waved a hand in front of her face, batting away my words as if they were pesky gnats. "Buy a DVD? Goodness gracious no. We have plenty of old movies on video. Surely you haven't seen all of them."

"At least two or three times, maybe more," I said, looking her straight in the eye.

"I've been meaning to talk to you about that." She squinted with eyes searching mine. "Too much television can ruin a person's eyesight, which accounts for so many youngsters having to wear glasses nowadays."

"She's right, Johnny. What's more, you spend way too much time with that gadget connected to your thumbs." Jed held out a calloused palm. "Put 'er there, son."

My Game Boy? No way, I'd die before giving it up, fall off the Earth's screen just like Mario or Luigi. I held the game behind my back and moved against the wall. Jed came after me, a devil's sneer filling his face.

"Help, murder, police!" was all I managed to yell before the old man bent me into a jackknife and pried open my fingers. "No, no, no! It's not fair. Somebody help me, please."

A few shoppers slowed down. Not one of them cared enough to stop. Even though Jed released me, he now had me backed against a wall, daring me to make a wrong move as he shoved Game Boy into a pocket of his overalls.

"I love you Mario … you too, Luigi."

"Shut up, you simpering dolt."

"Knock it off, both of you!" Delores said in a hissy whisper. "One of these busybody shoppers might call security."

"They ought to," I said, rubbing my fingers after Jed gave me breathing room. "Maybe Social Services will send me home."

"You are home, Johnny. It's what your ma wants."

I hated when Delores said that, at least once a day and maybe more. "So what am I supposed to do for fun?"

"Well, for starters—"

"That's it. I've heard enough," Jed said. "While you coddle poor Johnny, I'll get the truck."

I wasn't sorry to see the old man's denim backside shuffle away. Delores I could handle better than Mario or Luigi.

"You ought to be reading more," she said as the two of us took our time walking toward the exit. "I don't mean upstairs in your room, but outside in the fresh air and sunshine."

"Then rent me some new videos. How about one video for every book I read."

"Certainly not. Why your ma used to devour books, three or four a week, and during the winter even more."

And look where it got her, I wanted to say. "Come on, Delores, give me a break."

She lifted her head to the mall's open atrium where Jesus must've been watching because she came back with more than I'd expected. "You can pick from your ma's classic library. Of course, you'll want to start with *Robin Hood*."

Excellent, this was almost too easy. *Robin Hood* I knew backwards and forwards, having read the comic book and watched umpteen versions with Lark. So, I said, "Robin Hood, who's he?"

This made Delores's day. Some days it didn't take much. "Oh, Johnny, you're going to love the story. Reading opens up the mind to so many adventures. You just need to use your imagination."

Yes, my imagination. Besides *Robin Hood*, over the next few weeks I skimmed through the pages of *Swiss Family Robinson, The Legend of Sleepy Hollow,* and *Tom Sawyer*. While Delores fixed supper, I sat at the table and retold the stories as I remembered them from movies and comic books. What a sweet setup. Whenever I went shopping with Jed and Delores for items the farm didn't supply, she allowed me to rent a new video. Too bad I'd barely made a dent in the classics before running out of familiar stories. The next three trips to town ended with me leaving the supermarket empty-handed. The last time we drove home, I couldn't pretend it didn't matter. Instead I stared out the window and kept my mouth shut.

"We made a deal," Delores said. "No book, no video."

"Try one of those Jack London books," Jed suggested. "*Call of the Wild* is a page turner if ever there was."

"My eyes hurt from reading."

"Too bad, Johnny. I've been giving serious thought to returning your game but since you've acquired this visual impairment, we'd best wait a while longer."

Cripes. Poor Mario, the little guy needed me as much as I needed him. I closed my lids and called up the images of him and Luigi, their never-ending struggles to destroy Bowser and rescue Princess Peach. The little plumbers had been like family to me, that is, until Jed kidnapped them. The old fool didn't even know how to play the game. But he did enjoy playing with my feelings, brushing me off like crumbs from the table. So did Lark, but her I could excuse, even when she called me a little shit. So I'd tasted her blood, big deal. Me, her vampire kid, maybe that's why she hadn't phoned or sent a letter. Not even a lousy card.

Chapter 11

That night at B & B visions of Jonesy dancing in my head kept me from sleep lasting more than two straight hours. The sleep deprivation was nothing new but for a guy I barely knew and liked even less, last night's insomnia didn't make much sense. At breakfast with the same grub as served the day before, I'd barely made a dent in my oatmeal when Preacher Dave banged on a tin pie plate for quiet. After three more bangs and some prodding from Beefsteak, the preacher gave us an update on Jonesy's health, as near as I could tell, something about him having to stay in the hospital because of certain complications related to his diabetes.

"Dear God, save our brother from the fires of Hell and eternal damnation," Mandy yelled from her corner of the dining hall.

Her outburst spurred Preacher Dave to offer a lengthy prayer, more on the order of a mini-sermon for Jonesy's speedy recovery. By the time he'd said his amens and exited the hall, my food had slipped from barely warm into the don't-even-bother stage.

"Good riddance to Jonesy and his cooties," muttered Grumbler to my right. He nudged me to pass the toast plate so I did.

"That ain't very Christian-like," said this hugely overweight guy sitting across from him.

"Since when did you get religion, Fat Man?" countered Grumbler.

"Since Mandy." Fat Man stretched his equally fat finger within inches of Grumbler's face.

Some dude on the other side of Grumble chimed in with, "Show Fat Man those chops of your'n."

I cranked my head, just in time to see Mandy wallop Grumbler with her sack of worldly possessions.

"Don't you be talking in the negative about Jonesy," she yelled while continuing her assault on him. "He's as good a man as you'll ever find here or anywhere."

Grumbler threw his hands over his head while everyone at the table stopped eating and did nothing but stare, obviously enjoying the whole dominatrix scene between Grumbler and Mandy. I expected the cheering to start any minute. Interrupting a funfest was not my bag, especially when it involved entertaining the troops but this made no sense, which explained it happening at B & B.

Enough with the blood-letting, damn. I got up and separated the bitch from her worldly weapon. Mandy turned into a banshee, screaming as she came at me with a show of ten dirty claws. I wrestled her to the floor, but held back from pressing my thumbs into her throat. A set of polished shoes appeared in my peripheral vision, at which point I released her from my grip. She rolled onto her belly and licked the shiny shoes, which I realized belonged to none other than Preacher Dave. From behind I felt a pair of hands, twisting the neck of my tee before bringing me to my feet. Beefsteak showing how he earned his keep in a Christian manner—thanks for stretching my tee into a piece of crap.

While he had me in this puppet hold, Mandy made her usual feline recovery, by-passing the knees to an immediate landing on her feet. She belted out a sweet Jesus hymn while Preacher Dave wagged his finger in my face, showing me this nice pinkie ring, onyx and gold, with the stone turned inward so as not to attract the attention of his less fortunate subjects.

"Under no circumstances do we condone violence here at Bed and Bread," he said. "Especially despicable when it involves members of the opposite sex."

"Should I call the authorities?" Beefsteak asked, his fingers tightening the t-shirt knot.

"You got this all wrong," I tried to explain. "I stopped her from pounding on this guy." I reached over, put my hand on Grumbler's shoulder. "Right, Grumbler?"

"Lay off," he told me. "I'm here for the food and the prayers, nothing else."

"Liar, liar, pants on fire," Mandy yelled as she danced around me. "Your eyes tell me all I need to know. You're part of Satan's brigade. I knowed it from the minute you waltzed in here, so high and mighty."

Somebody say something. Zero, all I heard were the ravenous sounds of wolfing down food. Beefsteak released his grip on me and Preacher Dave backed away, as if there might've been some truth in Mandy's words.

"As much as this pains me, young man, I must insist you collect your belongings and leave immediately. You're no longer welcome here."

"What about the breakfast I didn't get to eat?" I exchanged glances with Preacher Dave and then fixed my gaze on the empty plate where I'd been sitting.

"Here at Bed and Bread we are not without compassion," he said. "After you leave, stop by the alley entrance. Cook will take care of you."

"Premium or standard fare?" Beefsteak asked.

"Given the young man's propensity for violence, standard fare seems more fitting."

***

Life, it couldn't get much worse when not even the homeless shelter wanted a guy like me. At least The Bish hadn't been there to witness my humiliation, to decide at that moment he wanted no part of me. Ten minutes later found me back on the street, more like the far side of the park, warming a bench while trying to not piss my pants over B & B's parting gift, a brown bag consisting of one apple, a carton of orangeade, and a peanut butter and grape jelly sandwich, none of which appealed to me, but when a guy's hungry anything will do. After finishing the standard get-the-hell-out-of-here meal, I stuffed yesterday's dirty underwear into the paper sack and with a single shot, deep-sixed it into the nearest trash can. The plastic-bagged toiletries I divided between my pockets and then leaned my head back and sucked up the sun's rays while trying to strategize my next move. At that point I drew nothing but blanks, a temporary setback waiting for me to resolve. Nothing, but nothing, would stop me from my paternal quest. I just needed an opportunity to push the right buttons. After another dry spell, the park bench talked to me with a slight bounce, announcing in the worst way another smelling dude sitting beside me. I opened one eye to the shitty nobody, a betrayer of lost causes—Grumbler.

"I wanna thank you, kid," he said, hands grasped between his legs, eyes on the skimpy patch of grass below. "You know, sticking up for me this morning."

"Too bad you didn't return the favor." I leaned over, shot spit into the dirt, and married the two with the bottom of my shoe.

Grumbler lifted his head and with an Honest Abe look, linked our eyes. "You're pissing in the wind, kid. It was me and Mandy and the gang what did you the favor. We set you up, for what you did for Jonesy. And you took the bite—hook, line, and sinker."

Like hell, get out of my face with your bullshit. "Yeah, well, you'll have to excuse me for not kissing your ass with gratitude."

"A kid like you, come on. Hanging out at Bed and Bread, or any other shelter, no matter how plentiful the food. You got the chops to play with the big boys, and real soon. Just you wait and see."

This I already knew. Did I look that pathetic? "Thanks for the pep talk. You'd better mosey back to your friends now."

"Not so fast, I ain't done yet. There's one more thing for Jonesy." He dug into his pants pocket, pulled out a paperback, and handed it to me. "He needs this, right away, I mean this very day, whilst he's bedded in the hospital but still has his wits about him."

The book was a Louis L'Amour western. Having read three or four of his and considering myself a fan, I opened it up. Taped to the inside back cover was a two-inch square packet, its contents anybody's guess.

"Pills," Grumbler said.

"What the shit for? Jonesy doesn't need these in the hospital."

Grumbler cocked his head, rolled his eyes. "Yeah, he does. He left them in my care. They're his safety net, in case last night didn't go as planned, which it didn't, thanks to you."

"So you're telling me Jonesy wants to die."

"Real bad," Grumbler said. "Those butchers at the VA, they want to dismantle him, starting with the foot and ankle. Pretty soon it'll be the other foot. From there, they'll keep working their way up his legs. He'll never know freedom again."

"Instead he'd rather die."

"Well ... yeah. So, you'll do this for him?"

"Sorry, I'm not interested."

"He's gonna die anyway. Let him pick the time. The place he already likes, clean white sheets and all. From there, he'll get a decent burial at Jefferson Barracks."

"Why me, I just met Jonesy."

"That's the beauty of it, no ties. Just deliver the book, is that asking too much? He'll take care of the rest."

"The guy's in a hospital, for godssake. He'll never pull it off."

"That ain't your problem." He shoved a note in my hand. "Here's the address and his room number."

I said nothing but opened the scrap of paper—big mistake because Grumbler took this as my acceptance.

"Thanks and don't you worry none about Mandy sending a curse your way," he said. "She saw in you what the rest of us didn't catch right off." He pushed himself upright and shuffled away.

I'd been had, but maybe in a good way. Decisions, decisions, what to do next: collect my belongings from the bus station or make the hospital delivery—fifteen minutes in the opposite direction, by bus and me not much of a rider. I fed the crumbs left over from my p and j to the waiting pigeons, all the while trying to ignore a horn beeping from the street. It beeped some more, annoying me to where I finally looked in the direction of an SUV parked curbside, its emergency lights blinking, and passenger window rolled down. I couldn't make out the driver's face but noticed he wore a hat on the order of Indiana Jones's.

He leaned over the shotgun seat and yelled, "Hey, Danner, bring your ass over here."

I took my time crossing the park but not until I stood alongside the vehicle did I realize who'd barked the order.

"You're still interested in working?" asked The Bish, his Indiana Jones hat too full-of-himself for the B & B persona.

"Yeah, I could use the money but not if it involves sweeping floors or cleaning toilets."

"Neither, but the job does involve a fair amount of traveling."

"Traveling I can handle. Of course it depends on where to."

"Here and there and maybe there but mainly out west, more to the point, Las Vegas."

If it sounded too good to be true, it probably was: that's what Jed and Dolores used to tell me, as if they'd been first to pass that gem along. Still, I couldn't help but drool over the idea of crashing Vegas. This could've been my big break, the opportunity to showcase any unrecognized potential.

"So, what do you think?" he asked.

"I might be interested."

"Mildly or otherwise?"

"Cut the bullshit," I said with a grin. "Where do I apply?"

"Right here." He stuck his hand out the window for me to shake. "Congratulations, you're hired."

"Just like that? When are we leaving?"

"Right now, last night I submitted my final adios to the shelter."

I surprised myself by having the balls to object. "There is one thing: if you're a smoker, I might have to reconsider."

"Gave up the suckers last year when I started coughing my guts out. Now are you with me or not?"

"Look out Vegas, here we come." I opened the door and started to get in when The Bish stopped me cold.

"Hold on," he said. "Aren't you forgetting something?"

"Nope, my stuff's downtown, if you don't mind stopping by the bus station."

"Later." He jerked his head toward the park. "I meant your book; you forgot it on the bench."

Forgot, I didn't think so. "It's not mine."

"Get the book, Danner. I'm not in that big a hurry."

Chapter 12

Way to go, Bish. He'd known all along about the mission of mercy, which made me wonder why he didn't deliver the damn book himself. Since we were already on our way to the hospital there didn't seem much point in arguing over which one of us would make the delivery. When we stopped for the red light on Twelfth Street, I opened up a different can of worms, one that had been bothering me ever since we met.

"Your name, The Bishop, it seems kind of formal, all things considered. Would you mind if I call you Bish?"

Tapping a forefinger on the steering wheel, he rolled the shortcut around in his mouth. "Bish … Bish … Bish … hmm. Yes, Bish will do just fine. And to level out the playing field, I'll call you Danner."

That he'd already done and without my okay so I asked, "What's wrong with Free?"

"It lacks upward mobility. You're practically grown-up; you need a grown-up name."

Yeah, right, at least my name showed the real me, now but not always. I decided to play along. "I'd like to try out Danner first, see how it fits."

"Whatever you say."

"If I don't like the fit, it's back to Free."

He pulled away from the light, beating out the car to his left. "Trust me, you're never going back."

"Samuel Dean Lawford, now there's a mouthful. How'd you come by it?"

"Long story short, my mother worked the Vegas strip. She was personally acquainted with everyone in the Rat Pack."

"The Rat Pack, never heard of them. They're an old time singing group or what?"

"Kid, you are young."

"Make up my mind. Before the light changed, I was grown-up, too old to be called Free."

Bish pulled a pack of cigarettes from his shirt pocket, tapped out one, and stuck it between his lips but didn't light up. "Old habits are hard to break," he said, turning onto Grand Boulevard.

"Tell me about it. Just so we're straight, I'm Danner and a Danner, same as my mom."

"Right, Emily Danner, a party girl I hardly knew."

"Not according to her. She said you beat the hell out of her."

He slammed on the brakes, nearly whiplashing my head. "She said what? I never hit Emily, not once, ever."

"So you do remember her."

"Like my worst case of poison ivy. End of discussion, today or any other day." He crushed his smokeless cig into the ashtray, reached for another, and pressed his foot to the metal. We went forward with a jerky motion. "Keep hammering me about Emily and you'll find yourself stuck at the V.A. with Jonesy."

"Speaking of Jonesy, you must know him pretty well and since I just met him, why don't you—"

"No, this is your assignment, one Jonesy and I expect you to carry out with the dignity and compassion appropriate for a Viet Nam vet such as him." Bish stopped along one side of the hospital and motioned me out.

"Didn't you see the sign?" I said. "There's a parking lot nearby."

"I prefer the street. Now make your delivery."

Jeez. I shoved the damn book inside my shirt, got out of the damn vehicle, and didn't bother telling the damn Bish goodbye. Nor did I stop at the damn reception desk where the clerk had her nose in the computer. Instead I hopped the nearest elevator, exited at Jonesy's floor and again without being noticed, followed the number signs, as if I'd made this route ten times before.

The room was a two-bed deal, one unoccupied and the other with an old guy propped up, an I.V. attached to his arm and wires monitoring his vitals. I dropped the book on the empty bed and said, "Delivery for Jones Alexander the Fourth."

"Not there, dimwit, over here."

"Jonesy?"

"Hell, yes. Who'd you think?"

I walked over and handed off the book to this guy I no longer recognized—clean-shaven and, well … clean. His head was wrapped in a plastic cap, the kind surgeons wear, in Jonesy's case maybe to contain any critters that hadn't bitten the dust. His eyes were roadmap bloodshot, as if he'd been on an all-night binge and his skin was casting an odd color I hadn't noticed during our short time together.

"Looking good," I told him.

"Lying bad," he told me. He flipped to the back of the book, scratched his fingers on the inside cover for a minute or so but couldn't release the packet. Disgusted, he half-tossed the book in my direction.

"Make it snappy," he said, "afore one of those nosy nurses comes a-strutting in."

I pulled the packet away from the cover, only then realizing what Grumbler had described as pills were two single-edged razor blades, which made more sense than Jonesy trying to O.D. while hooked up to a hospital monitor.

Wiped out from the minor exertion, he leaned back on the tilted mattress. "Wrap 'em in that paper napkin. Then pour me some water."

I did as he said, placed the package in his bedside table, and tapped the drawer. "One hand away whenever you decide on the close shave."

"Which won't be much longer, god willing. They scheduled me for surgery within the next day or so. Soon as the paperwork's in order, but with the red tape you just never know."

"Are you sure about this?" I asked. "It's not like they're holding you prisoner. Just check yourself out."

"And go where. Bed and Bread won't take me back with this damn gangrene chewing up what's left of my toes. All's I got are my friends there."

"And Mandy, she's your wife."

"Get real. She can't take care of me no more'n I can myself." He turned his head, stared at the wall. "The book's yours to keep. I already read it."

As if I could, with this day stuck in my memory. "You don't have to do this, Jonesy, you being a soldier who's probably seen worse than … than this."

"What do you know about life and death? You're nothing but a snot-nosed kid. Now pour the water and hit the road afore the nurse sees you."

I filled the plastic glass but let it sit on the utility table pulled up to his bed. "Maybe there's somebody you want me to call?" I asked.

The look on his face told me the question was stupid but he answered it anyway. "Not a living soul. I got my goodbyes in order, my will too. Did you see the flowers?"

They were sitting on the bedside table; I checked out the card. "Nice, from Bed and Bread. Preacher Dave led some prayers for your recovery."

"Ain't gonna happen, no way no how, he knows, they all know. Now remove yourself from my room. And don't forget the book."

He didn't have to tell me twice. I headed for the door but didn't get there quick enough.

"No, wait a minute," he said. "Hand me the blades. I want them close by."

"They're right next to you."

"Dammit, don't make me ask again."

I went back, opened the drawer, and showed him the folded napkin. "See, whenever you're ready."

"I don't want the napkin. Get rid of it."

"You want the blades loose in the drawer?"

"Afraid I might cut myself?"

"Okay, okay." I let the blades fall into the drawer and stuffed the napkin in my back pocket.

"I'm ready," he said. "Give 'em to me now."

"No, and don't ask me to help either. This is all wrong."

"It ain't for you to decide."

"Just hear me out. Slicing your wrists will never work, not with you hooked up to the monitor. It sends news flashes to the nurses down the hall, and once they see your vitals acting up, all hell will break out. Nurse Betty to the rescue before you have a chance to bleed out."

"Give me some credit. I'm going straight for the jugular. It'll be over afore Bossy Betty runs her sweet ass down here. Now gimme the blades—on second thought, blade. One's all I need."

"Plus a strong and steady hand, which you don't have and I'm not lending mine. You're going to blow this, make things worse for yourself." I had to think fast and came up with what I thought would be convincing. "The same thing happened to this guy I once knew. The razor didn't cut deep enough so all he got for his effort was a trip to the loony bin and a thin scar nobody noticed after the first week. Going for the jugular requires absolute determination."

"Which I have."

"And a sharp, strong tool, which again you don't."

He pressed two fingers to each temple and thought a minute. "Wait, don't go yet. I feel a thirst coming on."

I handed him the water. He drank half, emptied the rest on the floor, and pitched the plastic ware into the wastebasket.

"Not bad for an old guy, huh? Now, pass me the daisies." I handed him the vase. He sniffed, made a face. "I can't smell them."

"Neither can I. There's nothing wrong with your nose."

"Watch this." He took out the flowers, scattered them over his bed, and emptied the water onto the floor. The vase he slammed against his utility table, shattering the glass into pointed shards. "See, I don't need you or the damn blades after all."

Right, Jonesy. My hand shook when I pulled the napkin out of my pocket. "What about this?"

"Good idea, so's not to deter my determined fingers. You're free to go, Free, and thanks for stopping by."

This time there was no turning back but I did hesitate at the door. "So long, Jonesy."

"See you in the next life."

"Nah, I don't think so."

Chapter 13

As soon as Jed stopped bouncing the truck, I opened my eyes. We were back at the prison he called a farm and Rusty was running in circles, waiting for me to hop out. Naturally, Delores had other ideas; she couldn't stand seeing me idle for more than a few minutes.

"No playing with the dog, young man. Not until you give me a hand with these packages."

Damn, how'd she and Jed manage to get anything done before they had me as their slave? I carried her precious packages to the kitchen, and put everything away while she went to work squeezing a bunch of lemons for Jed's favorite cold drink. The old girl lived to please Jed. He lived to make my life miserable. And I lived for the day Lark would take me back.

Delores added just enough sugar to the lemonade, poured some in a small glass, and finished it off in one gulp. She was smacking her lips when I asked in my good-boy voice, "Is it okay if I go out now?"

"Why, of course, Johnny." Just like that she turned candy sweet. "About supper," she said, "would you rather have macaroni and cheese or chili dogs?"

"If it's not too much trouble, could I have both with three-bean salad?" I gave her the answer she wanted to hear. With any luck, she'd slice peaches and whip up her kind of cream which almost tasted as good as what came out of a can.

At last I escaped into the sun and played with Rusty, chasing each other dog crazy until we both collapsed in a heap. I put my head on his chest, leaned over, and listened to the steady beat of a heart filled with love. "It's just you and me, boy," I said, stroking his hair. "The two of us make a great team, don't we? Just like Mario and Luigi, we could conquer not one world but all six of them."

Rusty lifted his head, swiped my face with the velvety tongue I'd decided wasn't half bad. Never had I felt such love, not even when I was with Lark. I could've stayed there another hour but Delores started yelling about supper being ready. When she hollered, "*Now*, Johnny," I rolled to my feet and trotted toward the house. Rusty barked once and I turned to see him wagging his tail.

What more could any guy want, except Super Mario. And maybe the love of a half-way decent mom.

***

That night in my hotter-n-hell room I dreamed about Lark starring as the captive princess in Game Boy. I'd killed Bowser and was about to rescue her when a loud screeching pulled me away from my mission. I flipped onto my stomach, hoping to return to the castle and impress Lark. Then Rusty started barking, for real. Good old Rusty, he'd chase those outside demons away. But the screeching and barking didn't stop, even though the porch light came on and lit up the backyard. My bedroom too, along with weird shadows that creeped me out. I heard the kitchen screen door bang shut and decided not to wait any longer. I stepped into my shoes and headed toward the stairs. On the top step I tripped over the laces I hadn't tied and came crashing down into the kitchen, unlike my first day this time for real. Hunched over the table was Delores, wearing this crummy bathrobe she called her woobie and looking older than I'd ever noticed before.

"Don't go out there, Johnny. Jed can handle this without any help from you."

"Yeah, but Rusty might need me," I said, my words drowned out by all the screeching and yelping outside.

I ran out the door and followed noise that took me across the moonlit yard to the chicken coop. I skidded to a stop on seeing two shadowy figures. One was Rusty, teeth bared and going against the enemy: a wild cat—bigger, meaner, and deadlier as it ripped through Rusty's fine coat. I saw Jed too, raise his gun and fire one shot. One final screech ended the fight, luckily in our favor. Maybe Jed wasn't so bad after all, kind of like Super Mario defending the underdog. I passed the dead cougar on my way to Rusty. Blood seeped from my poor dog's wounds. I almost threw up on seeing his guts hanging out but that would've been an insult to our friendship. He was weak but managed to wag his tail when I patted his head.

"Careful, Johnny," Jed said in a low voice. "He's in shock and could bite you."

"Not Rusty, he loves me. Can we take him to the vet now?"

"It wouldn't change the inevitable." Jed cocked his shotgun. "I have no choice but to put him down."

I felt a hand on my shoulder, looked up to see the creepy Angel of Death in the form of Delores. "Let's go, Johnny."

"No! That's not fair." I pulled away and stepped back. "What's important to me, Jed always takes away."

"What he's about to do is considered an act of mercy, Johnny. You wouldn't want the poor creature suffering, now would you?"

I walked away, not with Delores but ahead of her, and didn't stop when I heard the shotgun blast that put my only friend out of his misery.

Chapter 14

Okay, so Bish hadn't deserted me. He was right where I'd left him, behind the wheel in a no parking zone, hat pulled down to shade his face. The motor was running and windows were rolled down, letting in hot air rather than sucking up the air conditioner, which told me he expected I'd be hung up for a good while. I slid onto the passenger seat and closed the door. He eased away from the curb and put the hospital behind us.

"You made the delivery?" he asked, pushing his hat back to where it belonged.

"As promised."

"And Jonesy?"

"Waiting for the nurse."

"Anything else?"

"Yeah, he told me to keep the book, that he didn't need it after all." I threw the damn think down on the space between us. "Next time, do your own dirty work."

"What's that supposed to mean?"

"It means I'm no fool and don't ever take me for one again or I'll show you a side of me you didn't think possible in the short time we've known each other. Now, unless you want to renege on our deal, I'd like to collect my belongings from the bus station."

I'd put Bish in his place and he knew it, which gave me the upper hand at least temporarily and maybe longer. Neither of us spoke on the ride downtown. He parked at a meter with time left on it and I went inside the depot to collect my gear from the locker. When I returned, he opened the back end by remote and I deposited my second-hand bags alongside designer luggage too nice for a guy working the homeless shelter. It occurred to me I knew nothing about Samuel Dean Lawford, other than in his former life he'd played around with Emily Danner and maybe helped create a kid neither of them wanted. Still, I climbed into the front seat again and banged the dashboard, as if to say 'Go.'

"We'll take the Denver route," Bish said. "I've never seen the wheat fields of Kansas."

"The wheat fields, aren't they kind of boring?"

No answer could've meant anything—yes, no, go to Hell. I let it go.

Bish merged into the traffic and soon picked up the Interstate 70 ramp. After passing the north side's old brick warehouses and industrial buildings, we moved away from the river and headed west. I could've made small talk about the city, and how Lark lived at the other end, but decided to let him stew over the veiled threat I'd made earlier. After a while he regurgitated two words I wasn't in the mood to hear.

"About Jonesy."

"Can we talk about something more uplifting, as in when and where we eat and how much you're popping for. I'm running on empty, except for a lousy peanut butter and jelly sandwich this morning. Oh yeah, I almost forgot—a mealy apple and some fake o.j. too."

"No problem, we'll stop after we cross the Missouri." He seemed to relax, and why not. He wasn't the one who helped a disabled vet off himself. "So what kind of food do you like?"

"Anything but organ meat or whatever you can afford. By the way, how much does this job pay and what am I supposed to do to earn it?"

"It pays one hundred a week plus expenses."

Cripes, I almost told him to pull over and let me out. "A hundred a week, what do you take me for? That's less than minimum wage."

"But more than you were making when we met three days ago. Did I mention the perks and bonuses?"

"Not that I recall. Actually, no, you didn't."

"First, your duties," he said. "For starters, I expect you to drive most of the time."

"That I can handle but not before we eat. I'm starving."

"So you told me already. There's a nice place in the St. Charles historic area, good food and—"

"Whatever. Just wake me when we get there. I didn't sleep so good last night." I slumped down in the seat and gave my lids a much needed rest. I could hear Bish fiddling with the dashboard buttons and soon got an earful of his music—my guess, Elton John. Not what I would've picked but what the hell, he was in the driver's seat. I'd already decided things would change when I set my sweet ass behind the wheel, in more ways than just the music.

Change in plans. Lunch wound up at a casino on the Missouri's riverfront, in a restaurant filled with pensioners who, according to one matching sweat-suit couple in the buffet line, preferred giving their money to the slots instead of grandchildren who hadn't learned the value of saying 'thank you.' Bish and I parked ourselves in a booth with cushioned seats. He picked at his food, moving it around the plate while I chowed down as if there was no tomorrow.

"You'll have to excuse me," Bish said, pushing aside his half-filled plate. "I have urgent business to take care of, but it shouldn't take long."

He disappeared, I figured to the john although we'd both pissed on our way in. What the hell, I figured. No point in wasting food he'd paid in advance for me to eat so I went back for a clean plate and filled it with a ton of seafood I hadn't bothered picking up the first go around. I relished each bite and then moved on to the dessert section. During my second round of desserts Bish showed up with a cup of coffee. He slid into the booth and glanced at his watch, a pricey one I hadn't noticed him wearing at the shelter, which made perfect sense considering the hypocritical factor of embracing poverty.

"Nice timepiece," I couldn't resist saying.

He glanced at it again. "Thanks."

"Are we running on a certain timetable?"

"Not exactly, though I would like to make the other side of Salina before dark."

I shoveled the last bite of pecan pie in my mouth and spoke before swallowing, just because. "You're talking Kansas, right?"

"Give the boy an A in Geography, an F in table manners."

I swallowed before apologizing. Jeez, it was déjà vu all over again, Delores without the Orphan Annie hairdo. I wanted to bust him but couldn't pass up the Vegas op. "With me driving, we can go even further."

"Salina works for me," he said. "Besides, I thought you needed your beauty sleep."

"The food woke me up, which by the way, thanks. I didn't expect such a spread."

"Just wait until you see Las Vegas."

By now I'd moved on to the cherry cobbler but didn't speak until I'd emptied my mouth. "Are you a gambler or something?"

"Both."

Bingo, I should've caught on before now. "So you were rolling the dice while I stuffed my face."

Instead of making a smart-ass comment, he stood up. I followed his lead, unsure of where it would take me, which pretty much explained my life until that moment. Wherever I went, trouble always dogged me, even when I did my best to avoid it.

My turn to drive, I adjusted the seat and mirrors, said a quick prayer to St. Anthony, a longer prayer to Sweet Jesus on behalf of Alexander Jones the Fourth, and hoped one more ghost wouldn't dog me all the way to Hell. Back on the highway after whizzing past the last of St. Louis's sprawling suburbs, we entered Missouri's countryside with Bish fighting to keep his eyes open. I held the speedometer to seventy but as soon as he started sawing logs, I let it waver between eighty-five and ninety. What a feeling, King of the Road, a first for me. Except for the hours it had taken to qualify for a driver's license, this trip would be the most time I'd spent behind a wheel. I glanced over to Bish, tried to imagine our being related. Nothing clicked, but at this point, I didn't care. Never had I felt so free, even when it was the only name identifying me.

An hour later at Kingdom City, Bish straightened up and turned his head to my side of the dashboard. "If a cop pulls us over, whatever the fine, it comes out of your paycheck."

"You wanted to make Salina."

"In one piece and without incident so make me happy."

I dropped down to the speed limit and changed the subject. "What about the Rat Pack."

"Ever hear of Frank Sinatra?"

"Who hasn't."

"Sammy Davis, Jr.?"

"Maybe … the black dude."

"Singer, dancer, actor, you name it; he did it better than anyone else. Sammy and Frank plus Dean Martin, Peter Lawford, and Joey Bishop made up the Rat Pack. A bunch of hip entertainers who hung out together and decided Las Vegas should pay them for what they'd been doing for free."

"Wait a minute—Samuel Dean Lawford, that's how you got your name?"

"Close enough, at least for this discussion. The Bishop was a fluke that came later."

"What about Sinatra?"

"Francis was my confirmation name."

"You're Catholic?"

"You have a problem with that?"

"Not unless you do."

Other than the close-enough origin of his name, I learned nothing about Bish while we traveled through the rest of Missouri. When he was alert and the satellite towers were transmitting in our range, he made phone calls from his cell, responding in a low monotone with one or two-word answers that made no sense to me without knowing the questions from the other end.

"You must have a lot of friends," I said in between calls.

"More like business associates."

"In Vegas?"

"And elsewhere. How's the gas holding up?"

Like clockwork, a beeper signaled 'nearing empty.' I took the next exit, pulled into a service station, and filled up with Bish's credit card while he checked out the convenience store. Later, I found him in the john, standing in front of the urinal. I positioned myself at the next station and whizzed a long and satisfying stream, waiting for his to match mine. I'd already zipped up before he finally released a sorry excuse of pinkish red. Blood, just what I needed. Damn, damn, and more damn.

"Maybe you should get that checked," I said although doctors are not my bag.

"Maybe you should mind your own business."

"No problem but just remember this: I didn't hire on to be nobody's nursemaid."

He should've given me some reassurance but countered with, "Be sure to wash your hands. I don't tolerate other people's germs too well."

"Same goes for me and don't you forget it."

Back in the store Bish loaded up with candy bars and snacks while I drew two large coffees-to-go, all of which he paid for at the checkout. By the time we'd hit the Interstate again the sun had lowered into dusk and Bish was fighting sleep again.

"Does this mean we won't for supper?" I asked.

"Nothing for me but if you must, make it 'to-go.'"

"Never mind, can we talk about my mother instead, just your general impression of her. Not about the two of you."

He sighed but straightened up. "Hell, it was ions ago."

"But you do remember her."

"Better than yesterday." He went quiet, seemed to be gathering his thoughts, those he wanted to share. "She was wafer-thin and exuded an air of innocence, that is, until she opened her mouth and released this unholy mix of sweet and sour sarcasm. As soon as someone challenged her, she'd switch to her vulnerable mode."

"Sounds familiar, she's toughened up now, put on a few pounds but still acts like the hottie she still is—not that it matters to me, her son."

"Emily with a kid, it's hard for me to imagine."

"Her too, she sent me away when I was eleven."

"Any regrets?"

"A few but none I care discussing. Anything else you recall … boyfriends, girlfriends."

"You really want to know? How's this, she was the epitome of a bitch in heat, with all the studs wanting to mount her. She enjoyed the attention and probably broke a few hearts."

"Including yours?" I wanted to rip it out, along with his smartass mouth. "Sorry, I agreed not to go there."

He slid down in the seat, tipped his hat forward, and said, "Wake me before the first Salina exit. I'll pick the motel."

Chapter 15

That night of the wildcat I lost the best friend I ever had, including Lark which isn't saying much. After Delores followed me back to the kitchen, she slid a pan onto the stove, fired up the gas, and tried to bribe my affection with this crap: "Sit, Johnny. Graham crackers and a glass of warm buttermilk should help you sleep."

Crackers and milk, all Delores could think about was comfort food. After her husband executed Rusty, give me a break. What did she take me for, a heartless jerk? I shook my head and dragged myself upstairs, all the while knowing morning would bring a hurt ten times worse than the one I now felt. I crawled under the bedcovers and must've slept because I didn't hear the rooster crowing, Jed's idea of a can't-fail alarm clock. Hours later after the sun messed with my sleep, I went to the window and forced myself to look outside. There at the farthest end of the back yard was a pile of fresh dirt where Jed had buried Rusty. No goodbyes, no last words, nothing.

Life goes on, that's what Jed said, which meant I still had to help the old man do chores. On the day of Rusty's non-funeral we worked in silence, ate in silence, and went back to work for two more hours before Jed excused me. We followed the same routine for weeks while Delores walked on eggs, afraid she might break me before Jed had the pleasure of doing it himself. Then one Saturday morning he cleared his throat and handed Super Mario to me.

"Maybe this will help, Johnny."

Thanks for nothing. I slipped the game in my pocket and that afternoon I sat under a tree near Rusty's grave and played for hours.

The next day Delores fried chicken and mashed potatoes for dinner, which usually meant she was buttering me up for another letdown. I braced myself for the worst when she brought out apple pie and ice cream. Two scoops over a gigantic piece of pie went to Jed, who always got firsties. Mine came next, a size smaller and easy on the ice cream. Then, Delores: pie only. She always left the crust, too many calories. After two quick bites, she set her fork down and hit me with this.

"We've been thinking, Jed and I, that maybe you need to get away, a change of scenery."

My heart banged against my chest. I almost pissed my pants but didn't make a big deal out of it when I asked, "Lark's ready to take me back?"

Delores's upper lip started to twitch. "That's neither here nor there. What Jed and I had in mind was taking a family vacation."

"What would you say to Branson, Missouri?" This came from Jed who didn't approve of having fun, especially when it involved money from his pocket. "That theme park, what's it called?"

"Silver Dollar City, I know some kids who went there." Could this be real? I pictured me eating my kind of food—hot dogs, French fries, cheeseburgers—and spinning on rides 'til the place closed for the day. I cracked my first smile since losing Rusty. "How soon can we leave?"

Jed swallowed the last of his pie before speaking, anything to make me wait. "Not 'til November, after the harvest."

Clunk went my heart.

"The harvest, no way. By then I'll be back in St. Louis, making my mark in junior high. Wait a minute, are you telling me ...."

"There's a fine school down the road," Jed said. "Taking you out for a few days in November won't be a problem."

Delores threw in her two cents; she always did. "That is, as long as your grades are more than satisfactory."

I knew it; I knew it. The best things in life always come with a price. This one came higher than I ever thought possible.

.

Chapter 16

Damn Bish, waking me up with the worst hacking I ever heard in my entire life. It started with a disturbing gurgle deep in his chest, then clawed upward to his throat before making a disgusting exit out his mouth. Repeat, again and again. A crappy infliction such as this did not belong in the company of civilized people, especially yours truly. Sick people most definitely not my bag, which I thought I had made clear when signing on with him.

And another thing: I should never have agreed to our sharing the same room even though he'd insisted on separate beds after the desk clerk had winked a 'sorry-no-can-do.' As for sharing the same genes with Bish, I'd pretty much ruled this out because there was nothing about his physical makeup I cared about inheriting for myself. On the other hand, his money and worldly possessions were distinct possibilities, as soon as I could figure out their bottom line. Bish hacked again, and then again, finally bringing up enough shit to ruin any chance of my eating breakfast in the immediate future. Some nerve, him criticizing my table manners back at the casino. I'd get him for that, some day but not this one.

"What the hell," I said after the coughing had quieted to a few spasms. "Since we're both awake, you want to hit the road now?"

He answered by flipping on the TV and scooting his back against the headboard, my cue to head for the bathroom so I wouldn't be subjected to his next spell.

Thirty minutes later with the sun to our rear and me behind the wheel, we pushed further west. Bish spoke his first words without the obscene hacking. "Sorry about the episode back there."

"Maybe we should think about separate rooms tonight, that is, if you can afford it." I wanted to hear him say money wasn't a problem but heard another hack instead, this one requiring a shitload of cheesy motel tissues to catch whatever his chest couldn't handle anymore.

"Don't let this bother you," he said into the tissues. "It's just a touch of emphysema that comes and goes."

Yeah, right. After it went, he straightened up and spoke with a clear throat. "I'm ready for some coffee and a decent breakfast. Take the next exit with a town nearby. The business district ought to have a restaurant or two."

"What's wrong with one of the chains off the Interstate?"

"Too ho-hum, I prefer the local eateries."

I gave him what he wanted: a folksy diner five miles down the road, where assorted locals whose clothing ranged from bib overalls to dress shirts with rolled-up sleeves had positioned themselves around the most prominent table, front and center. Whatever they were discussing—Bish figured politics and the price of wheat—petered into silence so they could focus on him and me, strangers invading their territory. Aliens, that's how they viewed us. I could see it in their faces. Me, yes; Bish, maybe so, maybe not, on him the verdict was still out. As we made our way to the only vacant table, he asked a passing waitress for water and two coffees.

"With or without?" she asked without the smile saved for customers she already knew.

"Regular without," I answered. The expression on Bish's face jump-started my day. I'd showed him another side of me, one comfortable speaking for both of us.

The waitress still hadn't cracked a smile when she brought the liquids or when she left with our order for the day's special—sunny-side-up eggs, sausage, cottage fries, and biscuits with gravy. Bish swallowed a handful of pills with his water and I braced myself for the next hack attack, which mercifully did not occur in the presence of others and make me his personal butt-boy. Our food arrived just the way I like it, steaming hot and with a bottle of catsup neither of us had requested, making our not-so-friendly waitress okay in my book. We ate like pigs and with every right. Except for snacks the evening before, we hadn't made contact with real food since the casino buffet Bish barely touched.

"A very satisfying meal," he said, mopping up the last of his eggs with a side order of toast, whole wheat no butter. He lifted his brow, waited for me to agree. "What say you?"

"Yeah, sure," was all I gave him, figuring my empty plate filled in the blanks, those words I didn't feel up to saying. In truth, the breakfast reminded me of what Delores used to make, and I was in no mood to ruin my day by going there.

After Bish paid the bill, we left. Just for kicks I cruised down Main Street USA where the stores hadn't come to life yet and only a handful of people were walking the sidewalks. Then through a residential area, nothing fancy but solid mid-America. Too tame for me, a guy intent on going places. On the edge of town where the houses were spread out to meet the wheat fields about to take over, I picked up speed, only to slow back down on seeing two people up ahead, running alongside the highway. The woman was blonde and barefoot. She wore a flimsy nightgown that showed every crease and curve. Following on her heels was this my-size but older, a jeans and t-shirt guy who kept lashing a long switch of wheat against her legs. All of a sudden they shot across the highway, making me brake to keep from picking them off. The dozing Bish now came to life with a jolt.

"What the hell," he said, leaning forward.

"Dude's beating the hell out of her, that's what."

They disappeared into the wheat and I pressed on the accelerator with every intention of putting the ugly scene behind us. After we'd gone a hundred feet, Bish found his voice, and said, "I suppose we should do something."

Yeah, him the gentle counselor for Bed and Bread, or me, the troubleshooter Preacher Dave had expelled. Just what I didn't need: a fistful of trouble. Still, duty called. I braked again, backed up the hundred feet, a first for me, and then sent us forward, cutting across the field in hot pursuit. Picking up speed, I plowed alongside the rippling wheat, giving the runners plenty of space. Bish braced his hand against the dashboard, so tight his knuckles turned white.

"Careful with the vehicle," he said. "I expect it to last me."

And me, leastways 'til we hit Vegas. I swung into a tight arc, slammed on the brakes, and offed the ignition before hopping out. Bish hesitated but only for a few seconds. We ran back to where the wheat had quit rippling and found the blonde splayed over a fallen stalk. The guy was leaning over her, his switch ready to strike while he yelled something about her cheating on him for the last time. He didn't even know we were behind him until I grabbed the switch and gave him what he was about to give her. Wailing on him felt so good I couldn't make myself stop even when his arms turned into strips of bloody ribbons, his t-shirt too. After a while he crumbled to the ground like a wad of Bish's used tissues. Blondie went bonkers, screaming as much for him as for herself. She rolled off the stalk and staggered to her feet.

After that I lost sight of her and then lost myself to a sharp pain in the back of my head, so unexpected I didn't know what to make of this goofy sensation that took over, carrying me to what I imagined as the limbo preceding death. Or maybe an ambulance transporting me to the nearest hospital in the boonies, or, considering my luck, the county morgue. Sweet Jesus, what a way to go, without getting paid or completing my paternal mission. My mission … what was it, I couldn't remember.

The so-called ambulance rolled to a stop, and just in time since my throbbing head could not have taken one more bump in the unpredictable road. Given the extent of my pain, no way could I have been dead, although it wouldn't have taken much for me to slip in that direction—straight to Hell would've been my guess since I didn't qualify for the pearly gates of St. Peter. Or wait a minute, was that good ol' St. Pete I heard calling my name.

"Wake up Danner, wake up. I hired you to drive, not sleep the day away."

My head, ouch, way too heavy to lift so I settled for cracking one eyelid to Samuel Dean Lawford, Grand Poo-Paw of the disadvantaged, sitting behind the driver's seat where I should've been instead of moaning in the back like a sore loser. It took all my energy to ask, "What happened?"

"Man, woman, wheat field."

"Him down, me up: what went wrong?"

"A classic case of spousal abuse: the misguided woman so terrified she couldn't accept our help."

"Our help—what did you do?" I stretched my legs as far as they had room to go since what had been their fetal position reminded me of an untimely birth, mine.

"Watch the window, please. The thought of footprints on it irritates me to no end. And to answer your question, I pushed you in the back seat and made a quick retreat before her man came to his senses."

I rolled to my back, taking my sorry noggin along for the ride. Bad move, I let out a yell and only then realized the cause of my unrelenting pain. The back of my head had sprouted a knot the size of an egg. "The blonde hit me?"

"Not exactly."

"I hit myself?"

"No, smartass, I used the tire jack, just once. It was the only way to stop you from killing her abuser."

"*Her abuser* deserved to die."

"And I deserve to ride shotgun instead of driving. So, are you up to the task or do we reevaluate our association here and now."

Time out for Bish whose raised voice initiated a hacking spell equal to any he'd presented so far. I cranked myself up and surveyed the area. A rest area surrounded by more wheat, meaning we hadn't left the state of Kansas yet, once again confirming the slowpoke's inept genes could never match the speedy superiority of mine.

"What gives," I said, returning to the flat-on-my-back position but with one hand cushioning the knot on my head. "A guy like me you can hire anywhere, Denver, for instance. A town that size and with that climate ought to support a decent shelter-house dude willing to work."

"You're absolutely right." Mr. Do-good dug into his pocket, pulled out a fat roll of money, and from the center plucked two bills. He threw them in my lap.

I expected a cool two hundred but wound up with two stinking twenties. Unbelievable, I held them up to the light.

"It's more than generous," he said, "considering this is your second day of employment and day two counts for zero."

"Like hell it does. Don't go pulling that shit."

"Then you're still with me."

"You saw what I'm capable of doing."

"And you saw what I'm capable of."

"With my back turned doesn't count." I sat up, helped myself to three Tylenol and a bottle of water from the hand he stretched out to meet mine which was kind of wobbly.

"Anything else?" he asked.

"Yeah, since you asked: about the coughing."

"I told you, it comes and goes."

"Well, the next time it comes, I might have to make it go by stuffing those precious twenties down your throat."

"And miss the next installment of Emily and me, I think not."

"It better be good, that's all I can say." I thought about saying more, and probably should have, but didn't feel up to the effort.

Chapter 17

Bright lights, flashy casinos, and luxury hotels competing for not only the high rollers but Mr. and Mrs. Joe Average and their brood of wide-eyed kids, that's how Bish described Las Vegas during our first cruise down The Strip. Oh yeah, Vegas rocked with everything I expected and then some. Even Bish looked better, what with him knowing his way around town, starting with our hotel, not the classiest but decent enough. Some of the help acknowledged him by name, which told me he'd camped out there before, maybe with a more dedicated butt-boy than yours truly, judging from the smarmy clerk's change of attitude when Bish negotiated for separate rooms. As it turned out the rooms were adjoining but far enough away that the hacking didn't bombard me that first night. Or maybe the cough had taken a holiday too. Or maybe my brain had grown used to it. Or to Bish, maybe he wasn't grating on my nerves as much as before.

Day Two in Vegas: in spite of the aching knot Bish gave me, my best night's sleep since the singular experience at B & B. Bish didn't bother knocking before entering, me still in bed and him already dressed and yakking about his need for morning coffee. I jumped in and out of the shower in record time, ignored the stubble below my soul patch.

Downstairs in the hotel coffee shop we hunched over the counter, eating waffles smothered with strawberries. I refused what Bish couldn't eat while he laid out his plans for the day, as in which casino he wanted to test his skill and how I wasn't supposed to leave said casino without first telling him. What a joke after being cooped up with him for a miserable sixteen hundred miles.

We took a taxi to one of the older casinos off The Strip where I wound up dipping into my own pocket to play the slots while he played Mister Big Shot at the black jack table. At the very least he could've given me some spending money. Not that I wanted anyone thinking me his boy-toy. Butt-boy was bad enough.

I win, as some gamblers say after the fact. I lost, and lost some more. Fifty dollars, to be exact, the limit I'd set per day until the someday when Bish decided to fork over my salary. After putting the bells and whistles of the one-armed bandits behind me, I found Bish where I'd left him hours before, playing Black Jack. He recognized me with a slight nod but his eyes never left the cards on the table so I leaned over and in a low voice told him I was taking off into the sunshine.

"And a temperature of one-hundred-four degrees," he murmured from the corner of his mouth.

"Dry heat, I won't even feel it."

"Suit yourself." He checked his watch. "Hotel lobby, seven o'clock sharp."

"A.M. or P.M.?"

"For supper."

"And maybe a show?"

"Whatthefuck!" he muttered, having just lost what started out as a decent hand.

Time out for good behavior; I backed off and disappeared into the streets of Vegas.

One hundred and four degrees of dry heat was still one hundred and four degrees of miserable heat but without the armpits dripping sweat. Before I'd walked to the first stoplight, two hookers approached me, one prettier than the other and both acceptable in my book. The blonde had wrap-around legs; the brunette's jugs had the eye-catching swing nature intended.

"How much?" I asked the blonde out of curiosity.

"Two for the price of one," she said. "One hundred of the sweetest dollars you'll ever spend."

The brunette wiggled her jugs. "Cash or credit card, you won't be sorry."

"I'm a little short. Could you float me a loan?" I showed her my empty palms, hoping she'd come down on the price.

Too late, the guy behind me didn't hesitate and off went the three of them, arm in arm.

Another missed opportunity. Hookers everywhere, like bees swarming honey, and me with pockets riding on empty, my crappy savings stashed in a hotel room across town. I thought about returning to the casino, asking Bish nicely for an advance on my wages. Even though I hadn't put in a full week yet, I'd done whatever he asked of me. And so far, he hadn't given me jack shit about his good old days with Lark.

Another time, maybe tomorrow, I squared my shoulders and kept right on walking, farther than I should have because the bands of tourists had thinned out as the neighborhood from the ancient era of Elvis grew seedier with each block, nothing worse than I'd seen before but not what I wanted that day. Yet, whatever the circumstances, trouble always managed to find me before I found it.

Had I not been walking with my head up my ass when passing a certain alleyway, I wouldn't have bumped into this Halle Berry lookalike. Nor would I have noticed her leopard-skin outfit showing off the goodies underneath, those girly essentials I had no problem imagining. Foregoing the hooker chitchat, she backed me against the nearest building, and sandwiched my face between her hands. She planted a wet kiss on my mouth, opened it, and shoved her tongue inside, a position she held until I raised a boner. Only then did she pull away.

"Wow. That was some kiss," I said, not wanting to think where her mouth had been before.

"Consider yourself lucky. I usually charge extra for the girlfriend experience but you're so damn cute, I couldn't resist making your day."

"Well, thanks I—"

"Cut the chatter. Just listen and nod, okay?"

I looked into eyes too old for her face, told myself to get a grip.

"Nod again," she said. "Pretend we made a terrific deal and you can hardly wait."

Pretend? Another female in trouble, did I not learn my lesson in that great state of Kansas? Never mind, I'd entered a new day in a different state. Nevada, where anything goes, Vegas, where everything stays behind when the perp leaves.

"Now walk with me," she said, slipping her caramel-colored arm through mine.

Had I fallen off the deep end? Allowing Miss Luscious Lips to lead me where anybody my age knew better than to go. Down a deserted alleyway with more cats than I could count—fat cats, scrawny cats, cats in windowsills, and cats on garbage cans. Luscious leaned into my shoulder. Her perfume sent me into next week; the touch of her hair brushing against my face made my boner ache. I wanted more, was determined not to goof up this incredible op. She stopped, in the worst of places, beside a quartet of garbage cans reeking from yesterday's fish special. Did I care? Hell, no. If I'd been wearing a watch, I'd've given it to her. Jewelry, still batting zero … unless, wait a minute, the diamond stud in my ear. Not unless she insisted.

Playing it cool, I opened with, "About your fee."

"Do me," she snapped back with, "here and now, before he kills both of us."

He … us … what? Trouble again, wherever I went. She unzipped my fly, at the same time backing me against another wall, maybe a garage. I was thinking blow job, her *modus operandi* on the run. Wrong. She jumped me, wrapped those long legs around my willing ass and gave me two minutes of the most disingenuous wham bam I'd ever imagined, all the while her lips locked onto mine, her tongue ramming deep in my throat, me ramming deeper into my new best friend. Even the cats got into the act, howling while I shot my pent-up wad. What a feeling, what a relief. I let out a yell when she released me, her feet grounded but leaving no more than an inch between our bodies. So much for Nevada's dry heat, I'd managed to work up a sweat, so delicious it soaked my tee and boxers. My hand couldn't stop shaking when I zipped my fly.

"Not so fast." She stepped back. "We're not through yet."

"About the money, I'm really sorry but …"

"Forget the money. Hit me."

"Hey, it wasn't that bad, not bad at all, leastways on my part. But if you weren't satisfied, give me a few minutes to recover and I'll try again."

"Idiot, I said hit me."

"No way," I said. "You're talking to the wrong guy."

Not in her book. She caught me off guard, running five long fingernails down my left cheek. Blood seeped into the sweat on my face until I wiped it away with the palm of my still shaking hand.

"Look, I'm sorry if I insulted you but …."

"Dammit, don't make me hurt you again." She stuck her face in mine, this time offering no kiss to rev up my engine. "Just hit me now and hit me hard, across the face like you really mean it."

"How can I mean what I don't feel? I may not look like much but I do have some standards."

Her face went soft; she couldn't have been more than twenty, if that. "Which is why I picked you, a girl can't be too careful. Please. He's watching our every move."

"He, who? The guy must be living inside your head 'cause there's nobody here but you and me and the screwed-up cats."

"You are so off base. The show's not over 'til it's over, and that's not yet. Now, for what we are about to do, I forgive you and you damn well better forgive me."

Before I could run away, she flew into me, claws poised like a jungle cat's which must've pleased our semi-domesticated audience to no end. One set of nails swiped my left shoulder, again drawing blood. When I grabbed her wrist, she caught my good cheek with the other nail set and drew fresh blood I didn't bother wiping away. Then she kneed me, not hard enough to send me to the ground but enough to show she meant business. After catching my wind, I did what she'd asked of me—slammed my open palm across her Halle Berry face. A moment of pain replaced the fear I'd seen before and made me feel worse than shit on a birthday cake with no candles. Another reason to hate myself, as if I didn't have enough already.

She staggered back on those five-inch heels but didn't fall. "Again, only harder and this time use your fist."

I closed in on her, whispered so the pacing cats couldn't hear. "Listen to me: As soon as you feel the tip of my knuckles, pull back and I will too."

"And you listen to me: my man's a sicko, one with sicko connections. Either you hurt me or he will, in ways you can't imagine and I never want to experience again. I'd rather take my chances with you." She reared her head and shot a load of sweet spit onto one of the wounds she'd inflicted on my face. "Do it now and do it hard. Now, dammit, we don't have all day."

So I did, three times in quick succession so as not to prolong the anticipation of pain. She crumpled faster than the dude back in Kansas. I rubbed my fingers into the moist saliva she'd planted on my bloody cheek. Those same fingers I curled into a fist and slammed it into the wall she'd backed me against. Again, only this time harder and with a passion I hadn't expected but fully deserved. My knuckles were scraped with blood and dirt but the healing grace of her saliva had already melted into my first wound and I couldn't ask her for more. Nor could I relieve this fresh load of guilt. I forced my eyes to the asphalt stained with god-only-knows-what, where she lay curled up, a battered baby who should've been bawling instead of me.

"You okay?" A stupid question, yes, but I had to say something.

Only the luscious lips moved. "Stop your sniveling and kick me. Pretend I'm a mangy cat foaming at the mouth, one who ripped out the heart of your best friend."

Rusty came to mind; I choked out a lame response. "No way, I can't." But I did. I kicked her again, but not as hard.

"Good," she whispered through a moan. "Now turn around and walk away."

"But …"

"Do not bend over. Do not offer me your grubby hand. Just leave and forget this ever happened."

Chapter 18

Ten weeks before the promised trip to Branson, okay I could hang on that long, what with junior high coming up and me helping Jed those hours before the sun set over endless fields of crops waiting to be harvested. I'd never been to Branson and other than this lousy work farm I'd never been anywhere outside of St. Louis, what with Lark having her heart set on being discovered, as if that would ever happen in Missouri, except maybe Branson and all those family bumpkin shows. I tried to tell her, but would she listen to me, no.

As for Branson, I kept thinking one thing and one thing only, Silver Dollar City and its wild coasters and water rides. Cooler than cool for people my age and older, all the way to Lark's plus another ten years or so. As for Jed or Delores, I didn't know for sure if they could they stand seeing their slave-boy Johnny having the most fun of his entire life. Give me a break. As far as I was concerned, the old folks could fork over some dough and turn me loose as soon as we got inside Silver Dollar's entrance. I'd meet them back there when the park closed, or not. Who knows, maybe I'd take a hike, maybe hitch a ride to Florida and join the circus. After all, working for Jed had taught me the fine art of shoveling poop and more poop.

Everybody has the right to a special day. Mine came in late August and had always been between me and Lark and nobody else. That is, until the year Delores decided to outshine her own daughter. The old gal went all out with country-fried steak smothered in thick white gravy, green beans with bacon bits, and my favorite macaroni with five cheeses which she called downright sinful due to the excessive calories. After eating thirds of everything, I still felt lower than the slugs I'd squeezed between two rocks stained with my earlier kills, those creepy crawlers that did more harm than good.

I was about to ask if I could please be excused when Delores brought out this chocolate cake topped with twelve candles, burning high enough to set off the smoke alarms we should've had but didn't because Jed couldn't bear to spend the money on what he considered an unnecessary necessity brought about by a government having nothing better to do than stick its nose into the business of decent folks such as himself. There I sat, trying not to smile through their off-key version of "Happy Birthday" that ended with something about me acting and looking like a monkey. Delores cut the triple-decker cake and handed me the first piece, a big deal on its own because Jed always came first. Of course, she made it up to him with a piece twice as big as mine. As was the house rule, we waited until Delores put a slice on her plate before digging in.

"You like?" she asked, clearly enjoying what Jed had referred to as a masterpiece.

"Yeah, it's pretty good." I changed the topic. What the heck, it was my special day, not hers. "Maybe Lark will call."

"Don't count on it," Jed said. "She has bigger fish to fry than a shrimp such as you."

"That's what you think." Backtalk, you bet, certain privileges came with my turning twelve. "Lark won't forget. This is my first birthday without her."

"Get used to it, Johnny." He shook a forkful of chocolate at me, scattering crumbs across the table cloth that I'd have to clean up later. "It won't be your last."

Thanks for nothing. I wanted to put my fist through the cake but Delores would've figured out a way of getting even. She always did, especially when I brought up Lark. Anyway this day, three hundred and sixty-five away from the big thirteen, belonged to me and no old fart and his masterpiece wife were going to ruin it. Not even Lark who probably forgot about the kid she dumped. My little man, she used to call me.

Well, I wasn't so little anymore. Five-six, according to the last time Delores stood me up to a doorframe in the kitchen and marked my height alongside Lark's on the day she turned twelve. She'd measured five-seven then, same as our last day together, the day I sunk my teeth into her. Of course, I had inches to go before I quit growing, another seven in my estimation.

I waited all day and evening for the phone call that never came, again making me look like the pathetic jerk we all knew I was. Damn Lark, damn Jed and Delores. Especially Delores for making me the best cake I'd ever eaten in my entire life.

***

Junior High in Podunk, USA, a big fat zero, unfixable—totally. What more could I say. Turns out there was no junior high or even a middle school for me, just seventh grade in a K through 8 Catholic elementary, with boys forced to wear prisoner-issue tan knit shirts and dark blue pants. Same shirts for the girls; they were condemned to wear their skirts below the knees so as not to encourage evil thoughts, or worse. As for me, I got stuck riding a yellow school bus with snot-nosed runts and no one my age worth hanging out with, which came as no surprise since I hadn't been surrounded by a ton of friends back home either. Looking after Lark had taken up most of my time until she outgrew me and latched onto a string of boyfriends who thought I took up too much of her time. That's what kids were supposed to do, I tried explaining to Lark. And how did she repay my honesty, by sending me away. Not one penny to my name and being held prisoner in an old folk's home.

Seventh grade in a new school, could it get any worse. I'd expected a bunch of country hicks and that's what I got, mostly farm boys who probably worked harder than me but still wouldn't have fit into my world considering the two dinosaurs yanking my chain. For putting up with Jed and Delores I deserved an Olympic gold medal and figured I'd earn one someday. No, make that an Oscar for best actor because I doubt they knew how miserable they were making my life.

Although I will give Jed this: as soon as school started he cut way back on my weekday chores, expecting me to spend those extra hours with my nose stuck in a textbook. I dragged out the study time, making sure I filled every minute so he wouldn't change his mind about me busting my butt. Delores jumped into the mix too, Miz Perfection, checking my homework, making me do it over and over until she couldn't find any more errors. In return, she always whipped up a decent supper—her words not mine. Working her was tons easier than working

Jed, who always narrowed his eyes to me, as if he wasn't quite sure what thoughts were tooling around in my head. Nor was I about to share them with the old fart. He didn't have a clue.

And then my life changed for the better, at least for a while. This girl, I guess she'd been riding the bus from day one but I didn't notice her until the third week when some kid shut me out of my usual seat, forcing me to head toward the back and find another. I first noticed the long red hair, on the order of Lark's but not as straight, and then those freckles scattered across her nose like cinnamon flecks on powdered sugar. She turned her face toward the window when I stopped at the empty seat next to her.

"Okay if I sit here?" I asked so she'd look me over.

Keeping her face to the window, she lifted her shoulders and spoke in the country drawl Southern Illinois diehards refused to shake. "Whatever, it's a free country."

"Same as me. Hi, I'm Free."

"Well, whoop-tee-do, aren't we all."

"Yeah, but I really am Free." The bus jerked forward, knocking me into the seat and against her. "My name's Free Danner."

This got her attention. She turned, showed me these green eyes sparkling with slivers of gold. "Free? You have got to be kidding."

"About what?" As if I didn't know.

"The name, it positively sucks. In fact it's positively stupid."

"Oh, yeah, well, what's yours?" Just like that, I had her.

"Rowena," she said. "It's positively beautiful; don't you think?"

I almost laughed but told her yes. She was positively beautiful too, in a way reminding me of Lark but nicer. We started talking, that is, Rowena did, mostly because I wanted to know everything about her but didn't want her knowing anything about me. She was an eighth grader who turned fourteen the week before. I couldn't hide the seventh grade thing but told her I was almost thirteen. Since she didn't say 'no way,' I figured she believed me. When we ran out of words, I pulled out my Game Boy, fired it up, and asked if she played.

"Not exactly, how does it work?" She leaned into my shoulder for a better view.

Hello, sweet dreams. I activated my thumbs, showed her all the neat things Mario could do, Luigi too, and how they fought to rescue the princess. Rowena caught on really quick so I handed over my guys and coached her on the tougher moves. For once the bus ride ended too soon. I slipped Game Boy back in my pocket, moved into the aisle, and let Rowena go in front of me. The bus driver, a grouchy bitch if ever there was, smiled at me right before we hopped off. Respect, I saw it in her face.

The school bell was ringing when I caught up with Rowena. It seemed right, me walking her toward the entrance. She even made a comment about me being really tall for my age.

"So was my dad," I said, "six-feet-three, maybe four."

"Was? You mean he's dead."

"Yeah, he died a hero. You probably saw it on TV, the bank robbery in St. Louis."

"Who hasn't—what a colossal bummer. If you ever need to, you know, talk …."

"Thanks, maybe you could call me sometime."

She did, but not until a week later. Same as our daily bus ride, I let her do most of the talking. But after she called three evenings in a row, Delores grabbed the phone out of my hand and went right for the jugular, anything to ruin what little life I had without her and Jed.

"Young lady whoever you are, do not be calling Johnny anymore," she said. "He's much too young for socializing with members of the opposite sex."

The opposite sex, I nearly shit my pants. Maybe that's what I should've done. It would've served Delores right, gave her one more thing to do since she took such pride in that brighter than white laundry she hung outside to dry. Instead, thinking faster than usual, I came back with, "Gosh, Delores, you didn't have to hang up on her. It was no big deal. She needed help with her homework."

"And so she called on you? That would be like the blind leading the blind."

"I don't think so." I pulled out two folded sheets from my shirt pocket, handed them to her. "Take a look at these."

Delores's eyes grew as big as cow patties. "Both A's, why Johnny, I didn't think you had it in you."

I laid it on thicker than the peanut butter Jed smeared over four slices of toast every evening after supper. "You helped me. I was trying to do the same for somebody else."

"Oh, Johnny, I should never have doubted you." She pulled me to her smelly boobs—ham and beans, a new favorite of mine but not on her. "The poor girl, what's her name?"

I had to think fast, pulled one out of my hat, the dumbest girl in class. "Brandi McAllister."

Delores stepped back and screwed up her face. "What kind of name is that?"

"How should I know? My teacher said we shouldn't judge others by their names or ethnic backgrounds."

"I couldn't agree more," she said and then chewed on her lip. Good, let her squirm for a change instead of me. "Although under certain circumstances it's best to stick with your own kind. This girl, you're sure she needs help."

"I already saved her from getting one F."

"The girl's name—now what was it?"

***

The next day on the bus I gave Rowena the okay to call again, as long as she used a different name. After hearing the name, she rolled her eyes and crossed her arms.

"Brandi, of all the stupid seventh graders to pick from, you picked one with a stupid name."

"It worked, didn't it? Delores feels sorry for anybody with problems."

"You are pretty smart." She grinned, showing me her pink braces. "When did you say you're turning thirteen?"

"Pretty soon," I said and then surprised myself by going in a whole different direction. "Have you ever been kissed? Because that's what I'd like to do before I make the switch."

"You're such a dope." She pressed her knee against mine, thought a couple of seconds before laying this on me: "Not only have I been kissed, I've actually done *it*."

"It as in *it*, you have got to be kidding." From there things moved faster than the rollercoaster I planned on riding at Branson. "So have I."

"No way, you're lying through those crooked teeth," she said. "But you still want me to show you, right?"

Chapter 19

Seven o'clock sharp, the hotel lobby, Bish had told me earlier that morning, which shouldn't have been a problem except it now required my hoofing it across town, a long, miserable walk given the heat playing chopsticks on my wounded face and psyche. Plus the curious stares of every person passing by, except the hookers who half-smiled, half-frowned, as if they'd already been there, done that. For them life really was the bitch I thought I'd been living until then.

Back at the hotel and in no mood for small talk with the know-it-all desk clerk, I lowered my head and slunk off to catch the elevator. At last, my room, a chance to regroup before meeting Bish. After an awesome dump I stepped into the bathtub, adjusted the showerhead, and let the spray pound cold needles into my flesh until it raised welts. While drying off, I checked out my face in the mirror and decided I could live with the damage. And if Bish didn't like it, screw him. Still naked, I flopped onto the bed, tucked a pillow behind my neck, and assumed the spread-eagle position. Forget about TV, forget about my empty stomach. I couldn't muster enough juice to click the remote or pick up the phone to order room service.

All I could manage were the crummy thoughts. This poor girl, this S and M hooker whose name I didn't even know, had crawled inside my head and my heart, sucking good and evil from every fiber of my lowly existence. We—she and me—had performed like pros for an unseen, unnamed person, whoever he was, for all I knew a troll living inside her head since he never came forward, never applauded a job well done. The more I thought about it the more I concluded I'd been had. Once again, forced to do someone else's bidding. And this time I'd been left with fresh scars to prove my stupidity—bloody cheeks, bloody knuckles, bloody soul. Some would heal fast; others—maybe so, maybe not.

Resolving zilch, I allowed myself a doze into the Branson of my kid dreams and from there, deeper and deeper into emptiness. Nothing, the absolute sweetest of a holding pattern surrounded me without making any demands on me. I could've stayed in limbo forever but not even nothing lasts forever, except heaven and hell, both of which I'd already tasted but wasn't ready for a total commitment in either direction. Ever so slowly I started tunneling my way out of nothing, clawing and scratching, fighting for a rebirth. It must've worked because I reached the scene of my infant baptism. Not a John the Baptist total submersion but a gentle sprinkling of water to the forehead … Lark beaming as she hovered nearby; baby-me in the arms of … of, I don't know, maybe Jed or Delores, who else would've cared enough to stand up for me, then. More water, way too much … hold it, a waterfall. Wrong as usual … a water pitcher, Bish pouring its contents over my wounded face.

"You're late," he said, as if I'd committed a crime.

He got that right. The egg behind my head was throbbing. I turned to one side, reached for the nearest pillow, and covered my face. "Give me a break, Bish. I had a rough day."

"So I see," he said, dumping more water. "Get up, get dressed. Ten minutes, the bar downstairs."

Short and snappy, some nerve. Here's to you, Bish Bitch. I raised my hand from under the pillow and flipped him the bird a millimeter second before the door closed, too late for him to have seen my in-your-face gesture. What a bite. I'd been delivering my end on a daily basis. He'd given nothing in return but empty promises. And Vegas in the late forenoon, I guess that side of Vegas counted for something other than dry heat. How about dry mouth, mine still tasting the warmth of Miss Luscious Lips, her tongue tickling every inch of mine. And what had she asked of me: too much, but it didn't stop me from going along with the sham instead of walking away from it. Why me, of all the low-down, mean pond scum she could've picked, why me. A sixth sense, maybe a yet-to-be-determined seventh sense capable of transmitting evil vibes to a chosen few. At least she hadn't asked me to kill her so as not to inconvenience anyone else. Been there, done that—almost.

An ice-cold long neck, just what I needed to settle my nerves. I rolled off the bed and dressed in five. Another minute took me into the hall and a non-stop elevator to the lobby and from there, the bar hopping with nondescript drinkers. I slid onto the stool next to Bish who was either pouting or too busy nursing his Manhattan and an unlit cigarette to acknowledge my presence. No problem. To the bartender I raised a friendlier finger than I'd given Bish only to have it dismissed when Bish mashed his cigarette into the ashtray and stepped down from the stool. Now there really was a problem. To hell with the job, I seriously considered punching out his lights.

"Better grab some peanuts," he said, shoving the bowl in my direction. "We're already late."

"You mean for the Surf 'n Turf advertised down the street, as in Lobster and Steak."

"Or fish filet and a Big Mac."

"Please tell me you're kidding."

He was, on both counts. I followed him outside where he hailed a taxi that carted us across town, beyond the seedy neighborhood of Luscious Lips and the shameful behavior I couldn't shake. To my surprise Bish handed me a cell phone, so we could stay in touch. Limited calls and no texting, the stingy bastard had no shame. While I figured out the system, Bish serenaded me with another hack attack. Even the cabbie shuddered from his front seat and only resumed normal inhaling when he stopped in front of a Hollywood-style apartment house, long past its prime but still holding on to a shred of mysterious dignity. Bish counted out some greenbacks, told our relieved cabbie to keep the change, and we stepped onto the sidewalk.

Miracle of miracles, his coughing took a break, how long was anybody's guess but on this a savvy bookie could've made a killing. We stood there for a minute with me taking in a mix of buildings from the fifties, adobes and frames, all worse than the one directly in front of us. On the chain-link fence hung this hand-lettered sign that cracked me up.

"City House," I told Bish. "This had better be good. Otherwise, what's the point of our being here?"

"Family obligations so don't embarrass me or make another ass of yourself."

There's a difference? I almost asked, but Bish had entered a twilight zone of calm piety. He opened the gate and started up the walk, expecting his starving Butt-Boy to follow, which I did to a narrow porch filled with folding lawn chairs no one occupied in spite of the cool evening. And then it hit me. This ho-hum sleeper had all the makings of an old people's home or a nursing facility, with the older-than-dirt residents gumming their supper of mushy peas spread over milk toast. And Bish, the do-gooder, making his rounds after a hard day of Black Jack, doling out dollar bills to the needy and deserted. Oh yeah, I'd been screwed again but not for long. I'd make him pay, in ways he never dreamed possible.

He rang the bell. We waited and waited, with me tapping my foot until he shot me a knock-it-off reminder. At last the door clicked. Bush pushed it open and we stepped inside to a foyer with poor lighting and a meowing cat perched on the corner pedestal needing a touch of greenery, as Delores the haphazard decorator used to say.

"What do you think?" I asked.

"About what: the state of the economy, global warning, same-sex marriage? Work with me here. In other words, shut the …."

Saved by the bell—actually a trio of look-alikes who popped out of nowhere, three abreast and heading in our direction. The brisk no-nonsense walk, the unrelenting discipline, the self-assurance faking as quiet demeanor, I'd seen it all before. No intros needed to tell me we'd entered a house occupied by those who still managed to demand and receive respect—brides of Jesus Christ dressed as modern-day nuns. The oldest of the three stepped forward, extended her hand to Bish.

"Good evening, Samuel."

"Nice to see you again, Sister Bernadette," Bish said with half a bow. What a suck-up. He turned to me and with a show of phony affection, placed his hand on my shoulder. "This is my assistant, John Danner."

"Sister Mary Fran is expecting you, Samuel." The nun scanned me with radar eyes, unsure of my worthiness, as well she should've been. "And John."

"Danner," I said, to which Bish squeezed my shoulder as he pushed me forward.

We followed Sister Bernadette, as quietly as the school children she probably taught before tackling Sin City and all its decadence. At the end of the hall she knocked on the only door and in reply to a muffled voice opened the door and allowed us inside without further supervision. I expected a stern but kindly nun-in-charge sitting behind the safety of her desk but instead saw one dressed in pale blue polyester, including the short veil barely covering her beauty-shop hair streaked with gray. High cheekbones, wide forehead and tight lips, her face could've passed for Ms. Trust Fund or former high-priced call girl. She stood up, tall and slender, her back straight as she met us half-way with opened arms that soon embraced Samuel Dean Lawford. Along with more hugs they traded in-between kisses while I shifted from one foot to the other, uncomfortable over an emotional exchange I'd never known. Sister Mary Fran took two steps back, worry lines creeping across her face as she scanned Bish's. Just wait until he coughs, I thought, clearing my throat until she noticed me.

"And you must be John Danner." Her eyes searched my battered face. "I see you've been involved in some type of altercation."

"More like a misunderstanding, Sister."

"Ah-h, one can only hope to your advantage. In any case welcome to City House."

I stumbled over a thank you and asked if once upon a time she'd taught Samuel.

"Everything I know," Bish replied with a smile I'd not seen before. "Sister Mary Fran is my birth mother, actually the only mother I can remember."

His mother—the far-out possibility of her being my grandmother, how cool was that.

Bish must've been read my mind. "Don't even think about going there," he said with a look more menacing than his words.

No problem, at least for the moment. I took another route and hit her with this: "So, Sister, you're in the business of rescuing people from poverty and shame."

"As of now only females, the very young and not so young and those in-between," she said, her tone matter-of-fact while evaluating me. "Nevada has legalized prostitution in a few counties, but not Clark, which includes Las Vegas. Nevertheless, it runs rampant here, a veritable haven for unscrupulous pimps. Their battered and abused often find comfort at our shelter."

I crossed myself, as much for her benefit as mine. "Thank God for shelters. Where would we be without them? In fact Bish and I first met at St. Louis's premier shelter."

She raised her brow. "Bish?"

"Sorry for the confusion. I meant Samuel. In St. Louis his friends and admirers call him The Bishop but I put my own spin on the name and shortened it to Bish. Which, I guess makes me more than a friend, or maybe less. We haven't figured that out yet but one thing's for sure, we're definitely not gay. In fact, we're straighter than the shortest distance between two points. Right, Bish?"

He answered with a hack attack, prompting Sister Mary Fran to pick up the phone and order a pot of tea. Great, just what the patient needed, but what about my stomach riding on empty.

"Excuse me, Sister," the schoolboy in me asked. "Please don't think me forward but is there any place around here I could get something to eat?"

She checked the no-nonsense watch encircling her wrist. It put to shame the Rolex encircling Bish's. "Of course, our dining facility is still open. And you, Samuel?"

He nodded through the pinnacle of his cough and she called the kitchen again, requesting tea be served in the Rose Room instead. On our way there Sister Mom walked between us, these two thorns flanking a rose, but she directed her conversation to Bish which made perfect sense given him being her son and me nothing more than an also ran. On entering the dining room, I expected a set-up on the order of B & B's but was surprised to find fifteen round tables covered with pastel tablecloths, matching napkins folded into tall glasses, and vases containing a single wild flower. Western hospitality with a southern flair but minus the mint juleps, it made a nice touch. About half of the tables were occupied, by assorted females who could've passed for anything from cheerleaders to housewives to the lowliest of streetwalkers. Without exception, they acknowledged Sister Mary Fran with a slight nod or wave of the hand. Not one of them seemed to notice Bish or me, the only males and definitely out of the loop.

Soup, salad, and sandwiches—as much as we wanted for one price, according to the waitress who poured the tea Sister Mom had pre-ordered. She didn't want anything else and neither did Bish who'd probably been chewing a deluxe steak around the time I was arguing with the deluxe owner of those luscious lips. Get over it ... her, I told myself, erase the whole sordid picture. I tried, I really did, but while I filled the crater in my belly, mother and son exchanged a long list of good deeds they'd accomplished since their last visit, each trying to out-do the other, which left me totally out of touch unless I counted back a few hours. Sister Mom or Bish wouldn't have understood the violence. Nor did I, after the fact.

"We must harness that wretched cough," she said while Bish stifled the latest hack with a handkerchief all but stuffed in his mouth. "First thing tomorrow, I'll call Craig Sloan."

"The head of pulmonology—don't bother. I've already seen his counterpart in St. Louis."

"And?"

"He referred me to the top oncologist."

Oncologist as in keeper of the Big C, I knew it; I knew it. As soon as Bish paid every dime owed me, I planned on saying adios and may we never meet again.

Sister Mom braced her shoulders against the back of her chair. "In that case, you'll see the top oncologist here. A second opinion can't hurt."

While she and Bish discussed the merits of nine-day novenas mixed with the complexities of modern science and pharmaceuticals, I finished off my pie a la mode but again refused what Bish couldn't put away. That cough, those germs, his mouth, no thanks.

My eyes were starting to glaze over until they latched onto a familiar face, with bruises visible from a distance of fifteen feet and belonging to the one female in Vegas I dreaded seeing again. She'd entered the dining room and was heading in our direction. Gone were the spiked heels and Jungle Jane outfit, replaced by sandals and a loose-fitting sundress, chocolate brown to contrast with her caramel skin. She'd ditched the hooker strut for oh-my-aching-soul, her body bent forward and eyes downcast. As she passed by our table the quick arm of Sister Mom shot out and stopped her cold.

"What happened?" Sis asked. "Don't tell me more trouble from that horrible man and his nephew."

"Precisely, only this time Everett fired his gun. The designated perp wasn't as tough as I thought."

"How fortunate for you."

"Amen and halleluiah unless the bruises fade too fast, then color me a fresh shade of black and blue. Now if you don't mind, I need a nice bowl of chicken soup."

Not once did Luscious look in my direction but there was no way she hadn't seen me, or heard the heart beating in my ears, so loud it kept me from opening my mouth to speak. I watched her walk away, the stooped posture having disappeared, making me wonder if it had been a show for my benefit.

"What's her story?" I asked Sister Mom.

"Twenty-three and from New Orleans, a Katrina refugee."

"She should've stayed in The Big Easy," Bish said.

"Too late now," his mother replied. "She's under the control of a pimp named Sugar Daddy. He boasts a stable of twenty or so hookers, all scared to death of him and rightly so. If the usual girl propositioning guy fails to attract enough clients, he raises the bar a notch. Big spenders don't flinch over the added cost of violent voyeurism. In fact, there's a waiting list to watch unsuspecting johns beat up the lovely hookers or else they both receive a nasty dose of corporal punishment."

"It's beyond obscene," Bish said.

Yeah, tell me. Visions of the afternoon, a broken collage of blood and humiliation bounced around my head. But when I spoke, it was in faked casual. "The girl you stopped, Sister Mary Fran, what's her name?"

"Your purpose for asking," she said while reevaluating the damage to my face.

"I might know her."

"Get out, from where?" Bish said. You'd've thought he'd known me all my life and couldn't figure out the connection.

"Here and there," I answered with a shrug, followed by a half-truth. "She looks familiar, from where I can't say. But what does it matter, unless she's working undercover."

"Not likely," Sister Mom said. "As for her Vegas name, Butterscotch should suffice—around here last names change faster than the liturgical seasons. As for her lifestyle I must warn you: stay away from her pimp. Sugar Daddy is meaner than mean, a bona fide servant of the devil."

"The police can't stop him?"

"The girls in his stable won't press charges; they're afraid of the consequences."

"What about you?" I asked, wanting to believe all nuns were invincible.

"God knows I've tried. Sugar Daddy retaliated with the vicious rape of one of our City House sisters, directly or otherwise, we still don't know because the perpetrator wore a pull-over mask. Nor was any DNA left behind. Without a positive I.D., the police can do nothing. We sisters do as much as we can in other ways: administering to bruised and battered, the emotionally-robbed and those with early-stage AIDS."

I held up one hand, showed her my palm. "Okay, I get the picture. But what I don't get is you and Bish … I mean, Samuel."

Ouch, I must've stepped over the line because Bish sucked in his breath. He held back a cough. The cannon ball Sister Mom shot in my direction could've melted steel. As it was, I felt like a slime ball for ruining Bish's time with her. She stood up, so did he. Followed by me, the years of respect and discipline etched in my brain.

"On that note I will say 'good evening'. You have five minutes to finish your meal," she told me, not Bish, "after which Sister Bernadette will escort you to the door. Until then, do not wander off on your own, or attempt contact with our residents, temporary or otherwise. They value their security and know better than to conduct business while under our protection. No exceptions, John Danner."

"Good night, Mother," Bish said. His lips brushed against her cheek but said so much more. "I'll call you tomorrow."

"As well you should. Do not disappoint me."

Chapter 20

Blind obedience had never been my strong suit especially when it involved the taking of orders from maternal figures, either biological or assumed. So, as soon as Sister Mary Fran left the dining room, I left my assigned table and despite Bish's hissed objections, headed to the one occupied by Butterscotch. I stood there, waiting for the lift of her head, the show-me face I purposely bruised. Instead she continued sipping soup from the side of her spoon, making me feel shittier than ever. But could I walk away, no. Not with my legs turning to sludge, my feet nailed to the floor. Since hemming and hawing wasn't my bag, I threw out a simple question.

"Can I sit with you for a few minutes?"

"If I said no, would it matter?" She didn't wait for my answer. "Okay, sit. Just don't hit me again."

Excuse me. As if the Cro-Magnon slug-out had been my idea, me the stupid tourist she'd picked up off the street. I took the seat across from her, and since time was running short, I pitched my best-in-a-pinch pickup line. "For what it's worth, I'm really sorry."

"Oka-a-y." Having emptied her soup bowl, she centered her spoon across the upper rim, and asked, "Anything else?"

"Yeah, give me a minute."

Tap-tap tippity-tat, not a good sign, her fingers telling me to make it snappy before she passed out from sheer boredom. I hate when people do that but Butterscotch, I'd've given a pass any day, any night. An idea had been tooling around in my brain for the past ten minutes, an eternity for a guy with attention deficit disorder. I decided to run my idea by her. "About this thing called revenge …."

"Hold on, who said anything about revenge? Not me, that's for sure." She glanced around the room—big whoop, as if our table talk mattered to anyone else.

"Hear me out," I said, lowering my voice. "Think about a thick, chocolate shake—"

"You had to play the race card."

"What's color got to do with this?"

"Chill out." She leaned forward. "How about this: do I look like a girl who does shakes?"

"Please, let me finish. As I was saying: you got this thick, chocolate shake—"

"Make it fresh strawberry."

"Okay, fresh strawberry. Add a couple of straws and a person to share with, and what's the pay-off? A taste so sweet you can't help but suck it dry."

"What has all this got to do with … duh, hello." She folded her arms under those sweet knockers. "You're talking about sharing, as in you and me?"

"And anyone else who wants a piece of him."

"Him as in my Sugar Daddy, are you out of your pea-brained skull? Sugar Daddy does not take kindly to those who mock his success."

"What about you?"

She extended one arm, palm down, and checked out her manicure while mulling over her next words. "I say, let's go one step further and kill the dirty, rotten, despicable fuck face."

"Uh … sure, if … uh—"

"He doesn't deserve to live, not after the way he disrespected me and a whole bunch of pros and laymen. There was this one john …."

"Stories from the trenches I don't need. Mine works just fine." I held out my hand, whatever it took to touch hers again. "By the way my name is—"

"Don't tell me. Knowing your name could be dangerous for both of us. I'll call you … Beauregard, Bo for short, as is capital B, little o."

What the hell … okay. Right now I needed the lowdown on Sugar Daddy.

Letting Butterscotch do the talking gave me the chance to observe a different chick from when we first met. This one had ditched the fake eyelashes and maroon lipstick for a scrubbed face, so drop-dead-gorgeous I wanted to make her my Princess Peach, forever and ever. Another time, another place, I willed myself to concentrate on her words, her take on Nevada's legalized prostitution, and how the lowlife pimps exploit their scared hookers.

"We're supposed to have certain rights. Sugar Daddy thinks otherwise. He controls a bunch of us. How many, I can't say for sure but he holds the reins so tight we can't take a sweet pee without asking his permission. Think Hitler minus the mustache. He doesn't tolerate outside interference. The moon and four seasons determine his moods—I swear the man's possessed. Whatever heart he once had—which ain't saying much—has turned so black it fell off the charts. Forget about his soul, lost to Satan on a stupid whim. 'Course, Sugar Daddy plans to reclaim it before the day of reckoning condemns him to eternal damnation."

"He told you this?"

"Once upon a mattress when he couldn't resist me. Now keep your mouth shut 'cause it's still my turn to talk. Paranoia rules the man's life. He never goes anywhere without his nephew Everett, a bastard in his own right and vile corruption of the inherited genes. Do not, I repeat, do not disregard the measure of Sugar Daddy's authority. The man has eyes in the sky and on the street. They're watching and waiting for us to make a wrong move so he can have himself some fun at our expense. Every morning without fail, or unless we've been excused in advance …"

She stopped mid-sentence, re-adjusted the expression on her face to schoolgirl, and offered a pleasant, "Good evening, Sister."

With those words, a firm hand to the back of my neck brought me out of the chair. That same hand rotated my body one hundred and eighty degrees and prodded me away from the table. Although I couldn't turn my head to Butterscotch, I managed to call out the name of my hotel.

"There'll be no talk of hotels," I heard Sister Bernadette say as we left the Rose Room. She marched me down the hallway and at the foyer she opened the front door and shoved me out. Bish was already on the porch, rocking in the chair and totally relaxed until Sister ended her bum's rush with an uncharitable farewell.

"Don't even think about setting foot in here again, Mr. Danner."

I could've invoked Sister Mary Fran's name, the possibility of our sharing the same DNA but I didn't want to cause her or Bish the further embarrassment he warned me about. Besides, I'd already squeezed more from the evening than I'd expected. What's more, my work wasn't over; it was just beginning, especially with Bish and his recreational pursuits, gobbling up the daylight by sampling one casino after another.

Chapter 21

It didn't happen overnight. *It* took weeks of planning, okay two to be exact. Two weeks of Brandi-faking phone calls and whispering on the bus to and from school. Two weeks of absolute trust, of making sure Rowena and me had all our ducks in order, as Delores would've said. The big day finally arrived with my stomach twisted in a dozen knots; I couldn't do my morning poop no matter how hard I tried. Like always, we sat together on the bus. We talked about stuff and more stuff but not about *it*. The anticipation makes *it* more special Rowena had told me over the phone the night before. Oh, yeah. At school I couldn't concentrate on English or math. Mrs. Thompson even asked if I wasn't feeling well, which later worked out in my favor.

During lunch I practically inhaled the meatloaf sandwich Delores had packed because, according to her, the cafeteria food was not fit for human consumption. 'No way' I said to the dessert she'd sent along—three gigantuous chocolate chip oatmeal cookies. I gave them to Mrs. Thompson and in return she gave me a bathroom pass. I hurried down the empty hallway, bypassed the boys' lavatory, and instead walked a few extra feet to the janitor's closet.

My heart was pounding when I opened the door and hurried inside, expecting to find Rowena waiting in the dark. Instead of a kiss, she kneed me in the balls. Or so I thought it was Rowena until I heard this guy say, "Keep away from my girl, you hear?"

My legs failed me and I hit the floor. The pain hurt so bad I wanted to yell but bit my lip instead. Although I couldn't see the kid, I figured him bigger than me, for sure his breath smelled like cafeteria nachos and cheese. Mine smelled like the meatloaf I threw up on both of us. After kicking me into a corner, he opened the door and left without closing it tight. The first voice I heard hurt more than my balls which were killing me.

"You stupid, Goofus," Rowena said in a loud whisper. "This was supposed to be a joke. You didn't have to hurt him."

"Him, what about me, he ruined my shirt," the kid whispered back. "You and me, we're supposed to be going steady. I gave you a promise ring. Sterling silver, bought with money I saved from my allowance."

"None of that has changed. You're still my Number One."

I still hurt but got up. I pushed on the door; okay I fell against the door. It swung open and caught Goofus on the nose. Blood squirted out and seeing it made Rowena scream, which threw me for the Fruit Loops Delores refused to buy. Rowena wasn't finished. She slid down the wall like a limp ragdoll but managed to keep her skirt where it belonged while I closed the door. A scene from one of Lark's old movies popped into my head. I yanked off my vomit shirt, pushed Goofus's head back, and held the shirt to his nose. My quick thinking made Goofus gag and me an okay guy in Mrs. Thompson's eyes when she came running down the hall and skidded to a stop in front of us.

"Good grief, what happened?" she asked, the last of my oatmeal chocolate cookie still clinging to her chin.

"I was leaving the lavatory at the same time this kid came in," Goofus said through my shirt. "The door hit me."

She lifted the shirt off of his face and scrunched up hers. "You're sure about that, Tyler?"

Tyler, okay Rowena's Number One boyfriend had a name. Goofus fit him better but I wasn't going for broke.

Rowena was still doing her ragdoll bit on the floor. She choked back a sob. Mrs. Thompson reached down, took Rowena's hand, and pulled her up.

"I might have to throw up," Rowena said.

"Not yet." Mrs. Thompson folded her arms. She looked at me, then Rowena, then me again. "Don't even think about lying to me, either one of you, because I have no patience for liars. Was this an accident?"

"Yes ma'am. Tyler told the truth." We both spoke the same words at the same time. How weird was that. I put my arm around Tyler's shoulder and felt him cringe. Out there in the hallway he didn't look nearly as big as he seemed in the closet. But he'd opened my eyes and now I knew the score. "Sorry about the accident," I said, squeezing his arm.

"Yeah, me too," he said with tears in his eyes.

After lunch period ended and I was back in class, all the talk centered on Tyler Jarvis, the eighth grader who thought his shit didn't stink. But I knew better and to prove it, I finished the day in my regulation shirt covered with his blood and my vomit, after telling Mrs. Thompson I washed most of it out. She didn't get close enough to call me a liar. As for Tyler, he got the afternoon off just so his mom could take him to Carbondale for x-rays.

Later that day after the final bell had rung and I was already in the hall, Mrs. Thompson called out to me, "I thought you'd like to know: Tyler's nose was broken but should be good as new after the doctor sets it. We expect Tyler back tomorrow."

"Yes ma'am," I said with a wave of my hand. "Thanks for telling me. I was really worried."

And still was. I hadn't counted on having to share Rowena with Tyler, or anyone else.

I needed a plan but didn't have one when I stepped onto the bus. Rowena was sitting in her usual seat, twirling a curl with her finger. But before I got anywhere near her, this eighth grader who'd never spoken to me before took his foot off the aisle seat, his way of inviting me to sit so I did. He told me his name and said he already knew mine, as did every kid in the school.

"They do?"

"You took out Tyler," he said.

"Not exactly, it was an accident."

"Sure it was."

Meaning give me a break, it was no accident. I didn't argue with him, just having the respect of an eighth grader—boy, what a feeling.

After the bus dropped me off, I walked with pride up the long driveway. Jed waved from his tractor, making me wonder if he already knew, and there was Delores, waiting at the kitchen door, a first for her.

"No need to explain about the shirt," she said, practically ripping it off my back. "Your teacher already called."

"It was an accident."

"And you lent your shirt to the injured boy, Mr. EMT to the rescue."

"Yes ma'am. If you don't mind, I'd like to start on my homework right away." I lifted my nose, glad to have it in one piece. "What's that I smell?"

"Roast pork with apples, just the way you like it."

What she really meant was: just the way Jed liked it.

Later at supper he kept eyeing me while I topped the crater of my mashed potatoes with thick gravy and let it trickle down to the moat I'd formed below. It could've passed for a chocolate sundae, almost. I was about to take my first mouthful when Jed said, "This boy with the injured nose, was there trouble between you and him."

"No sir, the only thing between us was a door." And Rowena, but Jed didn't need to know every stinking detail. Besides, Rowena wasn't a thing; she was … no longer my girlfriend unless she changed her attitude, which I intended to work on.

"'Cause if we're talking about a fight," Jed went on, "I wouldn't want you walking away from it, understand?"

"Yes sir, if ever there's a fight, I won't walk away."

Would he let it go? No, he came back at me with this: "In fact, maybe it's time to haul out the ol' boxing gloves, give you a few lessons in the art of self defense."

"Now, Jed, you don't need to show off your fancy footwork, leastways not at your age." Delores leaned over and piled creamed corn on my plate, making sure the pale yellow didn't mix with my gravy moat which would've ruined the whole picture.

"Sooner or later, the boy needs to learn," Jed said. "We don't want no sissy-pants carrying the Danner name, now do we?"

"I ain't no sissy pants."

"Am not," Delores chimed in. "We don't say 'ain't'."

I didn't mention the double negative Jed started, not that he would've popped me for calling attention to his bad grammar which Delores never corrected. So far, he hadn't laid a hand on me. But change was in the air, I could feel it.

"Sunday afternoon," the old man said. "Two o'clock in the barn, your first lesson."

That evening I was propped up on the bed while directing Luigi into another level when the phone rang. Instead of flying down the stairs, I stayed put and let Delores do the answering.

"Brandi has a question about math," she yelled up to me.

I went to the landing, English book in my hand. "I'm studying for a grammar test. She'll have to wait until tomorrow. Better yet, tell her to call Tyler."

"You mean the eighth grader who broke his nose?"

"Yes ma'am. I heard he's really smart and sometimes tutors the slower kids."

Chapter 22

Sugar Daddy, for sure not the run-of-the-mill pimp I'd seen in movies. No slicked-back hair, no alligator shoes with two-inch lifts, no fingers bogged down by gold-encrusted diamond rings, no teeth paved in gold or gold chains circling his rubbery neck, no pastel summer suit or white shirt stiffer than the starched doilies covering Delores's living room furniture. This dude was dressed for Vegas, a tropical shirt hanging over loose-fitting trousers, perfect for concealing his weapons of choice. I figured him around my height, maybe ten pounds heavier. Only the straw hat set him apart from the tourists, and his entourage of one, Nephew Everett, a mega version of his uncle and making a similar fashion statement.

Count me as one of many tourists on Freemont that day, wearing forty-something clothes I'd borrowed from Bish's closet and from his dresser, aviator sunglasses I wouldn't have been caught dead in otherwise. Sugar Daddy and Everett didn't even know we were breathing the same air when they stopped for a red light. Daddy removed his hat, exposing a sweaty bald head which Everett wiped with a handkerchief from his pocket. The light turned green, Daddy reset the hat on his head, and they took off across the street. Such devotion, I almost puked.

"Don't be fooled by Everett's lack of gray matter," Butterscotch had warned me. "Everett obeys on command. Just turned twenty-one and already he's psycho sick."

For me, not a problem, I'd dealt with his kind before, only younger versions. On the other hand, bringing Daddy down required a fail-safe plan, one I couldn't devise on my own, which made Butterscotch the perfect partner. Two days after the City House fiasco she'd called my hotel room. How she got my name I didn't ask; maybe one of the good sisters let it slip while praying for me. Butterscotch and I agreed to meet before sunrise on Sunday, behind a homeless shelter she visited now and then, not on business but to deliver donuts by the dozens. Her only contribution to the poor, she explained, putting her way ahead of me.

Earlier than early on the morning of our swap meet, I'd already dressed in black when Bish's latest hack attack sent familiar vibes through the wall separating our rooms. I held my ear to the door and waited another ten minutes for his steady Zs before slipping into the hallway. Sure, he'd be pissed to find me gone but I didn't owe him every minute of my life, awake or otherwise which is why I left the cell plugged into its charger. Out on the neon-lit streets it could've been mid-day, confirming Vegas never sleeps. I took a taxi to a seedy section the smart tourists avoid and had the driver let me out sooner than needed for added security. Ignoring the clutter of panhandlers and druggies, I hunched over for a two-block walk to the shelter, kept right on walking, and circled around to the rear.

No lights in the alley, just a faint odor of garbage mixed with the coolness of night before dawn, that priceless moment before morning yawns a new day and all hell breaks loose. I watched some mangy cat pawing at a doomed mouse until the shelter's back door swung open and out walked the incredible Butterscotch. Five-o-five my watch said, enough time for a quickie before attacking the nitty-gritty of planning. Bam! My bubble sprung an unexpected leak. Goodbye to the one-on-one, say hello to Butterscotch's tagalong.

Dulcie, she called herself, as in Dulcinea. Butterscotch introduced me as Bo. Okay, I got it, the whole intrigue bit. This Dulcie and I were running a not-so-easy-squinty-eyed scan of each other and she'd gone so far as to hiss at me when Butterscotch stepped in and told us to knock it off, that Sugar Daddy's eyes never went to sleep, anywhere, any hour—day or night.

Talk about paranoia.

Butterscotch slipped one arm through mine, the other through Dulcie's, and pushed us across the shadowy alley to this building ready for the headache ball. One by one we entered through an unlocked door, to an outsider looking as if a three-way was about to begin, the perfect set-up. Not gonna happen, that morning or any other with Dulcie playing number three. Even in the dark I sensed she was too meaty for my taste. But from the mission impossible angle teamwork was a top priority. No personality clashes, no in-your-face sarcasm. No problem; I'd been playing that game for years. Once again color me out in left field since Dulcie and Butterscotch already knew the pitch-dark building, relying on little more than their instincts and a pen flashlight. As we made our way through the hallways no one made a sound until Butterscotch let out a puppy yelp that stopped me cold.

"Hush!" Dulcie said. "You never felt a rat cross your path before?"

I'd felt the rat too. And smelled it, more than one and I don't mean the hookers. Them I had to trust, at least for the moment. I meant rodents, their odor so foul it had no place to go except through my pores and up my nose. Holding my exhale, I followed Dulcie and Butterscotch downstairs to a basement room once used by a janitor who'd probably quit out of desperation.

As soon as the door closed behind us, Butterscotch lit a fat candle and walked along with Dulcie while she inspected the closet-sized area. Taller than Butterscotch and shorter than me, Dulcie was dressed for limited success, in a tit-wringer top and red skirt with matching thong— not a pretty sight, especially between those two thunder thighs. Spaghetti strands of yellow hair draped around her quarterback shoulders. No amount of make-up could transform her less-than-ordinary face into anything close to pick-up quality, even if she hadn't been competing with Butterscotch in that gold and brown sundress.

Satisfied we were alone and the room wasn't bugged, Dulcie dropped her thunderous ass onto the only piece of furniture, a junkyard daybed, and patted either side for Butterscotch and me to join her. Bedbugs came to mind but when Butterscotch didn't hesitate about sitting down, I did the same.

"Been in the business long?" I asked Dulcie, my way of being polite.

"Three years," she replied, "all with Sugar Daddy."

How she ever pulled in enough johns to make a living blew my mind. "No kidding."

"No fun, but plenty of games and I, along with plenty others, have the broken bones to prove it. And just so you know: the entire stable is backing this project. Sugar Daddy has got to go—straight to Hell with no stopovers."

"Tell Bo about Teal." Butterscotch said.

Reverent as two Catholic school girls, they made the sign of the cross in unison. Not a first would be my guess. After a moment Dulcie spoke.

"Early in my career there was this young girl, no more than seventeen and barely surviving the streets when Daddy brought her into his stable. Teal wanted nothing more than Daddy's approval. She did whatever he asked of her, put in more hours than the rest of us, and not once complained about being his number one money machine. Daddy knew he had a good thing. He made Teal his pet, showered her with cheap trinkets until she started talking about returning to Oregon and making up with her family.

"'Sure, Baby,' that's what Daddy told her. 'But first, I need a show of love, how far you're willing to go for me.'

"Teal had never participated in The Game before; this would be a test of faith, like falling backwards into a set of waiting arms. Just three performances in three weeks, only three and she could go home with cash in her pocket. Poor thing, she agreed but right off the bat picked the wrong john, a pussy face if ever there was. Those wire-rimmed specs, a gentleman scholar—you know the type."

An image of Bish flashed in my brain, nah, no way.

"Don't think us prejudiced," Butterscotch interjected. "Some professors do have fire in their furnace. Others, burn on low and need a good stoking."

"Not this pussy face, he had neither," Dulcie said. "Backed against the fence Pussy Face just couldn't beat on her; and she wasn't smart enough to convince him otherwise. If only she'd been mean enough but mean wasn't part of her make-up. Daddy had been watching the failure-to-comply from his office perch, madder'n hell because he'd invited a big roller to observe as well. This I know firsthand because I was there too, my stomach turning flip-flops when Teal and her john ran out of the alley together. So disturbed was Daddy he sicced Everett on the two of them, right then and there. Teal's john may've escaped—no one knows for sure—but for Teal, time ran out faster than sand from an hourglass. The next day found her dead, her broken body dumped in Daddy's infamous Alley of Theatrics. Those in the know said our sister had been kicked to her death. A bitter lesson for all of us, one we will never forget."

"And one passed on to every hooker who joined Sugar Daddy's stable since Teal's expiration date," Butterscotch said. "Tell him the rest, Dulcie, Teal's afternoon in the alley."

"The big roller standing beside Daddy demanded a refund, which seemed fair enough. But Daddy's no pushover. Once he accepts money he ain't about to return it, regardless of the circumstances. Instead he offered up a sacrificial lamb, me. Five hours for The Roller to do with as he pleased. Suffice to say I still carry those scars, both inside and out."

"Which makes your stake in this bigger than mine," I said.

"And yours would be?" Dulcie asked.

I lifted my shoulders. "Not sure, the loss of pride, being forced to commit violence in order to prevent more violence." I didn't mention reinventing myself into a gutsy comic book hero who could've saved the day instead of blowing it. This sounded better: "Paybacks are hell. I call mine damage control."

"I so like your attitude," Butterscotch said. She slid off the cot, sank to her knees in front of mine, and said, "So, pay attention to this and no daydreaming. Whatever we start, we absolutely have to finish. Or else, Dulcie and you and me, we'll be finished forever."

Dulcie squeezed my forearm, as if checking out the muscle when she spoke. "You—whatever your name, and don't tell me again 'cause I don't want to remember it—you'd be doing more than accommodating a bunch of hookers. You'd be performing a civic duty, picking up the slack from those overworked and underpaid police of Las Vegas who couldn't be bothered nailing Teal's killers. I even sent them a letter with some clues but to my everlasting shame was too scared to come forward, with my family living in a neighboring state and all. Daddy and Everett, they make their own law and have long arms reaching far beyond the state of Nevada."

I started to ask a question but lost it when my mind headed south, in the vicinity of my crotch where Butterscotch's quick fingers were unzipping my fly.

Time out; she leaned back on her trim haunches. "Daddy issues the orders; Everett carries them out. These monsters are a danger to the community. Even the homeless aren't safe. There were these two men from the shelter, annoying, yes, but harmless ... you wanna hear about the mutilation?"

"Nah, I get the picture."

Dulcie stood up, feet spread and arms folded. "Then before we go any further, I need to know: are you in, all the way?"

I wish. Butterscotch was; that's for sure. She'd been prepping me like the pro I didn't want to think of her as, and Dulcie was starting to look way better than the first time we met.

"Well, what's it gonna be," Dulcie said.

"You two are making it hard for me to say no."

"Good," Dulcie said. "We'll take that as a yes."

Chapter 23

Butterscotch and Dulcie and me, a dynamic trio if ever there was; we parted that morning with me giving them an A-plus for the freebie they gave me. What's more, I'd developed a new respect for Dulcie and had to admit that sometimes skill topped physical attributes. Mission-wise, my teammates had more to lose in the payback than I did.

They told me Sugar Daddy ran his operation from a third floor walk-up, the same building that housed the girls in his stable. It was located at the end of what they called The Alley of Theatrics where cats and rats and stinking garbage discouraged curious outsiders along with those who knew the score. While Nephew Everett stood guard at the office door, his Grand Poobah uncle conducted business inside. One at a time, a steady stream of hookers presented themselves to Sugar Daddy. Seated behind his polished desk, he would engage them in a quiet discussion of their earnings over the past twenty-four hours, carefully recording the amount in a ledger while they handed over an envelope containing his lop-sided percentage. All quite civilized, unless Sugar Daddy questioned the reported income and demanded a greater share.

Arbitration, forget about it. Daddy never wavered. Any hooker who dared to object wound up in the Alley of Theatrics with some dumb-as-me fool, slugging it out for the enjoyment of the pimpster and his paying guests. But nothing stays the same for long, this thing called evolution; and if all went well, Daddy's game was about to evolve into nothing.

As was my lop-sided relationship with Bish; I'd about had it with him. So far, he'd paid me nothing but empty excuses and the loose change I swiped from his dresser while he was showering. He must've noticed but never complained because he knew better than to upset me after witnessing the anger management issues in Kansas. But the morning after Butterscotch and Dulcie was no morning for a showdown, what with me still reeling from the three-way. My first and better than expected, better yet, the promise of an eventual two-way between Butterscotch and me. But first, another first: my civic duty, ridding Vegas of Sugar Daddy.

"Everything okay," Bish was asking, along with his usual cough.

My bad for concentrating so hard I hadn't heard him open the door between our rooms.

"You bet." I smiled half-assed, my thoughts still with Butterscotch. "Since money's so tight, I might take a bus tour of the dam today."

"Excellent," he said. "As long as you don't forget your cell phone and the job you were hired to do, which means being here when I return. Six o'clock, no later."

Sieg heil! I gave his back the ol' Nazi salute as he left for his daily fix at the casinos.

Ten minutes later, a knock on the door. Room service compliments of Bish, I figured, checking out the hallway. Instead I hit my own jackpot—Butterscotch, pushing her way inside and ordering me to close the door. Before I could say a word, she backed me against the wall, much like our first meeting in the alley, but this time when we kissed, honey dripped from her mouth to mine. More than anything else, I wanted her. Against the wall, on the carpet, the sofa, the bed, anywhere and everywhere, I didn't care.

Instead she pulled away and tossed me a pitiful bone with this: "I'd offer you another on the house but I know you're too proud to accept charity."

No I wasn't. What little money I had would've been an insult to her fine body but that didn't stop me from exaggerating the state of my finances. "However much, just say the word and I'll pay it."

"Hush." She put her finger to my lips. "Someday soon we'll do each other for hours and hours."

"Just hours, that's all? How about the rest of our lives?"

"Yours or mine, be careful what you wish for. Anyway, back to business, we haven't much time. You know: Sugar Daddy and those eyes." She smacked her luscious lips together. "Pardon my thirst but I sure could use a sweet tea or something equally refreshing."

Now, before I finished what she started? Yeah, Butterscotch had her own agenda. I help myself to cokes from Bish's fridge and instead of playing with her, we played around with a few ideas on how to bring Sugar Daddy down. The best one revolved around Dulcie since he hadn't forced her to play The Game for weeks, not since the last john had enjoyed performing more than Daddy enjoyed watching, which must've been quite a stretch. Perfect.

But before we could finalize any plan, Butterscotch's phone rang. She answered on the first ring with nothing more than a greeting and listened while edging away from me and toward the door. She opened it when the call ended.

"Later," she said on her way out. "Daddy needs some reassurance. He thinks I went missing."

Just like that she was gone. Forget the plan; forget the revenge; forget the missed op.

***

Days of catering to Bish's every whim passed before the phone call I'd been expecting finally came, pulling me out of the shower as I preparing for another same-old-same-old evening. But instead of hearing Butterscotch's voice, it was Dulcie's that set me on edge as she rattled off a set of instructions relating to our upcoming meeting. She hung up before I could ask about Butterscotch.

Pre-dawn the next morning I again skipped out on the sleeping Bish, knowing he'd rag on me later for leaving without his okay or the cell. As if I cared, with him treating me like some junior high drop out. Close, yes, but I didn't owe him a play-by-play of my life story.

Again, I caught a taxi but to a different neighborhood, not as seedy as the shelter's but definitely on the fringe. Making sure no one was following, I covered three blocks in five minutes, arriving at All Saints of Las Vegas where a side door had been left unlocked. Inside, hazy lighting gave the place an eerie feeling or maybe it was the absence of bowed heads, me being the only person crazy enough for church at that hour. In one corner a bank of votive candles flickered, reminding me of another time, another life. Nearby stood an oak rack, stuffed with pamphlets for the taking. I helped myself, headed to the back pew, and genuflected before sitting down. A church for disenfranchised Catholics and other Christians so inclined I managed to read before giving in to a good sixty minutes of fighting sleep, my boney butt alternating between the seat and the kneeler.

During one kneeling phase my head was resting against hands hanging onto the forward pew when I felt the kneeler groan from added weight, Dulcie's. She was dressed in civvies, a t-shirt and faded jeans with gaping holes, and could've passed for a teenager showing off baby fat.

"Are we alone?" she whispered.

"Nobody but us sinners," I said, stretching my neck for a fifth mini-scan since arriving. "Where's Butterscotch?"

"Laid up at City House, Daddy hobbled her for straying too far from home."

"Dammit, Dulcie," I practically yelled through my whisper. "You should've contacted me right away."

She put her hand over my mouth. "And you'd've done what? Take him down with your slingshot? Whose fault do you think this is—yours, stupid."

I pushed her hand away. "My fault, how'd you figure that?"

"Idiot," Dulcie said, "for luring Butterscotch outside her safe zone. She was with you when Daddy called. He expected her back in a flash."

My blood topped the boiling point. I slammed the side of my fist against the pew. "How bad did he hurt her?"

"Foot-to-foot stomp, she won't be strolling for some weeks. Worse than the pain was Daddy dipping into her rainy-day reserve. For the record we hookers don't get compensated for time off."

"You think he knows about us?"

"Can't say for sure but we need to act fast before he does find out." She nodded toward the back wall. "Let's take our business into one of those."

"A confessional, it's just not cricket," I said in my best British accent.

"And you're not Austin Powers. God will give us a pass."

"You're sure about that."

"No, but the clock's ticking so what's it gonna be."

We entered a face-to-face confessional and she sat across from me, resurrecting a flood of memories worth forgetting.

"Amen," Dulcie whispered as an opener. "It's been months since my last confession and I'm still in the same profession."

"Cut the bull and show some respect."

"Sorry," she said, crossing herself. "Now, about Daddy, wouldn't you know, yesterday he raised this awful stink with me, all over a measly two hundred dollars."

"You held back on him?"

"The fool played right into my hands. Luckily, he has a big deal going down today so he scheduled my performance for tomorrow afternoon. 'Two o'clock in the alley,' he told me, 'and don't be bringing no soft-hearted mama's boy to make up for what happened to you the last time.'"

"Tomorrow afternoon? With that much lead time what's keeping you in Vegas? Leave today. Take a bus or a plane to anywhere."

"It doesn't work that way. Others have tried, and only a few have succeeded, which is why Daddy doles out our money one day at a time."

"I'll lend you the money." Okay, Bish's not mine since I didn't have any. Him and me, we were just another pimp and whore. "Better yet, I'll give it to you."

"And leave Butterscotch behind, neither of us would want that. Besides I adhere to certain principles, as do my sisters. Daddy's so mean he makes us pay extra until he locates the runaway. And when he does, look out, it ain't pretty."

"And if he doesn't?"

"Showtime, starring the most disabled among us but let's not dwell on the morbid."

Too late, I already pictured Butterscotch jabbing some clueless john with her crutch, ordering him to smash her good foot. Maybe she'd pick a jerk who relished the game, enjoyed beating up women, hookers or otherwise. Dulcie must've been reading my thoughts; with a flick of her finger she thumped my head. A wake-up call Delores would've called it.

"Stay away from Butterscotch," Dulcie said. "I mean this most vigorously. Girlfriend is taking a load off her feet so don't even think about distracting her. Besides, more pressing matters, the lifesaving kind, require our immediate attention." She reached into her gigantic handbag, pulled out a plastic sack, and handed it to me. "Your equipment for tomorrow, here's hoping it fits." Next from the handbag came a pen and spiral notebook. "My half of the plan's already coded and in place; it's been too damn long waiting for the other half, that being you, whatever your name. Which brings up another issue, before Butterscotch was hospitalized, me and her already decided you needed an expert sidekick."

I smelled a putdown. "No way, I prefer working alone."

"And I prefer a dude with some years to go with the muscle. We're talking about surviving the payback. So quit your whining and let's finish our business."

Chapter 24

Sunday afternoon, two o'clock in the barn, not where I wanted to be but didn't have much choice. Dust hung thicker than smoke in the bars Lark used to take me. She should've seen me now. Tickling my tonsils with my tongue made me sneeze. Not once but twice, and for nothing. Delores paid no never mind to my watery eyes. She was too busy helping Jed and me with the boxing gloves before hurrying out to her flower beds. As if the weeds couldn't wait. What she couldn't stand was the sight of human blood. Mine. For sure it wouldn't be her precious Jed's. Ice cold lemonade, that's what flowed through his veins. Sweet on her, sour on me. For sure, Jed was no dummy but neither was I.

There we stood, the two of us working our feet into straw covering floorboards as old as the barn.

"This way," Jed said, shifting his weight forward onto his right foot while holding up his right hand.

I copied the position and waited for his next words.

"Your left arm goes back like this," he said. "Wait a minute, I forgot, you're left-handed. Reverse the stance."

I fumbled around from one foot to the other until he finally said I got it right.

"And whatever you do, don't attempt a punch like this." He swung high from over his shoulder. "Understand?"

"I think." That's all he needed to hear. Before I could blink, he bounced the glove off my face. Did it again, only this time harder, giving me an idea how Tyler must've felt when the door hit his nose. Fortunately, mine wasn't broken, leastways not yet.

"Okay, your turn," he said, bending his face down to mine.

He let me hit him a couple of times. Easy punches, I didn't want to set him off. The next time I went for his face, he blocked my punch with his other glove, which until then hadn't been doing much except hanging out. Then he popped me, harder than the last time.

"Gotcha," he said with a grin.

Oh, yeah, but did I ever get him back. One, two, one—right in his gut, he doubled over, pain spreading across his wrinkled face.

"Why you little shit. You've boxed before."

"Never, I swear."

But I had seen plenty of movies, the first Rocky being my all time favorite.

***

On Monday I felt three inches taller when I stepped onto the bus. I must've looked taller too because Rowena waved at me from our usual seat. I started down the aisle when this really cute girl with a blonde pony tail asked me to sit down. She flipped her hair and batted her eyes and did most of the talking, mainly about do-good stuff, the total opposite of Rowena and definitely not my type. But what a feel-good, knowing Rowena was watching my every move instead of being a part of it. At school everybody but Tyler wanted me for a friend but not in the same way as Rowena. I let her stew for a couple of days, that is, until after school on Wednesday. She'd been hanging with some girls in the parking lot and when I got on the bus, she was right behind me.

"Pick a seat," she said, "around the little kids who don't know any better. We need to talk."

I passed up four girls who wanted me beside them before stopping at our usual seat, except this kid was already there, hugging the window. He might've been a sixth grader, I'm not for sure, but as soon as he saw me, he moved to another seat. Rowena scooted in first, then me. The bus was rolling onto the highway before she opened up.

"I don't like this, not one bit," she said. "By now we should be into our second week of doing *it*."

"Is it my fault you're going steady with Tyler."

"Not any more. We broke up."

"Your idea or his?"

"Who cares, but if you must know, mine. He's such a bully. Sorry 'bout that, I mean the other day."

"You shouldn't have told him about us."

She put her hand over mine, something she'd never done before. "I know and I'm truly, truly sorry. Can we start over?"

Anticipation, it was all I could think about.

***

Rowena swore the bathroom pass and janitor's closet would work again. Me, I wasn't so sure but couldn't come up with a better plan. We decided on the following Monday but on Thursday when Mrs. Robinson announced she wouldn't be in the next day, we decided to go with the substitute teacher.

Friday, same stomach ache during math, same cookie exchange at lunch for the bathroom pass, my wiener was about to explode when I opened the janitor's closet. No surprises this time, it was Rowena waiting in the dark, the only sound coming from her loud breathing. Before I could say a word, she backed me against the wall, unzipped my jeans, and grabbed what she called dickie-boy.

"Hurry up," she said, squeezing so tight I almost exploded from both ends. "We don't have all day, you know."

I barely squeaked out a simple question. "Shouldn't we kiss or something?"

"How's this." She stuck her tongue down my throat and without missing a beat managed to lift her skirt. That's when I realized she'd saved me the trouble of taking off her underwear, an important step we'd discussed more than once by phone and on the bus. Except for me putting one hand on her boob, Rowena made all the right moves, the heavy stuff, which worked out fine for both of us. *It* was over in less than two minutes and by then I'd forgotten about my stomach problems.

About Rowena, I couldn't say for sure but I guess she must've liked it because after that first day we met in the janitor's closet twice a week, a whole month of sweeter than sweet, until the day Tyler Jarvis caught me alone in the hall. He shoved me against the wall and told me to lay off Rowena or else he'd cut off my dick and feed it to the pigs. I knew they eat just about anything so I told him okay. Sure, I could've popped him and probably should have but I didn't.

The next morning like always I sat on the bus with Rowena. She smiled, held out her hand, and showed me this bracelet circling her wrist.

Cripes, I figured a gift from big-bucks Tyler, and me with no money to compete.

"Nice," I managed to say. "Did Tyler give that to you?"

"Tyler? No way," she said with a jerk of her head. "It's a purity bracelet from my mom. She made me promise not to have sex 'til I'm at least eighteen."

"What about you and me?"

"It's over, Dickie-boy. A promise is a promise."

Two weeks later Mrs. Robinson caught Rowena and her purity bracelet in the closet with Tyler and his dickie-boy. The principal expelled both of them. Just like that, Catholic school history. What a bite, if only I'd been the dude caught with her maybe Jed and Delores would've sent me packing. Instead, as Delores often said, I'd bitten off my nose to spite my face. What's really weird is how close she came to nailing the real me, a get-even squealer who sent Mrs. Robinson scurrying to the janitor's closet that day, all because of the unsigned noted I'd left on her desk.

Chapter 25

High noon the next day found me, John Danner the Second, behind a pair of shaded safety glasses, primed, ready for action, and minus the cell phone, again. No one, not even Lark, would've recognized me in the white carpenter pants, orange t-shirt with company logo, and Vegas ball cap covering my hair. All in all, it spelled construction guy. Expect my partner to be a look-alike, Dulcie had told me, and that he'd show up when I needed him most. Top Dog, she'd called him, making sure I understand my number two position.

But for now I was alone and marking time on Sugar Daddy's street when he left the building with Everett at his side. As soon as they turned the corner, I picked up my pace and walked into the neighboring building, a run-down apartment house undergoing a half-assed renovation begun that very day, thanks to Dulcie's connections. Two workers dressed like me were splitting for lunch; the other carbon copies smoking their joints didn't notice me slip my hands into a pair of surgical gloves and pick up one of the hard hats. Anyone of them could've been Top Dog, or not. After climbing up two flights of dusty stairs to the flat roof, I did a three-sixty of the neighborhood, said a prayer to Mother Mary, and made my first leap of faith onto the next roof. Mary came through for me; but considering what I was about to do only God knew how she'd feel about helping me on the return flight.

The building I'd left behind was a twin to the one I now entered, which gave me an immediate advantage. Finding Sugar Daddy's office, not a problem, it took up a good chunk of the third floor, the rest unfit for any business, legit or otherwise. I jimmied the locked door next to Daddy's office and found a room empty of furniture but filled with an oppressive heat known only to Nevada and the deepest caverns of Satan's Hell. Fortunately, and to Dulcie's credit, a breeze crept through the only window, its glass pane smashed and pieces scattered across the bare floor. By now I'd convinced myself that God was okay with this mission.

My only regret so far was failing to bring a good read for killing time because I had no idea when Top Dog would show or if he decided to pick his nose instead. After pulling ice packs out of my pockets, I put one behind my neck, the other two in my armpits. The hard hat I sat on while thinking about my future with Butterscotch. Somehow I couldn't quite picture us together for the long haul. Maybe she'd been right after all, about our spending hours together instead of an eternity. Either way I wanted time with her, just the two of us in a real bed with music setting the proper mood, maybe something by Coldplay. She'd probably teach me a move or two but I'd show her the softer side of love.

My daydream ended at one-thirty when Sugar Daddy and Everett returned, in a good mood from the sound of their muffled laughter seeping through the wall of cheap paneling separating us. Since I heard them, could they've heard me, the gasping for breath as heat sucked life from my two sorry lungs? Maybe, if they hadn't been so full of themselves. I considered moving further away but couldn't risk making any noise so I put my ear to the wall and listened. Making out which voice belonged to which idiot was not difficult.

"Dulcie better not disappoint me," Sugar Daddy said.

Everett came across dumber than a door. "Uncle Sugar, the rules that you and you alone created say we cannot control what john she happens to pick."

"Yeah, I been thinking 'bout those rules. They may need revising in the near future."

"Amen, Uncle, it is your game."

"You remember Butterscotch's jellyfish from some days ago?"

"You talking 'bout the weak-kneed scaredy cat what nearly pissed his pants?"

"That be the one, Nephew. My eyes and ears tell me Jellyfish and Butterscotch were seen talking afterwards, all friendly-like."

"That ain't right. She knows the rules."

"My sentiments exactly, we need to rectify the situation before it goes any further, but how?"

"Give me time. I'll think of something."

Weak-kneed scaredy cat, I'd show Sugar Daddy and his nephew my knees and then some. Beads of sweat mixed with anticipation were popping out on my forehead as I waited for The Game to begin.

Showtime: Dulcie came strolling down the alley with Mr. Tourist wearing a loose-fitting shirt, cargo shorts and hiking boots. Nice touch, the way she caught him off guard, backing him into the fence, just as Butterscotch had done with me. After a sixty-second wham-bam-thank-you-ma'am, she slapped him and he came back at her with the flat of his hand. From there they went at each other like two alley cats but without the screeching. I couldn't tell the real from the fake and was beginning to worry if there were any pulled punches when Dulcie finally slumped to the ground, her body quivering. Mr. Tourist didn't stop with a few kicks. He turned into an animal, unable to stop and seemingly enjoying every moment.

"Whoa," I heard Sugar Daddy tell Everett. "Get your ass down there before he kills the ugly bitch."

"Aw-w, that ain't fair. It's been a long time since we seen us a final performance."

"Go on now. She's too good to let die, anyways not today."

"Whatever you say, Uncle."

After hearing the door close, I slipped on my Barack Obama face mask and waited. Act Two: Everett came running across the alley to rescue Dulcie but Mr. Tourist had other ideas. He turned on Everett, my cue to visit the adjacent office. Making no sound, I opened the door and went inside, my heart pounding so hard Sugar Daddy must've heard it.

There he was, standing at the window, totally into the scene below and unaware I'd invaded his space. That is, until I drop-kicked him from behind, well almost. Somehow on the way down, he managed to take me with him. Before I could smash my fist in his mouth, he was on top of me, his thumbs under the mask and digging into my throat. Sweet Jesus, I couldn't breathe. My eyes were trying to pop their sockets. All I could think about was ripping Barack Obama off my face. I was about to pray when I heard a thud and felt Sugar Daddy keel over, relieving me of one burden.

Top Dog to the rescue, he was my five-inches-taller and fifty-pounds-heavier lookalike, right down to the Obama mask. I was fighting to regain my breath when he jammed his fist into Sugar Daddy's glasses and ripped them broken from his eyes, then relocated the bastard's nose to his left cheek. Sugar Daddy never uttered a sound when Top Dog kicked in his ribs but instead rolled to one side, as if offering up his best kidney. After smashing it, Dog rolled him back and went for the other one while I scrambled to my feet and watched because two against one wouldn't have been fair. Although I did wind up with Sugar Daddy's blood on my gloves, how I'm not sure. Had it not been for the warning below, a rock crashing through the window, Dog would've finished him off, snuffed the life from him. But a second rock sailing through changed his mind.

With no time for a final check of the alley scene, I followed Dog into the hallway.

"You go your way, kid, and I'll go mine," he said, until that moment the only words I heard him speak. "And next time don't play the revenge game until you've earned yourself some chops."

Chops, you bet. He should've seen them in Kansas. Dog disappeared down a long hallway. After making sure nothing of me was left behind, I hurried back to the roof, slipped off the mask, and buried it deep in one pocket.

"Mother of Mary, stay with me," I prayed, taking my second leap of faith. She must've because I landed with bent knees onto the twin building. I went down the steps faster than I'd gone up them, again no one noticing as I strolled through the first level. Outside, hands in my pockets, I slipped off the gloves smeared with Daddy's blood, lowered my head, and casually zigzagged through a few crummy streets before reaching Fremont and the strolling tourists.

When I was sure no one had followed me, I hailed a cab, climbed into the back seat, and whistled a made-up tune until I had the cabbie drop me in front of a casino ten blocks from my hotel. From there I walked to a movie theater, bought a ticket to the latest James Bond flick and in the restroom, ditched the construction clothes in favor of my tee and jeans underneath. Only the steel-toed boots remained, and they didn't look out of place in a city where anything goes.

Chapter 26

Time out: day one after Sugar Daddy's downfall. I entered Danner's version of *going to the mattresses* which consisted of hanging out at the hotel pool by day and by night watching pay-for-view movies in my room. No porn, thanks to Bish the Pious who blocked my access to the adult channels. Again, this junior high image of me he couldn't shake unless he needed the grown-up me for companionship. On the plus side, he did keep his distance, having bought my song and dance about fighting a mega case of diarrhea. It also kept him from noticing the twin bruises on my throat or the annoying static in my voice. Butterscotch or Dulcie: not a word from either, a good sign which meant they had no reason to detour from our original plan.

As for Sugar Daddy, he had his own version of the mattress, laying on one while fighting for every breath in the ICU of Las Vegas Hospital. About Everett the Stupid, all I knew for sure was he crawled out of the alley alive, which made my skin crawl. Dulcie and her pseudo John should've finished what they'd started.

On my fourth day of lying low, I stirred from a sound sleep, unable to ignore a knock-knock from the adjoining room. "What!" I finally yelled, my throat having returned to normal.

"Sorry about the disturbance," Bish said through the door. "But I didn't think you'd want to miss the fireworks."

As if I hadn't seen several versions before. Feeling generous, I rolled out of bed, stepped into my briefs, and crossed over to Bish's room. I joined him at the window but instead of your run-of-the-mill fireworks, I witnessed a cloud of red smoke mushrooming into the sky, bringing a weird sensation to the entire city. And an even weirder hack attack from Bish, forcing me to help him into the bathroom where he assaulted the toilet bowl with tar-like blood, I figured for my benefit. Anything to compete with the fake diarrhea I'd described in nauseating detail.

Forget about sleep. We got dressed, went down to the street, and along with everyone else, oohed and aahed over the glowing atmosphere and distant sirens. After a while Bish started yawning so we returned to our rooms. Falling back asleep, not a problem. I pictured myself with Butterscotch, making the most of those hours she'd promised. Forget eternity or a week in paradise, I was in for the short haul.

Later that morning before I'd fulfilled all my dreams, more knock-knock followed by desperate pounding, Bish yelling for me to come over right away. I considered going naked, giving him a heart attack but instead slipped on a clean tee and boxers. He was sitting on the edge of his bed, bent forward while watching TV, some reporter with long dark hair detailing news about the spectacular fire that had destroyed City House.

City House, dear God—any place but there. Maybe God was sending me a message. If not God, Everett the Devil, I pictured him with a can of gasoline, body still aching as he limped from room to room, tossing fuel over furniture and curtains, flames shooting up to destroy Sister Mom's refuge for hookers. What about Butterscotch, she owed me.

The reporter went on about Sister Mary Fran, the founder of City House, how she managed to escape, as did four other nuns and seven temporary residents. Two people in the house did not survive—the stern though much beloved Sister Bernadette and a young woman whose name was not revealed pending notification of kin.

Panic set in, all but crippling me. My knees buckled; I slid to the floor, back against the bed. Bish's hand gripped my shoulder, squeezed harder and harder as together we endured another of his hack attacks. My heart started pounding when the phone rang. He answered with a *Yes, Mother*, another *Yes, Mother*, followed by a *God rest her soul, Mother* before the call ended.

He leaned over, the stubble on his face rubbing against mine. "The young lady you were talking to the other evening, I'm sorry, she didn't survive."

I said nothing but went back to my room. I knelt before the bathroom's porcelain god and gave up the remains of a late-night burger and fries. Having nothing left to sacrifice, I stepped into the shower and released the hot water. The stall became my refuge, the absolute of nothingness, until Bish came in and found me huddled under water gone cold. Without saying a word, he helped me out of the wet underwear and into bed and then left me, not quite alone but with a new set of demons.

The next day in The Alley of Theatrics, police discovered Everett dead, his throat slashed from ear to ear, rats lunching on the open wound and surrounding flesh. Meanwhile across town, Sugar Daddy's condition had improved to where the hospital transferred him to its not-so-critical section. Two days later a student nurse fainted when she found him in a situation similar to Everett's but minus the feeding frenzy.

During Everett's descent into Hell, I was attending the funeral Mass for Sister Bernadette, the former Maureen O'Dell of New York City, and during Sugar Daddy's descent, I was escorting the remains of Hooker Butterscotch, the former Theresa Saint Pierre, to the Vegas airport for eventual burial in a cemetery on the outskirts of New Orleans. But Top Dog, that's another story, him being from Oregon, the brother to that young hooker named Teal who never made it home because Sugar Daddy had kicked her to death.

***

That night with Bish snoring louder than a lumberjack's chainsaw, I plugged my ears with bits of tissue and vegetated in front of the TV, staring at god-only-knows-what movie flashing on the screen for god-only-knows-how long. I'd come to this fork in the road, forced to make a decision in the name of self-respect. No more Mister Nice Guy, I'd allowed Bish far too much leeway. He'd responded by pushing me to the limit; now my survival instincts told me to push back. I debated between leaving with all his money or just my lousy salary before he woke up, or leaving with his money before making sure he never woke up again. I imagined myself holding a pillow over his face during his next attack, gently ever so gently letting him drown in the phlegm he didn't have the strength to bring up. What to do, what to do. I fell asleep before reaching my decision, giving Bish a timely reprieve because right after I woke up, he handed over two weeks salary. Plus another fifty for no reason whatsoever.

"I'm taking Sister Mary Fran out to dinner tonight," he said. "You'll come with us?"

As if food could fill the empty pit in my heart. "I won't be hungry."

"You're sure about that."

My silence answered for me.

He couldn't leave it alone. "You want to talk about last night?"

"Not now, maybe later." Maybe never, what did he know.

"Sure, kid ... Danner, whatever you say."

I should've taken him up on the offer to talk, played on his sympathy but that wasn't my style, leastways not then. What's more, percentage-wise I was ninety-nine and nine tenths positive that his sperm had not contributed in any way, shape, or form to my DNA. And although Sister Mom would've made an amazing grandma, I just couldn't see her and me on the same team.

Still unsure about my current situation on the street, as in a reversal of the Sugar Daddy payback, I hung out in my room all day, except for two trips to the coffee shop where I charged my purchases to Bish. He didn't return until ten that night. I was already in bed but not asleep since I'd slept away most of the day. I waited another hour before switching on the TV and kept the sound low, again unaware of which movie flickered from the screen and not wanting to be alone with my Butterscotch thoughts on what I coulda, shoulda, woulda done—if only I hadn't been so wrapped up in playing Superman-to-the-rescue.

As for Dulcie and her tough actor-john, I hadn't heard from either of them since the souring of our sweet revenge. Nor did I expect to, ever again.

***

The next morning Bish asked too nicely if I'd join him for breakfast. Half-starved and having nothing better to do at ten o'clock, I agreed without his usual arm twisting.

"Pick a decent place," he said. "You and I deserve a special treat."

"You pick. I'm still in mourning."

Bellagio's, his choice not mine, it didn't get much better. Out of respect for the City House tragedy we skipped the super colossal buffet and instead chose the most casual of dining—bacon and eggs, same as our hotel coffee shop, but served with fine china and man-sized utensils at triple the cost.

After finishing my last triangle of toast, I turned down Bish's offer for his leftovers. Poor slob, he just didn't get it. "How's your mother?" I asked.

"Already talking about fundraising for another City House," Bish said, "Like Phoenix rising from the ashes, you know what I mean?"

"I'm not stupid."

"Did I say otherwise?"

"No, but you were thinking it. I'm quite the reader, not because of Lark but her mom, the only grandma I've ever known which is not to say that couldn't change in the near future."

"Not while you're here in Vegas."

"You wish. Phoenix was a mythological bird, destroyed by fire, only to rise again."

"Close enough," he said. "I should be so lucky."

"Only if you believe in reincarnation."

"I'm not ruling it out. In fact, I'm not ruling out anything. Now, how shall we spend the day?" He pulled out a quarter from his pocket, flipped it in the air, and I called heads. "Congratulations, you've won a day with me at the casino."

"Great, there's nothing I'd like better than watching you lose my future earnings."

"Relax. Yesterday dealt me a good hand so I've decided to pass my luck on to you."

He dug into his pocket for a fat wad of greenbacks and peeled off some C-notes. Six to be exact, half of which I blew away within hours on the slots at Caesar's Palace with no one asking to see my I.D. Not about to lose the other half I wandered over to the blackjack area, stood back, and for the next two hours silently cheered Bish through a winning streak that mercifully ended while he was still ahead.

Since Bish was riding high, I agreed to dinner with him and Sister Mary Fran. He and I took a twenty-minute cab ride away from The Strip and wound up at the kind of restaurant he could easily afford after his black jack success. At first I didn't recognize good ol' mom, already seated in a candlelit corner of the dining room and dressed in civilian clothes that must've set her back a few bucks. After a ceremonial wetting of the cheeks, we sat down.

Our waiter came by, introduced himself, as if any of us cared, and suggested we start out with cocktails, which Bish rejected by going with white wine plus fruit and cheese. This was the Vegas I'd expected from

Day One. I was totally into the evening and determined to milk it for everything I could, quite a stretch considering my current state of mind.

"Would you like to talk about Butterscotch?" Sister asked me. "I'd be happy to share her finer moments."

None of which could compare with mine, I told Sister thanks but I'd rather talk about her. "Or, we could talk about me," I added as an afterthought.

I glanced at Bish, enjoyed watching him squirm over the possibility, however remote, of him being my sperm provider and his mom, my grandma. She glanced at Bish, more amused than annoyed.

"Samuel, what have you been telling Danner about me?"

"Nothing," he said, "other than the origin of my name, which intrigued him."

Sister Mom's laughter took a good ten years off an already perfect face. Unlike her previous reaction to my interest in the family history, this time she opened up. "The Clan: Samuel for Sammy Davis, Jr.; Dean for Dean Martin; and Lawford after my dear friend Peter. I knew them first as a showgirl at the Sands and later when I got into trouble, they came to my rescue with a fistful of money—pocket change to them but to me the lifeline I desperately needed. An abortion or a baby—the choice belonged to me and no one else." She warmed Bish's hand with hers. "I've never regretted my decision."

"What about the other guys?" I asked, breaking up their touchy-feely. "Sinatra and Joey Bishop, I mean."

"Well, after Samuel's birth I decided he'd have a better life with a loving family which I was in no position to provide in the foreseeable future. So, I give up the baby I dearly loved, allowed him to be adopted through a private attorney. I knew the couple—wonderful people whose last name happened to be Lawford—no relation to Peter, who adored me and I in turn, him. Although I felt confident Samuel would be raised in a loving home, I couldn't erase the horrific guilt of my actions, not only those leading to his conception but the aftermath as well. Only drugs and alcohol could ease my pain until a casual acquaintance, a former hooker whose judgment I trusted, suggested I accompany her on a weekend retreat of quiet reflection. It was during that time I had a mind-altering experience, an epiphany which changed my life forever after. As for Samuel, he received a wonderful start in life."

Again her hand warmed his, applying just enough pressure. "Right, darling?"

"If you say so, Mother."

"Trust me, you were happy. Unfortunately, neither of your adoptive parents had an extended family and when they were killed in a plane crash—"

"Goodbye home sweet home, hello orphanage," Bish said. "Not that I'm complaining."

More adoring glances between Sister Mom and her child, just color me the outsider. One who knew his place, I waited until she returned to her story. "Samuel was a delight and loved by all. At first I told no one of our relationship when I was assigned to the same orphanage but felt it was God's will that I should have him in my presence every day."

"What about Sinatra?"

She raised her brow. "Use your brain, John Danner."

"Oh, yeah, I get it—Sister Mary Francis."

"Joey Bishop wasn't really involved," she said.

"The Bishop came about years later," Bish said, "at Bed and Bread in St. Louis. The guys thought I projected a certain reverence."

Little did they know, or me, allowing myself to get stuck with His-less-than-holy Reverence.

Sister Mary Fran ordering a vegetarian plate didn't stop me from ordering the eight-ounce strip steak, or Bish from the chicken noodle soup he had a tough time finishing even with her practically spooning every slurp into his slack mouth.

"I've made an appointment for you with Allen Bloomberg, head of oncology at the university," she told him.

"Thanks, but I'm through seeing doctors."

"Don't be ridiculous. You've always been a fighter."

"One who knows when to throw in the proverbial towel."

"I can't stand seeing you like this."

"You won't have to; I'm going away."

"Not before I mount my fund raiser to rebuild City House. I need you here so I won't have to worry about your being elsewhere."

Oh, yeah. They were mother and son, all right.

"I'll keep in touch," Bish said, squeezing my hand as tight as she'd squeezed his. "And should any problems arise, be assured my good friend Danner will rush me to the nearest medical facility."

Good friend, more like Butt Boy number one and two. Thanks for confirming what I didn't want to hear that day or any other. I'd been demoted to playing nursemaid to a dying man.

Chapter 27

Vegas without Butterscotch I could've done without. Ditto for a homicide investigation possibly leading to yours truly, the instigator who didn't follow through with an outcome that should've ended better—thanks but no thanks. Bish must've sensed my edginess because one day while we were eating breakfast at the hotel café, he dangled a brochure about Montana's Big Sky Country in front of me. I took one look at it and caved like cardboard under an elephant's rear end but didn't let on.

"Montana, that's a long way from here," I said, returning the brochure to him.

"But you have nothing better to do with your time. Come on, admit you're intrigued. The whole mountain scene is absolutely incredible. Trust me, it'll blow your mind."

"Scenery's for old folks. I'm more of a sun and surf guy." More like a wannabe, I'd yet to see the oceans or a single Great Lake. "Give me water activities designed for the fit and trim." Of which I considered myself to be and Bish not. Hurting his feelings hadn't been my intention, I just wanted out. Montana would go on my list of dying-to-see places but not with a dying man. "Maybe you should find another driver."

"We'll leave tomorrow morning," he said.

What? Now his hearing was failing.

"After a good substantial breakfast," he went on. "I know how much you like to eat."

"Yeah, so long as it's not me doing the cooking or cleaning up."

"Shaving supplies, et cetera, the selection is significantly better here in Vegas than where we're going," he said, pushing back his chair. "We'll shop now, after I pay—unless you want to pick up the tab. That'll free up the rest of the day for casinos."

Bish's idea of a better selection wound up being one of Vegas' many Walgreen's, as if no such box store could be found in Big Sky Country. Inside Walgreen's it was Bish's show and his wallet. Me, I just pushed the cart while checking out chicks in skin-tight pants and off-the-shoulder blouses. Bish focused on the crowded shelves. Shaving cream, razors, deodorant, shampoo, soap, aspirin, hydrogen peroxide, rubbing alcohol, bandages—a lifetime supply which raised the checker's eyebrows when Bish asked her to separate his five-to-one ratio from my few items.

Back in the parking lot we, meaning I, loaded up the SUV's back end. The efficient Bish was already belted in his seat when I climbed into mine. The edginess I'd been trying to ignore was toying with those muscles behind my neck and across my shoulders. Bish, on the other hand, was energized with Mountain Dew anticipation. He tapped the dashboard, tapped it again.

"Let's go," he said. "The casinos await me."

Not yet Mister All-About-Me. I decided to clear the air before starting the engine. I looked through the windshield, eyes riveted on this old geezer passing by instead of on Bish who didn't have a clue about the doubts ping-ponging my head.

"How long you plan on holing up in Montana?" I asked.

He gave some thought before answering. "As long as it takes."

It, I knew all there was to know about *it*, I'd lived with *it* twenty-four/seven. "As long as *it* takes—what do you take me for?"

"Don't make me say the words that brought us together, starting in St. Louis and now moving on to Montana's heaven on earth."

"Speak for yourself. What's in *it* for me? I could leave right now and never look back wishing I'd stuck around for *it*. There's nothing stopping me, you know. I don't owe you a thing."

"Except maybe your life."

I grabbed the front of his shirt and twisted it high into his neck. "Don't give me that. Lark would never have accepted sperm from a jerk like you."

His face turned blotchy as he squeaked out his next words. "You didn't know her then. You think you know her now but you don't. Not in the same way I do."

I reared my fist back, ready to pulverize his sickly face when someone else's fist banged on the windshield, followed by a white bearded face taking a good look at mine.

"Hey, fellows," the old geezer yelled. "Take your fight out of Vegas."

He didn't move on until I released Bish's shirt, which prompted another hack attack, along with enough blood to fill two man-sized tissues. After finishing, Bish told me to leave, that he didn't need me anymore.

"For once you got something right." I popped the rear door, did the same to the driver's side, and planted my Nikes on the parking lot. I felt this immediate release, freeing me from the pathetic jerk.

"Wait," he said while I was yanking my Walgreen bag from the back end. "Don't leave like this."

"What other way is there?"

"Stay with me and I'll make it worth your while."

Sweeter words I'd never heard. And a nicer handwriting I'd never seen when Bish signed over the title of his SUV to me that very afternoon. My first vehicle—damn right and at a price I was willing to pay. Or so I thought at the time, until my neck spasms acted up again. I pulled into the front entrance of MGM and agreed to meet him in the lobby for dinner at seven.

"Our last night in Vegas," he said, handing me one of his credit cards, a first. "We'll take in a show, your choice."

I rolled the card between my fingers before returning it. "Nah, that's okay. Just dinner works for me."

Back at the hotel I left my supplies in the SUV and carried Bish's to my room. The door to his room needed some TLC before opening to me, a skill I picked up during my years in Juvy. Those bags of lifetime necessities I set in the middle of Bish's bed before helping myself to ten thousand dollars of his casino winnings, greenbacks he should've been more imaginative in hiding instead of using the hotel's cold-air duct and picture frames and the hidden panels in his locked suitcases. His specially-engineered designer luggage, I should've asked Bish to pop for a new set for me. Oh well, too late for any more freebies, including the cell phone I left behind. After shoving my clothes into my crappy bags, I took the service elevator down to the basement. No point in sending up red flags by exiting through the main lobby, not with Bish a favored guest who preferred the hotel safe for most of his cash and me nothing but a bottom feeder, his lowly butt boy.

Let him find a new butt boy. Any down-on-his-luck-no-clue would've jumped at the chance before knowing the score. I didn't want anybody taking advantage of Bish but wasn't about to wait around, making sure no one did.

Chapter 28

Oh, yeah. Color me free, free as my former name and not one ounce of guilt. Money earned, money paid. It worked for me. I drove back east with a three-by-five photo of Bish tucked in my pocket, one taken at the casino right after he won all that money, so on top of the world a bystander wouldn't have suspected the man was hanging on by a thread, knowing someday soon he'd be cashing in his chips for the last time.

Two days later I hit St. Louis mid-afternoon and parked down the street from Lark's apartment. The key she'd given me no longer worked so I figured out another way inside, through the basement window I'd unlocked before she shoved me out the door, literally. But that was then and this was now. I wasn't much older but a whole lot smarter.

Lark nearly flipped when she came home and found me waiting in the living room.

"You changed the locks," I said after we sort of hugged.

"Out of necessity," she replied, her lip quivering for no good reason.

It's not like I'd ever hurt her, not really.

Some things never change; she moved away from me, and said, "A woman living alone can't be too careful."

"I could change that, move in and keep out the crazies"

"You think? I don't."

Instead of arguing, I changed the subject to one she couldn't resist. "How 'bout we go out for supper, just like we used to do. You pick, any place but Hector's Mexicana."

"No problem there. Immigration sent him back to the wife and kids in Matamoros."

I stepped back, held up my palms. "Whoa, don't blame his deportation on me."

"And don't go putting words in my mouth. Some law-abiding hypocrite in the Emergency Room ratted on him to the police and one thing led to another."

"What can I say? Some things work out for the best."

"Some people never change, Free."

"Speaking of changes, I go by Danner now."

"Just Danner, since when did you decide on the singular?"

"A wise man once told me that I didn't come free and he had the paid receipts to prove it. I gave up on Free when the name quit working for me."

"Well, I'm a Danner too. Long before you ever were and don't you forget it."

As if I could.

She plopped down on the sofa, lit a cigarette, and crossed her legs before giving me her version of the birds and bees. "This whole parenting thing, trust me, is not what it's cracked up to be. It's not rocket science either. First the guy plants his seed; then the woman bears his fruit. Just like that they're stuck, at least one of them, usually the female until she can figure a way out because kids are not what they're cracked up to be either."

After two long drags from her cigarette, she crushed it into the ashtray and lit another. "Take me, the only offspring of parents who should've remained childless. What did they know about love, not a damn thing, them and their strict rules about not doing this and not doing that. Unless it involved work, then it was all about do, do, and more do-do. We all knew I wasn't cut out for the farm life but did that stop Ma and Pa who were already old when I came into the world. Hell, no. They worked me harder than Cinderella minus the stepsisters and definitely with no Prince Charming sweeping me onto his great white stallion and carrying us off to a faraway castle. I knew I'd have to find my prince elsewhere."

She snuffed the life from that cigarette and folded her fingers into a church steeple, waiting for my input which didn't take long.

"I'm still hungry. You got anything to eat?"

"Not a crumb, you got any money?"

She spoke with a get-real look, "On your nickel or mine?"

"More like a dollar, I'm paying."

End of discussion, hello belated Mother's Day, a first for me, taking dear ol' mom out to dinner.

We dressed for the occasion, her showing off in a slinky, above-the-knee outfit and me in tight Levis and a western shirt, courtesy of Samuel Dean Lawford. Naturally, as soon as Lark noticed my leather boots, she exchanged her spiked heels for below-the-knee alligator boots. As if footwear could resolve the issues bugging us for years.

"I assume we're going by taxi," she said.

"You assumed right." This was not the time to bring up my SUV parked down the street. I passed the phone to her, the yellow cab number she knew by heart.

Red Lobster, Lark's choice. Table instead of a booth, my choice—front and center so there'd be no doubt as to who was paying. Our waitress regarded Lark and me as a kinky couple. In a way, she was right. Lark chose a fancy mixed drink, strawberry served in a stemmed glass. I thought about a cold longneck but settled for lemonade. We both ordered the lobster special, another first for me, which gave her the chance to play mommy-know-it-all, instructing me on how to extract every bit of meat from the shells.

We ate more than we talked, which suited me fine since Red Lobster was not the time or the place to discuss the real purpose of my visit. When the bill came, I made a show of paying in cash, knowing the waitress in Lark couldn't help but notice the fat tip I left on the table.

After that, we kicked back in Lark's living room. Me, on the sofa with my legs propped on the coffee table; Lark grounded in front of the second-hand velvet, her legs yoga style, twisted into a pretzel. She told me to pick out a video, whatever I wanted to watch. Anything to avoid a meaningful exchange, the woman wasn't fooling me.

"Not tonight, maybe tomorrow." Meaning I planned on overnighting. Our eyes locked for a brief instant, neither pair comfortable with the other. I handed her Bish's casino photo. "There's this picture I want you to see."

She examined it for a long time, running her fingers across the glossy finish as if trying to redirect his image to her twisted brain. "I'm supposed to know him?"

"Samuel Dean Lawford, Sammy from way back when. Come on, Lark. Last month you named him as a potential sperm provider. The two of you partied together."

"Did I say that? Gosh, I don't know, Free."

"You mean Danner."

"Yeah, I keep forgetting. Now where was I?" She held up the photo. "Hmm, maybe a one-night stand ... maybe not; it's been eons ago and you can't expect me to remember every guy who fell head over heels for me. Besides, this could be anybody, any wannabe big shot."

"After a big win in Vegas," I said. Her eyes lit up, right before I let her down. "Too bad he lost it all a few days later."

"Too bad I'm not feeling the love."

"You said he was one of three possibilities."

"Did I say three? Hmm, not to brag but considering my undeniable popularity back then, there might've been more."

I snatched Bish's photo from her fingers, stuffed it back in my pocket.

"Don't get yourself all bent out of shape," she said. "You asked; I answered. What more can I say." Lark unwound her pretzel legs, got up, and after a lazy stretch, she strolled into the kitchen with me on her heels. After pulling two beers from the fridge, she twisted off both caps. "Just what we need to take off the edge, okay?"

As if two beers were all it would take. She held out one of them to me. I did the unexpected, knocked it out of her hand. Foam spilled onto the floor.

"How 'bout this instead," I said, slamming her against the fridge. Her sleepy eyes flew open. She caved under my forearm; I propped her back up. Oh how I wanted to wrap my fingers around that quivering throat, squeeze until those eyes popped like pulp from grapes, same as Sugar Daddy had done me. Tears began welling in her eyes and triggered raw nerves in my gut.

"Think, Lark. I want names—first and last. And I'm not leaving until you give them to me."

After she croaked an okay, I stepped back. Rubbing her tear-stained cheek, she came up with the two she considered most likely: Blake Turner and Mitchell Compton.

"Trust me," she said. "You wouldn't want Blake, a convicted murderer who'll never set foot outside Sing Sing."

"What kind of moron do you take me for? Sing Sing's been closed for years. It's a museum now."

"You're confusing me." She backed away as if I might hit her. "Okay, okay. Blake resides in a California prison, which one I'm not for sure."

"Not for sure or don't know."

"Don't know and don't care."

"Who'd he kill?"

"I don't have the foggiest. It's not like we were friendly at the time."

"Don't mess with me, Lark. Who'd this Blake kill?"

She twisted her mouth, all the better to think up a plausible lie. "It might've been a convenience store clerk or the owner of a drycleaners, some ghetto in Southern California."

"As in Los Angeles?"

"How should I know. We're talking a lifetime ago."

"Yeah, my lifetime. You don't know how many times I've wanted to kill you."

"And you wonder why I sent you away."

"I was eleven and needed you."

"An incorrigible eleven, who was I to argue with the case worker."

"God forbid you would've sided with me. So back to Blake Turner, how'd you meet him?"

"After picking up my high school diploma, I high tailed it to the big city, my take on St. Louis at the time. Boy was I ever naïve. As soon as I stepped off the bus, I ditched the duller-than-dull Emily name and turned myself into Charity for no reason other than thinking it was a name people would remember and think kindly of me."

Right, I slid my hand over my mouth and coughed. "And Turner did."

"Not exactly, I'd been waitressing for a few months, barely paying the rent while saving up for modeling school when I received a last-minute call to work a banquet for this downtown hotel, which is where I first met Blake Turner. Six-feet tall and under the sorry impression he was Mr. Hollywood, what a knucklehead. He kept running his fingers through his straight-from-the-salon feather cut until the banquet captain threatened to make him wear a hairnet if he didn't stop. That evening we were so busy nobody gave Blake a second glance, that is, except me, a big turn on for him I hadn't expected given my tender age. By the time we were passing out the split lemon cake to ho-hum conventioneers, Blake was brushing up against me, feeding me a line about a career in modeling. Music to my ears, I took the bite, an Adam and Eve reversal if ever there was."

"Yeah, I know the feeling."

"No you don't. Anyway, Blake cracked me up. He couldn't pass up a mirror without checking out the eye creases he swore added years to his then twenty-eight, and nothing I said could convince him otherwise. He ran with what he called an artsier-than-thou crowd and brought me along, a plus for both of us since I needed the right contacts to jumpstart the modeling and he needed a pretty girl to complete the Ken and Barbie picture. Lots of parties, lots of booze and rec drugs with bohemian types who dressed in black and read poetry or made fools of themselves trying to improvise, let the good times roll and boy, did they ever.

"Blake soon heard the siren call of Hollywood and wanted me to tag along, but first things first. I needed some glam shots for my modeling portfolio. He said he knew a guy who knew a guy. I played along, did what I had to do, unspeakable things, and where did it get me? No friggin' where. I decided to drop Blake, not all the way but enough to make Mr. Hollywood realize he'd no longer be starring in the life and times of Desiree Danner, the name he dreamed up in place of Charity. But, before I could act on my decision, Blake took me to another party, where I met … well, Sammy and Mitchell Compton."

"You knew Blake before Sammy."

"Hmm, I guess I did."

"And Mitchell Compton's the other guy you couldn't remember from before."

She eased onto a chair at the table. "Only because I don't want you getting mixed up with him either."

"Okay, what's Compton's story?" I sat across from her, swiped crumbs onto the floor, making a clean place to rest my elbows.

"He came from money," she said, half apologizing.

"No problem. I can live with that."

"Don't be so sure."

"I won't know until I meet him."

"You won't like him; he definitely won't like you. Besides, he doesn't live around here."

"Just tell me where. I've got wheels." Bummer, I hadn't meant to let that slip.

She cocked her head, viewed me in a new way, one I'd not seen before. "You … a car, since when?"

"That, Lark, is none of your business."

"Take me with you." She leaned over, grabbed my hand, and held it to her bruised cheek. An obvious attempt to lay guilt on me, okay, I did feel bad about coming this close to smacking her. But she'd smacked me plenty of times and paybacks are hell.

"More than anything else in the world, I absolutely need a vacation," she said. "We could travel, see the country together."

"As in You the Misunderstood and Me the Incorrigible, no way could I inflict that Vacation from Hell on either of us."

She let my hand slip through her fingers just as she had done with my childhood. "Get over it. You were a crybaby then and you're a crybaby now."

Chapter 29

Southern California—the ocean and beaches, palm trees swaying in the breeze, and everywhere the most beautiful girls I'd ever seen, except for Butterscotch but she was history now and forever. Before hooking up with a bronzed babe or even learning how to surf, I decided to check out Blake Turner, mainly to rule out the murderous dude who could only spell trouble for me and then to concentrate on Lark's third possibility who sounded more like my kind of guy.

Using the City of Angels as my home base turned out to be a money pit and not wanting to blow all of my recent earnings, I put myself on a strict budget which meant staying at this cheap motel near the main library. What a cram-jam of info overload, I scrolled through the computer's criminal archives for days before moving on to the courthouse and newspapers where I nearly went blind doing the same. I nearly lost my mind too, what with the A.D.D., my attention deficit disorder.

Two weeks of cheap fast food and useless research netted me nothing but a big fat zero. By the end of each day I was too wiped out to hit on any chicks, even those in the immediate hood who walked and talked like the pros they must've been.

So I took the more direct approach—one I should've tried from the gitgo—I went back to the library, logged onto the Internet, and googled Blake Turner. Duh, just color me stupid. Found my man on the first try.

This Blake Turner was most definitely my Blake Turner, and not a bona fide convicted murderer but a make-believe one, a level B character actor with a skimpy profile of his name listed on a few movie credits, so far down the list few people bothered reading it; Blake Turner, who twenty years before had portrayed an angry sociopath convicted of killing a handicapped convenience store clerk, in a movie that must've gone overseas or straight to video because I'd never heard of it. Me, John Earl Danner the Second, possible son of a card-carrying Screen Actors Guild member, already I felt connected and could hardly wait to meet the man. Or for him to meet me, whichever gave me the upper hand. As for Lark, had she been anywhere within a hundred miles I'd have tracked her down, wrapped both my hands around her scrawny neck, and choked every breath from that mouth filled with lies and more lies.

More research told me Blake Turner lived in one of those non-celebrity-yet-over-priced neighborhoods in the Valley, Sherman Oaks to be exact. I figured him as a coffee-away-from-home guy, which accounted for my parking around the corner from his Spanish-style house at seven o'clock one sunny morning. Sure enough, thirty minutes later his overhead garage door opened and a purple Alpha Romeo backed down the driveway. I followed the car for several miles to a stand-alone café called Avery's. After my guy parked, he checked out the rearview mirror and ran a comb through his salon cut. He stepped out of the sporty car, exuding Hollywood, that's for sure, I'm guestimating six foot, one sixty-five. Casual shirt and shorts made his California tan pop. Dark hair, no sign of gray, which could've been nature's way or the bottle's, either way I didn't object to self-improvement. Nor did I discriminate against aging hunksters.

Blake Turner paid no attention to me following him into the packed eatery, where over-the-hill waitresses were carrying platters loaded with tropical fruits, egg white omelets, and not one sausage link or slice of bacon or toast lathered with creamy butter that Delores swore by. Walking toward the back, Blake nodded to several eaters and when he slid into the last booth so did I, planting my butt directly across from his.

He looked at me from a wrinkle-free face and asked the obvious, "Do I know you?"

"Not exactly but I know you." I stuck out my hand and while he shook it, introduced myself as Danner, nothing else. His hand was soft, the nails trim and buffed to an understated sheen. A gentleman's hand, Lark would've said. An actor's hand was one she hadn't described to me. Nor a murderer's, damn her for wasting my time.

"You're in the business or trying to get started," he said with an I-could-care-less expression.

"Neither but I'd still like you to hear me out."

A waitress came by, poured him a green tea and aimed for my cup. Blake put his hand over it, told her I wasn't staying. I slid the cup out from under his hand and told her I'd changed my mind and would like some tea.

"The usual?" she asked Blake while filling my cup.

"Make that two," I said, adding as a Bish afterthought, "and put both orders on my bill."

"That won't be necessary," Blake said.

"Please, as a favor to me."

What could the man say, nothing without making a minor scene which didn't seem his style. By the time our waitress wiggled her hips away, his attitude had changed but it still smelled phony. "Look, if I sent you a wrong signal, I'm sorry," he said. "But I only swing in one direction—toward beautiful women."

I couldn't help but smile. "Good. That's one thing we have in common."

For the next few minutes I played this game of "Name My Mom" to his blank face before we finally connected today's Lark to yesterday's Emily, aka Charity, aka Desiree.

"Desiree, Desiree Danner, if memory serves me right, that lovely name came from my brainstorming."

"Desiree, she didn't keep that one for long. She didn't keep anything for long."

"Or anyone, as I recall. Better eat your omelet before it gets cold."

Breakfast turned out better than I'd expected. Or, maybe it was the company. Blake Turner gave me a ton of attention, none of it directed toward Lark which didn't bother me because my whole life had been about Lark this and Lark that. Blake even discussed his acting career, in particular the movie with him playing the sociopath killer.

"Which is how Lark described you to me," I said without thinking. "I expected to find you warming a prison bench."

"Why am I not surprised? Even when I knew her, she confused make-believe with reality."

"Yeah, that would be Lark."

He pushed his plate of half-eaten food aside. "Not that I want to lead you down the path to certain Hell, but here goes: have you ever considered a theatrical career?"

"Funny you should ask because I place acting at the very top of my career choices."

"Then you've had lessons."

"Not in the formal sense, by the seat of my pants if that counts for anything." For me acting had been everything, what got me into trouble and out of it. "Also, some modeling but so far I don't have an agent."

"And you're how old?"

"Twenty-two, made my grand entrance seven months after you left St. Louis."

He threw back his head and laughed. Nice teeth, every one of them near orthodontic perfection. "I should've guessed; you think I'm your long-lost dad."

"Lark thought there might be an outside chance. I'm not pushing anything, just trying to narrow the possibilities."

"I like you … Danner, but trust me, no way in God's Sequoia Forest are you my offspring. That would be as miraculous as the Immaculate Conception."

"Then you'll take a DNA test?"

"That I'd have to think about," he said, grabbing the check I knew he would. "Look, I have two gigs coming up, one out of town toward the end of the week, the other for a few hours tomorrow. You're welcome to tag along on the later, strictly as an observer. Unless you're tied up elsewhere, tracking down numerous leads."

I met him head-on with my best phony baloney. "You're suggesting that Lark … Desiree hopped from bed to bed, that she used men?"

"Sorry, the comment was beneath me. I can only speak for our time together. We were tighter than a rubber band stretched beyond its limit. One of us had to let go so we both could survive."

"Who let go?"

"We both did but I let her think otherwise. It was easier that way. So, are you game for tomorrow? How much you'll learn, I can't say but if nothing else, you will come away with some new perspectives." I nodded and he scribbled the address on a slip of paper. "It's in the

Valley, not far from Burbank. I'll meet you in the parking lot, one o'clock sharp. You need directions?"

"I'll get them off my GPS." What used to be Bish's; I hadn't given him much thought, only when I climbed into his … my SUV and switched on the engine.

Chapter 30

A gig with Blake Turner, oh yeah, I pictured anything from a scene in an action movie, a chick-flick comedy, even a slice and dice horror. Worst case, hard or soft porn—what little I'd seen was off-the-wall corny. I preferred my action live with real girls, slow and easy with me in charge, just the opposite of Butterscotch.

I knew it, I knew it. From the moment I pulled into the parking lot, I knew Blake Turner had set me up. Except this was no joke, at least he didn't think so. There he stood, beside his Alpha Romeo, chatting with a fifty-something man and woman. Actors, I figured. And like Blake, their skinny bods dressed in California bold sure to wow the residents of Venture Haven, a retirement community of which I wanted no part, not even for a single afternoon of old-fogey entertainment. I should've hopped into my SUV and pulled away before Blake saw me. Too late, he waved me over. I went with feet dragging, the story of my life.

"So glad you could make it," he said before introducing me to Marsha Hollister and Doug Evans. Easy names to remember and close to the front of the alphabet, probably not the names their parents had given them.

"Would you mind?" Marsha asked. She shoved a fancy hatbox into my chest, expecting me to grab it. On top of the box she dumped a manila envelope. "The music, too, Doug and I can manage the rest."

The rest, what rest? Not a thing in anyone's hands except mine. I'd been relegated to Prop Boy, better that than Butt Boy.

"Didn't I tell you this would be an education," Blake said, leading the way through a garden lined with palm trees and flowering shrubs.

"Only if I'm part of the act."

"Not unless you have a union card," Doug said.

"How do I get one?"

"Same as everyone else: by acting."

Or maybe by replacing some smart-ass actor who just happened to collapse when no one was around to see what happened. A rabbit punch could've sent Doug into la-la land. Not too hard, not too soft, but just right.

"On another topic," Blake told Doug. "Max called to say he might be late. And don't ask 'how late' because I have no idea whatsoever."

"Oh, man," Doug said. "This is the second time in two weeks."

My grand debut; every actor has to start somewhere. As we made our way into the complex of single-level stucco buildings, old people were popping up everywhere—working the sidewalks and paths with canes, walkers, and wheelchairs, others being pushed by grinning orderlies who deserved a medal for doing a job no one else wanted. A woman rounder than she was tall came out of the main building and greeted us like we were returning magi.

"How wonderful of you to come again," the social director told Blake and his entourage of two, okay, three including Prop Boy. "We've gathered your many fans in the salon where they're having a sing-along in anticipation of your arrival. And what are you gracing us with today?"

"Scenes from "A Streetcar Named Desire and other works by Tennessee Williams," Blake said. "Plus the usual romantic duets and depending on the time, a bit more of Mark Twain."

"I just love your interpretation." She clapped, dug one finger under the ring of bracelets squeezing her chubby wrists. "Wonderful, wonderful, let's not waste another minute."

We followed her into the building and down the hall to a lounge where the old folks were seated theater-style and finishing a song I'd never heard before. The window shades were slanted into a closed position, creating shadows that made the raised platform with small piano seem almost professional. After relieving me of the props, Doug and Marsha started arranging them on the platform table while Blake took on the role of typical man-in-charge by doing jack shit.

"What about me?" I whispered to him.

"Can you play the piano … never mind, here comes Max."

Dressed in a clown suit, I'm not kidding. He gave Blake a thumbs-up and headed for the bathroom.

"Not bad," I said, "two gigs in one day."

"I've done as many as four," Blake said.

"Wow. That must've been some workout. So what about today? I know I could act if given the chance."

"Excellent," he said. "You play the shill. Find a seat in the audience and applaud like crazy if there's a lull or should the urge move you, whichever comes first."

Already the urge was moving me. To get out, fast. As I was backing away, the social director bounced her boobs against my back and motioned me to the one empty seat, second row middle. I found myself wedged between two heavyweights. Both women, one tucked her flowered dress under a pair of massive legs and the other once-overed me through eyes on the verge of calling it quits. Not liking what she saw, she blew a fat raspberry in my direction. Any chance of escaping disappeared when the clown returned as a piano player and parked his butt on the bench. Overhead lights dimmed the room. The actors faded into their positions. The audience chatter hushed to a few whispers, and a magic I never expected took me to another place. To scenes from movies I'd watched with Lark and even Delores, and songs that didn't do much for me but obviously made a difference to those around me. Live theater, I'd never viewed it before but already wanted more, only next time with me on stage, drinking in the applause.

After each performance I led the clapping and at the end I would've stood to demand more if it hadn't been for the raspberry fart with rheumy eyes falling asleep against my shoulder, just like that without a single snort or warning whatsoever. Or so I thought until the lights came on and some guy behind me poked her with his cane. Getting nothing, he poked her again. This time she slumped over, head first into my lap. Dead, there was no denying it.

Ms. Social Director and her staff earned their money that afternoon, ushering the old folks out before most realized one of their own had passed into the next world. Blake and Company did their part too, assuming new positions out in the hallway, shaking hand after hand marred by ugly spots and crippling arthritis while I remained seated so as not to disturb the singular dead. One prayer I gave her, okay two plus a sign of the cross in my head, more than generous all things considered. After the lounge had emptied out, two orderlies pushed away the chairs around me, lifted my lap companion onto a gurney, and wheeled her away.

When I glanced in Blake's direction, he crooked his finger to me. I didn't hesitate to answer his call.

"You could use some fresh air," he said.

"What about the props?" As if I cared.

"Not to worry," he said, motioning to his company of two talking to each other.

I walked into the sunny day with Blake, his chiseled profile showing me a strong jaw and firm resolve. I couldn't read his feelings but my head was spinning with theater and film, old people and death. It just didn't get any better or worse. As we followed the same path we'd taken earlier, neither of us said a word until Blake asked what I thought.

"I'd like to think the old gal died happy."

"Of course, she did. But I was referring to the gig as a whole."

"Not bad, not bad at all." I reached down, plucked a flower, and shoved it behind one ear.

"You're too kind," he said. "I wanted you to see the down side of acting, what happens when the movie parts dry up and Social Security hasn't kicked in yet."

"Until it does, I guess you make a living entertaining old people."

"Yes and no. The live applause keeps me sharp and keeps me in spending money, not that I'm hurting for cash, but most of my earnings come from residuals, commercials, voice-overs, inspirational tapes, and audio books. Ever listen to one?"

"I'm a reader not a listener."

"And a wannabe actor, which is why you must pay attention to voice patterns, not just the words but how they're spoken." He put his arm around my shoulder and continued the fatherly advice. "Hang in there, Danner. You'll find your niche someday."

We stopped in front of my SUV. "Nice set of wheels," he said, dropping his arm to pat a fender.

"I earned it the hard way but it's all mine, free and clear."

We leaned our backs against the fender, neither of us ready to leave. Blake seemed to be debating some problem in his head and must've resolved it because he finally said, "Look, this may be a bit premature, but if you're really interesting in acting, you ought to consider a portfolio—headshots and full-length."

I didn't mention the modeling Lark and I used to do. To hell with her, this was my time to shine. "You got any contacts."

"Indeed, I do. The photographer I have in mind demands top dollar but his results are fantastic. All the big names swear by him, especially the younger guys—Timberlake, Efron, Grenier. You'll need an appointment, of course. Figure six weeks from today, this guy's incredibly busy."

"Six weeks, no way, I'll run out of money before then."

"Perhaps I could make things happen sooner, if you give him an advance toward the photo shoot."

"How much are we talking about?"

"A minimum of five thousand," he said.

I left him leaning on the fender and clicked my remote to open the driver's door. "Thanks but I'll shop around for someone more affordable. About that gig later this week …."

"A big one, out of town and no, you're not invited."

"Then how about lunch after you return. My treat, for sure."

"Lunch and dinner belong to my wife, unless I'm working."

Damn, I hate competition, no matter what level. "I should've known. You're married."

"Tell me about it. To Hell-On-Stilettos," he said with a roll of his eyes, "even when we're involved in one of my favorite pastimes, hunting mushrooms."

"Heels in the woods, I'm impressed." Yeah, by her stupidity, I pictured blonde, inside and out. "Any kids?"

"Not a one and that includes you. Nevertheless, you're starting to grow on me so watch your step. Scary, isn't it?"

"Not for me. I've been to Hell and back."

"I figured as much. You remind me of myself at your age but minus the soul patch and ear studs. Look, I really do want to help. How about I put up two thousand toward the photos and you put up three. You can pay me back and yourself by working as a movie extra."

Exciting, you bet. I tried not to show it. "You're sure you want to do this?"

"Absolutely, I wouldn't have offered if I didn't. We'll breakfast at Avery's tomorrow before I leave for my gig. Bring the money then."

Chapter 31

My first autumn without Lark, as if she cared, a Saturday starting out like any other Saturday in late October, the trees washed in orange and the air smelling like Halloween couldn't wait for its turn to roll around. And after Halloween, look out. Silver Dollar City, here I come even if it meant dragging along Jed and Delores.

"Johnny! Quit your daydreaming," I heard Delores yell from a row of gigantic mums where she was pulling out weeds while I loaded pumpkins onto the back of the truck.

I straightened up, and yelled back, "I can't fit another pumpkin on the bed."

For an old lady Delores moved pretty fast, bringing with her a bunch of flowers. She handed them to me along with another order. "These go in the kitchen, you know, in the painted bucket I keep under the sink."

"After that, can I take a rest?"

"Depends on what Jed has in mind. Make sure you ask first."

She climbed into the cab and headed toward the road, to her produce shed I painted the week before, bright yellow to attract customers passing by. A Saturday like this meant lots of sales and an empty truck by nightfall. Hey, I was starting to think like a farmer.

Back at the house I took care of Delores's mums her way, cutting an inch from the stems before sticking the whole bunch in her special bucket I filled with water. The arranging she could do later. Since I'd been neglecting Super Mario, giving him some attention seemed only right. We'd just moved into the first level when Jed found us on the couch.

"Do I need to separate you two again?" he asked and then answered for me. "No, I didn't think so. Five minutes, meet me in the barn."

There went my minutes. His five happened in the bathroom, a mid-morning dump that always ended with him lighting a single match when the tightwad should've lit five or six. Think Silver Dollar City, I told myself while burying Mario deep in the cushions. I was waiting in the barn when Jed caught up with me, his mood way better than before the toilet duty. Now he couldn't wait to involve me in his next project—the dreaded alfalfa.

"There's hay to move upstairs." He pointed to a wide opening in the ceiling. "And don't even think about sneezing." Like always, he took the best pitchfork for himself and handed me the one he described as his favorite. "You know the routine, Johnny, same as before. We work as a team."

You bet, me pitching hard to keep up with Jed, and Jed pitching harder to make sure I didn't. It didn't take long before hay flew onto a tarp; the tarp we rolled into a bundle and dragged up the ladder. I led the way, better my backside in his face than his in mine. Upstairs, the too-sweet smell of alfalfa bombarded us; its fine dust creeping into my eyes, making them itch and water. Jed knew but did he care, no. And neither did I care about him. After thirty minutes of pitching and climbing, his face was ten times redder than mine felt. Sweat rolled from his forehead, also a plus for me. On our last trip up to the loft we stayed there and moved the hay around with our forks, me on one side of the hole, Jed on the other. To pass the time I started whistling, but after a while Jed told me to knock it off.

Okay, I thought about Branson instead, pictured myself conquering the water slide and roller coaster just like I'd conquered Mario's many enemies. I could've gone on and on with my daydreams but Jed pulled me back into the barn.

"Take a … break whenever … you … need it," he said through a huff and a puff.

I kept on working but hit him with this: "About Silver Dollar city, you think Lark might want to go with us."

Jed stopped. He leaned on his fork and scrunched his eyebrows into a frown. "Give it a rest, Johnny. Emily doesn't want you. Never did. In fact, had it not been for me and Delores, Emily would've flushed you down the toilet when you were no bigger than a shriveled-up turnip."

This time the old man had gone too far.

"That's not so," I said. "You're nothing but a stingy two-faced liar!" I slammed my fork into the floorboards and squared my shoulders. "Me and Lark, we love each other in ways you'll never know. Yeah, real love between a guy and a girl. She told me I was the best fuck she ever had."

There, I said what I'd felt for months. And Jed went ballistic.

"Why, you little bastard!" he yelled, spit flying into a spray of alfalfa dust. The fork fell from his hand. A vein popped out on his forehead. Snorting like a bull, he stumbled toward me.

What happened next should never have happened nor did I make it happen. All I know for sure is this: Jed came after me but never got there. One minute he was tripping over his feet; a second later he'd disappeared—headfirst down the opening that separated us. I leaned over his favorite pitchfork, saw him laying on the hard ground below, face up and not moving.

"You okay, Jed? Jed, answer me. Jed?"

When he didn't, I hurried down the ladder. Jed's red face had turned the color of ashes. His eyes were wide open, staring but not seeing, and soft white foam spilled from his mouth. I didn't touch him but ran to the house and called 911. Then I hopped on the old bike Jed had fixed for me and pedaled to the highway. Delores took the news pretty good until we got back and she saw Jed zonked out on the ground. She cried when the paramedics came. Cried even more when they finally loaded him into the ambulance. She was still crying when she climbed in beside him.

Between sobs she called out to me. "I don't know when I'll be home so you do the best you can. Okay, Johnny?"

I nodded and waved and watched the paramedics close the door. After the ambulance drove off, I finished the chores, which took my entire afternoon. That evening I played Super Mario until my eyes burned so bad I went to bed before ten o'clock.

For weeks Delores spent every day at the hospital overseeing Jed's care, which gave me the run of the house, not that I took advantage of it. When I wasn't in school, I did my own chores and helped a rotating team of neighbors milk Delores's cows and harvest the rest of Jed's crop. Food was never a problem, not with the farmers' wives supplying me with casseroles, cakes, and pies. Twice, I tried calling Lark but her phone had been disconnected. Maybe she needed money. I thought about asking Delores to lend her some but decided the timing wasn't right.

At last came the day I'd been dreading. The same paramedics who took Jed to the hospital brought him back in the same ambulance. After getting him settled in a special bed, they shook Delores's hand and hurried out the door. Now the old man really did look old, and hate filled his eyes once they fastened on me.

"We need you, Johnny, more than ever," Delores said when the two of us were in the kitchen. "Jed can't feel a thing below his waist. Nor can he talk, thanks to the stroke he suffered after his fall."

"How long before he can walk again?"

"Never, Johnny. This is as good as it gets."

"What about our trip to Silver Dollar City?"

"Not this year. We'll just have to wait and see. I'm really sorry."

Cripes. She was sorry—what about me. My world still belonged to Jed, only now the old man controlled it and everything else from his bed.

Chapter 32

The next morning at breakfast Blake finished his omelet while the waitress poured more green tea, winding-down time I put to good use before handing over my three thousand bucks toward the photo shoot.

"Can we talk about Lark ... uh Desiree."

Blake glanced at his watch, nice but not in the same league with Bish's Rolex. "I suppose so. What do you want to know?"

"What she was like back then, in St. Louis when you dated her."

"Young, yes; naïve ... I don't think so," Blake said. "She thought of herself as Cinderella and called me her Prince Charming. I took her to this party in the Central West End, a transitional area of newly rich crowding out the old-money. I can still see our *numero uno* host, a blonde-headed stud flanked by two gorgeous babes."

"Mitch Compton?"

"Desiree told you about him? I'm not surprised. She was hanging on my arm until I introduced her to him, an arrogant prick working in his daddy's construction business."

"Just like that." I snapped my fingers. "She and Mitch hooked up?"

"Not quite. While Mitch was preoccupied with his small harem, Desiree made friends with his bartender buddy, a Joe College nerd she immediately enchanted."

"No kidding." Lark and Bish, whatever the connection, it blew my mind. "So, where did that leave you?"

Blake shrugged. "Prince Charming wound up sharing the stage with King Midas and his ugly toad bartender. That's when I hit the road to Hollywood."

"Some fairy tale, huh, not all of them have happy endings."

"That, dear boy, depends on your outlook."

After slapping a twenty on the table, Blake got up, which was my cue to do the same. Out on the parking lot, he brought up the photographer, said he'd be seeing him on location the following week. "So, are you still interested in the photo shoot?"

"You bet." I forked over an envelope bulging with cash. "Here's hoping nobody gets the wrong idea about this transaction."

"Not to worry, I've been hanging out here so long I'm like one of the family."

Like family, maybe he'd include me in his, the real one lacking a kid, although I no longer considered myself one but knew how to milk the sympathy angle. We shook hands and agreed to meet again at Avery's on the Monday after Blake finished his gig.

The in-between time I used to my advantage, taking in all the latest movies, two or three per day, which really dug into my reserve, what with the soda, popcorn, and Milk Duds. Still, compared to college a cheap education and worth every penny, not just studying the stars but all the character actors and extras so I'd have a head start when my turn finally came.

After hours of practicing facial expressions in front of my motel mirror, I was primed and ready for my Monday meet at Avery's. But did Blake show up, no. He didn't show up on Tuesday either. I thought about asking the waitress if he was sick but decided a home visit made better sense. Meet the wife and turn on the old charm, let her see what an asset I'd be to their childless family. Blake must've wanted me for his son or he wouldn't have encouraged me to enter the acting profession. And if the DNA test didn't work in my favor, he could still introduce me and my portfolio to a high-powered talent agent. Already I was envisioning myself as the next rising star.

On Wednesday after sleeping in, I by-passed Avery's and went directly to Blake's neighborhood. After parking near his cul-de-sac, I exited my SUV and almost fell into a swarm of bike-riding kids who'd taken over the sidewalk and street. If staying focused hadn't been my prime concern, I'd've given them a closer view of the concrete pavement. Instead I headed toward the arc of the cul-de-sac where the Turner house sat. Nice sod, but the trees and shrubs needed a good haircut. I thought about making Blake a deal, once we were better acquainted, yard work in exchange for room and meals while taking acting lessons and working as an extra. After punching the buzzer a total of four times, I was considering my break-in options when the door opened part way.

"Mrs. Turner? Mrs. Blake Turner?" I said to the lady of the house, a this-side-of-fifty cougar with awesome boobs spilling out from an extra tight tee.

She didn't speak but nodded with a tangled mop of big hair, as red as Lark's but from a bottle instead of the genes. Cuddled in her arms was this fluffy canine mop, a pink bow stuck on top its head. I held out my finger to the little dog's pink tongue. After two friendly licks and one not-so-friendly growl, she chomped down hard enough to draw blood.

"Shame on you," the lady scolded.

Me or the vampire bitch? I wasn't sure but while rubbing my wounded flesh, I introduced myself, and added, "The son of an old friend of your husband's."

"And who might that be?" she asked with attitude.

"Lark Danner …" Mrs. Turner shook her head and kept shaking it while I recited the litany of Emily Danner … or Charity … or Desiree.

"Never heard Blake reference any of them," she said, "kindly or with malice."

"Four names, one person. Once upon a time she and your husband knew each other in St. Louis."

If it hadn't been for my Nikes blocking the threshold, Mrs. Turner would've slammed the door. "Sorry," she said. "You have the wrong Blake Turner."

"I don't think so. Could we please talk about this?"

"Today's not a good day; in fact it's the absolute pits." She screwed up her face with a look that spelled tears. "Come back in a month or so."

Obviously Blake hadn't told her jack shit about me. She tried shutting the door again, this time ignoring the potential damage to my foot.

"Please, I won't take up much of your husband's time." I crossed my heart, twice for good measure. "I promise."

"Damned right you won't because I wouldn't dream of letting you do otherwise."

Bingo! She opened the door wide, allowing me to follow her tight ass teetering on five-inch heels down the hallway and into a casual area, I guess the great room. Two banks of framed eight-by-ten black and white glossies decorated the wall. The photos didn't tell me much about Blake Turner the man I wanted to know better but plenty about Blake Turner the actor passing himself off as a tough gangster or whacked-out addict. Again, I felt a connection since I now considered myself an actor of sorts but one lacking the training Blake could help me achieve.

Mrs. Turner waved me to a cushiony white sofa covered in see-through plastic that farted when I sat my butt down and with every move thereafter.

"Fifteen minutes, that's all I'll allocate to you." She sank into a plasticized chair angled with the sofa and motioned to the coffee table parallel with my knees. Other than a few naked branches and not much else the only items on the table were a wooden box painted with an Asian theme and a half-empty box of tissues. I looked at her; I looked at the boxes.

"Have I missed something?" she asked. "You did want to see my husband."

Duh, I didn't want to believe the obvious, no way, no how. I thought about shedding some tears but instead slammed the heel of my palm against my forehead. Blake in a box, how could he do this to me? I had to think fast, salvage what I could from what little time we'd spent together. Time, hell, what about my three thousand bucks. What about my portfolio, my acting career. "My apologies, Mrs. Turner, I didn't know … uh."

With that she opened up the wa-wa floodgates. "Two days residing in this damn box, his mini-coffin. In life we were practically inseparable."

I passed the tissues. She took two, honked into one.

"How long were you married?"

"Twenty years of near perfection." The second tissue she used to dab mascara seeping from her eyelids, all the while going on about the late great Blake Turner. I clung to every word, hoping for a mention of me, of the money I'd shelled out.

"Was there a write-up in the newspaper?" I asked. Not that it would've mattered with me too busy learning my new trade.

"Not a damn word, after all those years he gave to the profession." She honked again, took a deep breath that lifted those awesome boobs.

There'll be a memorial service later, after I pull myself together, which could take months given my current state. What I regret more than anything else is Blake wanting a houseful of kids. Sure, I wanted them too but not as much as he did. He was a giver, my Blake—such passion, such generosity.

Such opportunity, one I couldn't pass up. Dollar signs were registering in my brain, if only she'd let me play my hand. Her story felt too perfect but having no choice, I let her ramble.

"How devastating all those years ago, Blake learning he could never father a child due to a wandering case of mumps traveling down to you-know-where, those magnificent jewels we both loved beyond words."

She glanced at my crotch; I came back with, "Did you ever consider—"

"Adoption, sure, I harbored no qualms whatsoever. However, Blake snuffed out that idea quicker than pee whizzing on a freshly lit match, never mind about my maternal instincts, no indeed. In the end we settled for dogs. Right, Snooks?"

She squeezed the bitch; the bitch growled at me. Had it been just the two of us, Snooks and me, I'd have shut her up for good. One twist of the neck and Snooks could've joined her master in the box.

Mrs. Turner shifted in her chair, producing the usual plastic fart when she crossed her ankles. "Now, tell me again—your connection to my dearly beloved Blake."

"He and my mom were friends, a long time ago … well, less than a year before my birth. Since I was planning this trip to L.A., she asked me to look him up, just to say hello."

"Hello? That's all?" The face behind her make-up lost its color. She arched her eyebrows. "Or maybe to deliver a one-liner such as: 'Mommy wants to hook-up with you again, one last screw for old time's sake.'"

What'd I say? The wrong thing, I guess. Mrs. Turner's gates opened again and splish-splash went a flood of tears. She grabbed the little coffin, shaking what remained of Blake Turner from his final resting place.

"Did you hear that message, you bastard? Another one of your lays sends her regards. Will this charade never stop, not that I should care since at last you belong to me and no one else. Every sliver, every fragment, every bit of dust—mine, all mine. And how about this: I sold your half of the Forest Lawn plot you treasured. So, when my turn rolls around you're going into a bigger box with me. Just think: the two of us together for all eternity."

I passed more tissues and waited until she calmed down before trying another angle. "If you'll excuse my asking, ma'am, how did Mr. Turner die?"

"Food poisoning—oh how Blake loved the hunt, mushrooms, that is, especially those growing wild in the hills around L. A. He prided himself on recognizing the poisonous and non-poisonous varieties and shared his knowledge with me. We were quite the team, Blake and me. Unfortunately, his last meal came from some frozen mushrooms I picked, although I didn't share that particular piece of information with the police investigating his death." She patted every inch of her nose, all the while looking at me. "You won't say anything, will you?"

"Not on your life." Okay, so I'd lied. I wanted to rip off one of those stilettos and hammer her face until it turned into a serious case of raw hamburger.

"The nerve of this last chippy, phoning my Blake and warning him to watch out for some crazed weirdo who thought he sprung from Blake's remarkable loins." She uncrossed her ankles, leaned forward, and searched my face. "As if there was any money to inherit, only bills I'll have to work the rest of my life to repay. Did I tell you that I'm an established actor?"

"No ma'am, but I figured as much. What I mean is because you're so pretty."

"Well don't get any ideas about my putting out because I firmly believe in a respectable period of mourning. In spite of all I said, deep down my Blake was a good man, a decent provider. Had it not been for the five thousand dollars he hid under the mattress, I don't know how I would've covered his cremation expenses."

My three plus his two, and nothing to show but a box full of bones. I wanted to kill the bitch and the growling vampire cuddled in her arms. Instead, I separated my ass from the plastic and stood up. Mrs. Turner did the same.

"Now where did you say you hailed from?" she asked.

The airhead had forgotten and I was not about to remind her. "Just blew in from Vegas," I said. "Now if you'll excuse me …."

"But your fifteen minutes, they aren't up."

"Yes, ma'm, but they are awful close. And I'm thinking better I should leave now than outstay my welcome."

"You're sure about this?"

"Never been surer."

Chapter 33

The California crapshoot turned out to be a huge waste of time, Bish's money, and high hopes that didn't pan out. An unfortunate set of circumstances the late Blake Turner would've called the fiasco he created, one I had no intention of repeating without the assurance of megabucks. Sure, I'd sworn off Bish, vowed I'd never fall into a similar situation again, and yet I did. In Vegas I found him warming a counter stool in the hotel coffee shop, took the stool next to his, and stumbled through a humbling apology while he crisscrossed his spoon through a bowl of oatmeal without bothering to eat any of it. His eyes had retreated into their sockets, his skin corpselike, but we didn't discuss the nitty-gritty of his future. His big concern was where I'd been.

"First to St. Louis and then L.A.," I said, "in search of my sperm provider."

"L.A.?" He half snorted. "I guess Emily must've sicced you onto the pretentious Blake Turner, what a joke. Emily dumped him for me."

"Really, I can't imagine why."

"He took more than he gave, for that matter so did Emily."

"Don't we all," I said. "At least Blake took to me right away. He would've paved my way into showbiz if his wacky wife hadn't offed him, or so she confessed to me."

"You saw the body, read his obit?"

"Not exactly, but I heard his ashes rattling in a box."

Bish gave me this you've-got-to-be-kidding look. "You're such a dope. How much did they take you for?"

They, as in Blake and the wacko wife? What a colossal dumb-ass I'd been, falling for a rank con when I should've been playing my own. The only part I wanted to believe was Blake's infertility. No way did I want a father so despicable he'd cheat his own son.

Bish's eyes lit up, his skin came to life. He downed the last of his coffee and signaled the waitress for more, allowing me time for further groveling.

"About the money I borrowed—"

"The money you took, ten fucking thousand to be exact."

Damn, I didn't want to blow this. "You can have what's left—about a thousand give or take."

"Easy come, easy go, eh? Here's the deal, hotshot. Walk away now, with nothing and that includes the SUV. Or, stick with me and the thousand is yours, plus another ten. However long it takes. And don't play dumber than dumb. We both know how this is ending."

"You still thinking Montana?" I asked with my heart racing.

"Haven't stopped, but if you agree to my terms and then bullshit me with another sidebar to California or elsewhere, I swear when I die you'll already be in hell, waiting for me to arrive."

Yeah, and then waiting on him, kissing his ass for all eternity.

I took the Montana deal.

***

Bish set his final destination for a mountain cabin in the middle of Montana's nowhere, a speck on the map between Butte and Missoula. But first we needed supplies. He directed me to the only grocery store within umpteen miles of what he referred to as paradise. His condition had gone further south in the few weeks since we'd shopped Walgreen's. This time we both steered the grocery cart through narrow aisles, me doing the pushing, him hanging on to it for dear life when he should've been driving the store's only motorized handicapper had it not shot craps.

Before he got too carried away with the whole menu bit, I set him straight with, "Don't expect me to do the cooking."

"Relax. I'm not fussy."

Yeah, but where did that leave me. Bish didn't care, a typically selfish me-first trait I'd seen before in the dying. He started grabbing canned goods off the shelves so I did too, making sure I picked what worked for me—beef ravioli, hot tamales, and corned beef hash. He went for the Spam and baked beans—good luck getting me to open either. When it came to good eats I had certain standards which didn't include old fart food. Delores would've called my choices a generational thing. She thought she had me figure to a T but what did she know. Not the real me for sure.

"Can you do eggs?" Bish asked, half-leaning, half-standing at the dairy case.

"If I get hungry enough and we've run out of cereal."

Into the cart went four dozen eggs, plus butter and evaporated milk, canned biscuits, bacon and sausage, loaves of bread—enough to feed a small army or maybe two teens for a few days. He paid in cash, leaving me to wheel out the cart and load up the SUV. After starting the engine I turned off the air conditioner and rolled down my window, part way only to avoid another hack attack from Bish. I breathed in the rugged scent of Montana and thanked God bringing me there.

Several miles out of town the road narrowed as it hugged the side of a mountain. To Bish's right a drop-off, so deep I didn't want to think about seeing it any closer. To my left water from above trickled down through the rocks and tangled brush and young evergreens before rolling onto the two-lane highway.

"Those trees are lodge pole pines mixed with spruce and Douglas fir," Bish said.

"Uh-huh, thanks for the botany lesson."

"You mean dendrology, the study of trees."

"Show off." Not now, not with me creeping out, so little road and nowhere to go if another car came toward us. At least our lane had the mountain advantage. As we turned with the bend, Bish straightened up and pushed his back against the seat.

"Slow down, slow down," he said in a low voice. "You're about to witness nature at its best."

Slow down, hell. I brought us to a complete stop and set my lights to flash.

Deer jam, on the road ten feet in front of us, two does and two little fawns, babies who hadn't lost their spots yet. The mamas glanced up, moved quickly to pass by me, so close we could've rubbed noses before they dashed up the mountainside with feet barely touching the rocky surface. The fawns they left behind—nature at its best, oh yeah, I'd lived a similar scene. But didn't expect what followed. The little guys sunk to their bellies, heads down and skinny legs splayed over the pavement.

"What's going on?" I whispered.

"The instinct to survive," Bish said. "They think they're hiding from us. Play along and enjoy."

You bet. Bish rolled down his window, held out his cell phone, and captured the moment on camera. I wondered what happened to my cell phone. Maybe he'd get me another one, if I played along.

I heard snorting to my left, does calling out to their young. The obedient fawns wobbled to their feet and scampered off, taking the same path as their mamas before. The innocence of nature, what a sight, one I wouldn't soon forget. But then a horn beeped from behind, ordering me to move on. Instead of a flip-off to my rearview mirror, I shifted into drive and stepped on the gas pedal.

Bish broke the spell when he asked, "What are you thinking?"

"The usual: how much further before we get there."

"Liar," he said.

No point in arguing; he'd nailed my thoughts. If ever there's a poll asking for the ideal place to die, I'd have to vote Montana.

We drove another hour, high into the sunset of a mountain, before arriving after dark at our Big Sky hideaway, a two-room log cabin once owned by a sheepherder, according to Bish who perked up on seeing it through the beam of my SUV's headlights.

"This place better have running water," I grumbled.

"Not only faucet-wise but a flush toilet," Bish said, "power-generated electricity too, all the modern conveniences except TV, computer, and telephone."

"What? Those are my lifelines to the outside world."

"Mere distractions, take it from one who's enjoyed many moons in seclusion."

Without a butt boy, I almost asked but figured it no longer applied to our current situation. "Cut the Indian jive. How many months in one outing, give me a number."

"Okay, at least six. This is where I learned to meditate."

"Meditate? That's what you plan on doing?"

"Hell, I don't know. I'm down to the wire, taking one day at a time. Now help me unload this truck."

"Hey, a little respect please. *This truck* as you refer to it happens to be the SUV of my dreams."

Bish didn't give me any lip. In fact he seemed okay with the deal we'd made. I figured, what the hell, nothing or nobody lasts forever.

We soon settled into a comfortable routine, with me doing all the work while Bish parked his scrawny ass on the porch rocker and depending on the time of day, observed the sunrise, high noon, sunset, or a sky full of the brightest stars I'd ever laid eyes on in my entire life. Which made me realize how little of life I'd experienced outside the confines of my own world. Our cabin reminded me of a gangster's hideaway, straight out of a movie set but this was for real, not make believe. Other than the big bedroom, which Bish used exclusively and with no argument from me, there was an okay bathroom—shower, no tub—plus a kitchen/living combo. I slept on the pullout, under a grandma quilt. The only heat source came from a stone fireplace that kept me thinking about the wood I might have to chop in the near future, depending on my tolerance for the state of Bish's health once the weather turned bitter. As it was, to take out the chill in July we needed a fire every night and those fires were using up wood someone else had already provided.

One morning after Bish had finished off the two pancakes and sausages I'd put on his plate, he decided to take a hike, literally.

"With or without me," I said, not caring one way or the other since I'd already been going out on my own every day.

"Suit yourself."

I went along, more out of curiosity, to see how well he managed which turned out better than I'd expected, in fact not bad at all. I followed his lead upward into a dense forest of lodge pole pines and after ten minutes, we approached this clearing and a herd of long-horned sheep grazing on meadow grass.

"What the shit," I whispered.

"Don't spook them," Bish said.

I counted fifty sheep, from the young nudging their mamas to proud rams patrolling the outer rim of the herd's grazing. We stood there motionless, observing their every move while Bish leaked tears I tried to ignore. Then a bugle erupted nearby, almost causing me to piss my pants.

"Moose," Bish said. "Damn, I should've brought my whistle."

Oh, yeah, his moose whistle. More grunt than whistle, Bish loved playing with it. We waited ten minutes for a sighting that never came. I could've stayed longer but Bish was leaning against a tree with his eyes starting to droop so I suggested we hit the path before carrying him became my only option. I wasn't too far off because the last hundred yards before our cabin required him hanging onto my arm and from there, my shoulder.

"Thanks for the close-up," I told him after we were back inside. "I've never seen anything like it before."

"You're not alone, Danner. Most people die not knowing what they've missed."

Hello, he hadn't told me anything I didn't already know. And, I'd made his day as much as he'd made mine.

Chapter 34

The next two months ranked in the top three of my entire life, what little I'd experienced up until then. Every day brought a new adventure, with or without Bish, but most often with him because health wise, he wasn't getting any worse or any better. When we weren't exploring the area on foot, I'd drive us thirty minutes in any direction, stopping along the way so we could get out and walk until he said enough, reserving what strength he had left for the return.

Back at the cabin he taught me to respect firearms, how to fire not only a shotgun better than Jed did but also a handgun, and the proper maintenance of these weapons. Soon I was outshooting him in target practice. From there I graduated to taking out some rabbits, even though they weren't in season. So what, we were no different from nineteenth-century pioneers surviving off the land. What's more, I didn't have to nag Bish about taking one more bite of rabbit stew. Hands down, the best I'd ever eaten, maybe because I first soaked the rabbit in beer before letting it simmer long and slow.

Every few weeks we'd go into town and while I stocked up on supplies we could've done without, Bish got his prescriptions refilled, which took way longer than it should have and made me wonder how he was spending his time. Then one day after whizzing through the grocery store, I hurried on to the pharmacy, expecting to find him still there, passing time with the town's old farts. Instead, the pharmacist rolled her Asian eyes toward the back door. I went out, didn't see Bish or anyone else so I walked across the alley, my instincts carrying me to the rear entrance of a two-story building, the only one with its door painted red. I knocked, called out Bish's name, and to my surprise the door clicked open so I pushed on it and stepped inside.

"Please take a seat and activate the TV," said a female's pre-recorded voice. "A service representative will be with you shortly."

Television, I hadn't watched the tube for months. Nor had I missed it, something I never thought would happen. I sat down on the leather sofa and checked out the room—more leather furniture, pine walls decorated with Western art, an Indian rug covering wood floors. It took me a minute to realize where I was, another for Bish to come down the hall, his step full of vigor, his face flushed with the aftermath of what must've been good sex.

"You're next," said the woman trailing behind him.

Not so fast. I waited until she moved in closer and opened her robe. What I saw didn't impress me. She wasn't a total turn-off, just not my type, as in too much make-up, too much belly fat, and two little boobs. I pulled a Bish, coughed long and hard into my hands while considering my options. The best I could deliver on short notice was, "Not today, maybe some other time."

"Don't be a momma's boy," she said. "I'm running a special today: buy one, get the second half-price. Your friend already picked up the tab for both of you."

"A little bonus for not being a total asshole," Bish said, his weight barely denting the leather as he plopped down beside me. "Go ahead. I'll wait for you here, maybe take a short nap."

"Make it a long one," she told Bish and to me said, "The name's Lilly." She pulled me up by one hand before I had the chance to refuse her again. I watched her long black hair swing with each step as she led me down the hall to a door painted with yellow and blue wildflowers, the kind I'd seen scattered across the mountains. She turned, looked me over from head to toe.

"Nice boots," she said.

"Hand-tooled leather, a gift from … Sammy."

"I figured as much."

"It's not what you think."

"Whatever. The boots stay in the hall, house rules."

I braced myself and after she yanked off the boots, we went into what she called her special room. The shades were drawn, country western music filled the air, and while I was taking in the surroundings, she caught me off guard with a knee to my groin. Hard enough to bring tears, but not hard enough to double me over. She knew her stuff and out of respect for the memory of Butterscotch, I didn't retaliate by showing her mine.

You ungrateful bastard," she said. "That's for humiliating me in front of Sammy."

I didn't have to fake the cough that came with my next words. "Sorry, I didn't mean to hurt your feelings."

"Just so we're on the same page, I don't offer half price deals to anybody, not even a long-standing customer such as my good friend out there. For what you are about to receive, he paid double and I intend to give him his money's worth. You savvy?"

"Considering our initial contact, I don't think I'm up to much receiving."

"Quit sniveling about reinvigorating your manly charm. What I take down I put back up, thanks to certain healing powers inherited from my Lakota ancestors."

My first Indian style, little did I know. She shoved me against the wall, one hand undoing my belt and fly while the other held my mouth to receive a kiss wetter than the saliva of a panting St. Bernard. Next she ripped down my jeans, ordered me to step out of them, as if it hadn't occurred to me on my own. One jean leg was still tangled around my ankle when she dropped down to the hardwood planks, pulling me with her. Instead of attacking my mouth, she repaired what she had damaged, shocking me into an amazing revival I didn't think possible on such short notice. For the next thirty minutes, we covered every inch of the bedroom floorboards, mostly with her still in charge and me loving every minute of playing the underdog. Afterwards we took a hot shower together, a nice touch that ended too soon for me when she switched off the faucet and ordered me out.

"That's it, end of story. No more fun this afternoon," she said, throwing me a towel. "I carpool with another mom and today's my turn to pick up the kids."

She disappeared, leaving me to dress alone. After I'd finished I found Bish on the sofa, stretched out to his side and facing the back. I nudged him with the toe of my boot and when he didn't stir, I tapped his shoulder.

"Hey, good buddy, wake up, time to hit the road."

He gave me nothing, no flutter of eyelashes, no gurgling from deep within, no pulse beating from his neck or wrist. Dammit, why now and here of all places. Choking back an unexpected sob, I knelt beside him and was half-praying, half-cursing, when Lilly came prancing through, wearing jeans and a baggy shirt, her long hair pulled back in a ponytail, and no makeup.

"Show's over, boys. You gotta skedaddle before I can."

"You go on. I'll lock up."

"No can do. It's against the house rules, my rules."

I stood up. "In that case, we have a serious problem. Bish … Sammy … he's either comatose or dead, I'm thinking dead."

"Shit, not on my watch." She bent over, pressed two fingers to the side of his neck.

"I already checked there."

"Shit, shit, shit. We … you … get him out of here. Both of you … now before I leave … before my old man comes home from work."

"You're married?"

"Hey, did I ask about your private life. I don't even know your name. And don't tell me; I don't want to know."

Right. "Five minutes, that's all I need to bring my vehicle around and move him inside."

"Okay, okay, but make it snappy. I'll text my kid to hang tight."

Instead of backtracking through the pharmacy I shot down a side street to where I'd left the SUV, and minutes later parked in front of Lilly's building. She was waiting at the open door, finger pointing to her watch. We propped up Bish between us, walked outside as if he was stupid drunk, and pushed him into the passenger seat. After arranging him in an upright position, a single tear slid down Lilly's cheek. She kissed a row of her fingertips, touched them to his lips.

"Adios, Sammy, I'm going to miss your tender touch and all the other niceties. You'll always be tops in my book."

I drove away, nice and easy, and when I checked my rearview mirror, Lilly was gone. What to do, what to do, I couldn't think straight. I rolled down the windows, turned on the radio to Incubus playing "Wish You Were Here," which was pretty ironic even though the lyrics didn't fit my situation. I was free again. But who to thank, God or Bish, I wasn't sure. Either way, I'd been given a pass, relieved of offing Bish, something I knew he eventually would've asked of me, figuring I owed him because of the SUV and money. Or maybe I'd have done it on my own because I couldn't stand seeing him suffer any longer.

Some miles from town I parked alongside a clump of trees, and opened a can of warm soda from under the seat. I looked at Bish, unsure if his soul had left his body yet and when the physical effects of death would take over, hopefully, not on my watch because I couldn't stomach nature at its worse. Movies were one thing; virtual reality too, but real life didn't cut any slack. Bish had been gone for only an hour, give or take, and already I missed him. I leaned over, took his face between my hands.

"Speak to me, Bish. Give me some kind of sign."

Again, what I'd expected: nothing. So I took charge and did what seemed best for both of us. I drove back up the mountain I'd learned to love and the cabin I'd shared with him. Now to the practical matters: money, money, and money. Sure he had plenty, but where? I rummaged through every drawer, every shelf and cupboard, behind every wall hanging, within every photo, to locate his total cash on hand—forty-five thousand in assorted bills—all the while debating whether to bury him under the pine trees or ship him back to Sister Mary Fran for a proper Mass. Catholicism and motherhood won my vote. Besides, I didn't have a shovel and couldn't see myself going down the mountain to buy one and then having to come all the way back up.

What more could I have ask for. That night God stayed with me when I drove to Butte, Montana. The Big Sky's stars were not shining brightly on the city, neither were the welcoming lights of Limestone Gardens. Those I shot out before driving into the mortuary's circular driveway. After stopping in front, I wasted no time in getting out, and did the same for Bish. I helped him to the double door entrance and laid him out with some difficulty considering the stiff he'd become. Arms folded and wearing his best suit, a pinstripe I wouldn't be caught … never mind. Stuck to the lapel was my unsigned note with instructions to contact Sister Mary Fran in Las Vegas, along with a promise that money for his burial expenses would be forwarded to her. The next day I kept my word, with a cashier's check for ten thousand dollars Fedexed from miles away in Billings.

Losing Bish really hurt, more than I ever expected. In my own twisted way I'd been right about not wanting him for my real dad because he made a better substitute. That way I couldn't blame him for not being around when I needed him most, those years centered on no one but Lark and me. But now he was gone and as Delores would've said, with every lemon you need enough sugar to make a tall glass of lemonade, words of wisdom proven true more than once. All that was behind me now; Bish had moved on to a better life in a different dimension and I was determined to do the same in the here and now. About the remaining thirty-five thousand Bish couldn't take with: I guess Sister Mary Fran could've used the entire amount, what with the shelter burning down through no fault of mine and her other charity work. But given my current lack of finances, I needed the money more than she did since her building was most likely insured. Nuns can be pretty anal about the nitty-gritty of life and deep-pocket donations.

    Mission accomplished, I hit the road again, this time my business taking me to Florida.

Chapter 35

Two back-to-back life experiences and neither of them ending on a high note, I didn't need another. This time I did my homework and had a plan in mind before rolling into the Sunshine State. Florida's Panhandle welcomed me with sand whiter than snow, graduated shades of sea blue water, and palm trees beaucoup, some four stories high, others more like house plants living in a jungle. Phase three of my search, and what I'd hoped would be the end, had taken me to the Destin area, waterfront communities designed for any Joe or Jane willing to pay mega bucks for a small town atmosphere without having to associate with small town hicks who couldn't afford to live next door.

It didn't take long for me to get the lowdown on Mitchell Compton, building contractor and upright citizen, a recent widower and father of three—a son in elementary school, another in junior high, and a daughter one year behind me. Double bummer, according to his wife's obituary, they'd been married two years before I was born. Oh yeah, Mitch Compton had some *'splaining* to do. Perfection I didn't expect, just honesty. On the plus side I was impressed with his financial know-how and figured there'd be enough money for all the kids he sired, even an outsider like me, that is, if I qualified.

Qualifying for a laborer's job in construction—no problem in a state that didn't have a union to say I wasn't qualified for a backbreaking, eight-hour day or that I hadn't inherited the right to work from my father or my grandfather or my brother or an uncle. America, the land of opportunity and opportunists, you bet, but finding a job was still the hardest part, given the lousy economy. Since Compton Construction Company was number one and only on my list of places to work, I took the direct approach by making friends with the company's gofer, who said he hated working there. I didn't bother asking him why, just forked over two hundred bucks and suggested he look elsewhere for work or I'd report him to cops for growing weed in his backyard. Hello, I became the new gofer for carpenters working on a seaside gingerbread sitting on a postage-size lot that cost a cool million plus, go figure. My pay was a notch above minimum, enough to cover the rent on a studio apartment without digging deeper into my reserve.

During my second week on the job Mitch, as everyone called him, came strutting through the construction site in his tailored jeans. Although sweat had stained the armpits of his knit shirt, the incredibly muggy day didn't seem to faze him. He walked with the assurance of a guy who'd spent time in the military, his back unyielding, stomach flat. We wouldn't have met then if I hadn't made sure he saw me busting my butt. Literally, right in front of him, pushing a wheelbarrow piled with concrete blocks mixed with mortar and stucco that no one except yours truly could've managed. That is until a block fell out, barely missing the tip of my steel-toed boot.

"Sweet mother of god," he yelled. "What the hell do you think you're doing?"

"Sir?"

"Drop those handles and deliver your sorry ass to me."

Yes, master and sperm possibility. I came running, stood before him front and center.

Mitch Compton had not yet lost the macho features of his youth—pronounced cheekbones, skin tanned and lined from years in the sun, eyes hidden behind a pair of shades with a price tag higher than the monthly rent on my studio. What I saw of the hair his hardhat didn't cover was thick and wiry, sandier than mine but streaked with gray. He introduced himself and warned me about overloading the barrel because the last thing he wanted was another workers' comp claim, which was how the guy before me lost his job. Nice.

I all but clicked my heels and saluted him. "Sorry 'bout that, sir. It won't happen again. I have this habit of striving too hard, sometimes beyond my realistic capabilities. One hundred ten per cent, that's my goal, every day."

"Rain or shine, what dedication," he half-snarled.

"Thank you, sir."

"Shut up, I know a bullshitter when I see one. Believe me, I've seen them all, none of which are currently employed by my company nor are they allowed to breathe the same air I breathe. From now on, whatever your name is and if you have half a brain you won't tell me, stay out of my personal space or you'll be taking your one hundred ten percent elsewhere. Do we understand each other?"

Sure we did; me more so than him.

Chapter 36

Alone and lonely most definitely described me to a Florida-T, not a good thing for a healthy guy trying to make his mark in the land of sun-drenched babes. On the plus side, there was no one I wanted to hang out with more than yours truly but with nature calling, more like howling, I felt the urgent need for female friendship. Please, no more hookers, just a normal guy-girl thing. Since I'm not much of a drinker and smoke bothers my allergies, I ruled out the bar scene; perfect for showing off my construction muscles but not the place for girls I wanted to meet. Grocery stores were supposed to attract single females—nope, too old for me. Ditto for the cougars, too close to the Blake Turner fiasco I couldn't forget. Church was another option. Sunday Mass, nice girl, respectable family—wouldn't have been a problem for me but for her, maybe. Okay, definitely a problem since I didn't come with a decent resume. I shelved the church bit for now and instead resorted to my comfort zone, where I should've looked from the gitgo, the local bookstores.

Ten days later I let the girl of my dreams find me.

I was staring out the window of Duffy's Books when this yellow convertible pulled into the strip center lot and parked two spaces to the left of my SUV. Miss Priss got out, wiggled her legs into a comfortable stretch, and with a single flip of the head, adjusted her shoulder-length hair—blonde, the color of wheat. Her white lace-trimmed top hung loose over tight black capris, nothing out of the ordinary but on Miss Priss, more than extraordinary. She moved like a dancer, never wavering in a crisscross of high-heeled sandals. Oh yeah, she was quite the honey; and me, I could smell the money. Money mixed with honey, a combo better than cheese topping a chili mac.

Not wanting to blow my only chance, I stepped back, and observed her peruse the center front displays, respecting each book with a certain reverence I couldn't help but admire. From there, she headed to the fiction area, oblivious to me trailing one aisle across and two rows behind. While I checked out books with no intention of buying, she browsed for what she must've considered the perfect one. Fifteen minutes passed before she picked a current bestseller, a good choice and one I'd already read. After paying for the book, she wandered over to the in-house café, bought a latte, and made herself comfortable at the only vacant table. A table for two, it couldn't get much better. I made my move.

"You're a fan of Grisham?" I asked. She answered by propping her book on the table and opening it to Page One. Easy does it. I cleared my throat and gave her another chance. "Don't make me stand here all day."

Smooth move, it worked, sort of. She swiveled her head, forty-five degrees in my direction. From there she started a ho-hum appraisal of my worn jeans, working upward to land on a face that didn't leave as much an impression as her just-purchased bestseller. She yawned, turned the page, and took another sip of coffee.

Another brush-off, nothing I hadn't experienced before but given my poor track record one I'd never learned to accept without trying a different approach. "His latest is a snoozer, trust me."

"I don't trust you," she said, eyes fixed on Grisham's words. "Nor am I interested in letting you be my friend. Now, if you'll excuse me ...."

Whoa, just what I needed, a testy bitch—not. I backed off, and should've cut my losses but instead retreated to the café counter, bought two lattes and two biscotti wrapped in cellophane. I brought my peace offering back to her table and without permission, invaded her personal space by sitting my butt across from hers. My boldness got her attention, as did the goodies. Without so much as a thank you, she peeled off the wrapper of one of the biscotti, dunked it in her coffee, and took a single bite of decadent chocolate. I was hoping for an Adam and Eve moment but had to settle for attitude.

"Nothing—and I do mean nothing—about you appeals to me," she said. "Your hair needs a professional styling, your teeth need an orthodontist, your nails need a manicure, and your bod needs a designer makeover. Furthermore, you stink to high heaven. No offense, it's the cheap cologne. Ugh, if there's one thing I cannot stand, it's cheap. I don't come cheap, nor do I associate myself with anyone or anything that's cheap."

The cologne I'd lifted from Bish? The cologne he wore whenever we went to town, give me a break. I tuned back to her running-off-at-the-mouth. Those heart-shaped lips I wanted to shut up with a kiss she'd never forget but she was still talking about me and I couldn't resist listening.

"You are beyond zero, a negative with no hopes of ever crossing into the positive. To be perfectly blunt, you—whoever you are and don't tell me your name because I don't want to know—are nowhere in my league. And there is no chance in hell of your ever getting past the first rung of my league. Do I make myself clear?"

One more person who didn't want to know my name, what was it with me, or maybe it was them. This one ended by taking another bite of biscotti, a delicate sip of coffee.

"Could you please be a little more specific?" I asked.

The next ten seconds felt like sixty but produced a better response than I'd expected. She choked up, erupted with a spray of biscotti-tainted coffee across the table to desecrate my cheap T-shirt. I came back at her with, "I'm sorry, what league did you say you were in?"

She blushed, unable to speak for a good fifteen seconds. "*Touché*, my bad for listening to any part of the garbage you dished out so pathetically."

"If that's the best you can do in the way of an apology, I guess I'll have to take it."

"You'd better because this conversation is most definitely over."

"Can I at least tell you my name?"

She glanced at her watch, stifled another yawn, this one a fake. "Go ahead but make it quick."

"John Danner, but those people I connect with are allowed to call me Danner."

"Really, how generous of you."

"Is that your way of saying I'm not cheap?"

"It's my way of saying goodbye." She stood up and tucked her book under one sun-tanned arm.

"Wait, don't go yet. There's still the coffee I bought."

"Enjoy. I only have ten minutes to collect my brother."

Not yet, I stood and blocked her path. "Collections first, at least tell me your name … please."

"Morgana … Morgana Compton."

"Morgana, that's awesome," I said as she passed to my right, "Morgana as in Morgana Le Fey, one-time fairy and half sister to King Arthur of Camelot."

"Now I'm awed," she replied from over her shoulder.

Morgana, daughter of Mitchell Compton, possible half-sister to John Danner of Nowhere, she hadn't told me anything I didn't already know.

Chapter 37

What better way to establish a connection with the man who could be my father than to first establish a connection with the daughter who could be my half-sister. Other than my name Morgana Compton knew zilch about me. I, on the other hand, already knew where she lived—at home with her family and driving the MX-5 Miata from her sixteenth birthday five years before. I also knew her as a hungry reader who usually stopped by Duffy's on Saturday morning after swinging by the soccer field to deposit ten-year-old Chad the Younger but not twelve-year-old Evan the Older.

Fast forward another week to Duffy's where I Morgana gave me a rundown of her Saturday routine, one I already knew but preferred hearing it from her lovely lips. Same table, with an invitation I didn't have to squeeze from her. Pass the biscotti, please—you'd have thought we were hanging out at a café in Italy.

"I've put college on hold," she said over a second coffee, "not that I mind. Daddy's so busy making money he needs help with the boys. We're all a little nutty, fighting this emptiness that won't go away, or maybe we're not ready to let it go, I just don't know. Did I tell you? Mommy died last year."

Bummer, another fact I already knew but didn't let on. She talked about the late Rachelle Compton, one-time socialite from Mobile, and how much she missed her. The brothers did too, as much as I'd once missed Lark, for me a lifetime ago.

"Losing her must've been really tough on your father," I said.

"Poor Daddy, he adored Mommy. This may sound cheesy but she was the syrup on his waffles." Morgana blinked her eyes, ridding one of a single tear. "Say something, anything before I shed a waterfall."

"Death or desertion," I came back with. "Either way we're talking about a sense of abandonment."

"That is so true but not what I wanted to hear. What about your mother."

"She deserted me."

"Then your father raised you?"

"Never in the picture, a mystery which I intend to resolve in the near future."

"Good luck with that. So, tell me about your childhood."

Hers I already knew. Christmas in Aspen, Easter in Rome, August at the family cottage in Maine, they hadn't been back since the mother abandoned them when she died. "What's to tell, relatives who tried but couldn't deliver … a miserable situation that only got worse with time. But here I am, talking to the prettiest girl in Florida … make that the entire USA."

"Don't make statements you can't back up. Where did you go to school?"

"In Illinois, it's kind of complicated. For the record, I'm a streetwise college dropout with survival instincts and sometimes I have to ask the real me to stand up. Scary but true."

Okay, so I'd exaggerated the college bit and then some. But this was about selling John Earl Danner the Second—ASAP, before the holidays because I couldn't see myself spending Thanksgiving or Christmas with a Super Mac and fries.

We bumped our fingertips, nice. Maybe my touch worked the same for her. I'd sprung for a manicure earlier in the day, from a Thai nail technician who offered me a blowjob in the bathroom for the bargain price of forty dollars. But when I came back with thirty, she huffed and puffed and blew me out the door.

"Sorry about my being such a bitch last week," Morgana said. "Will you forgive me?"

"Maybe, if you'll let me take you on a real date."

"A real date, no. And don't take it personally. Between Evan and Chad, they take up most of my time."

"On a Saturday night? Come on, you can do better than that." I showed her my buffed fingernails. "Look, no more gook. I clean up pretty good."

"Well, it's a start, minor but nevertheless admirable." She thought for a minute or so. "There are several great movies playing at the cinema across the street. Meet me at nine, in front of the box office and maybe we can agree on one."

"How 'bout I pick you up at home and meet your dad the old-fashioned way."

"Daddy? Not a good idea. He wouldn't like you. In fact, he'd probably hate you."

"Right, I'm not in his league."

She laughed. "For now be satisfied I'm letting you into mine."

***

Our first date couldn't have turned out better had I planned it myself. We agreed on the movie, a romantic comedy—R-rated for language not explicit sex since I didn't want to start something I might later regret considering our possible kinship. Afterwards Morgana insisted on picking the restaurant, a hole-in-wall seafood dive, away from the price-gougers meant for tourists. We ordered a pitcher of sweet tea and shared a platter of crab legs, and didn't stop until we'd sucked the shells clean.

"Are we having fun yet?" I asked her, pouring the last of the tea into our glasses.

"More than I ever expected," Morgana said. "I'm glad I let you talk me into this."

That smile, those eyes, I didn't want the evening to end. "What about your brothers?"

"Sleeping over with friends and I hope having a ball because when the boys are happy, I am too."

"Let's hear it for the boys. Sorry I couldn't resist."

"Bette Midler, James Caan, right?"

"Show-off, now about your dad ...."

"He's quite the movie buff too. Although he'd never watch one with … someone like you. What I mean is a perfect stranger."

"An easy fix, whadaya say?"

"No, no, and no to your ever meeting him, don't make me say it again."

"Okay, okay, I won't."

***

Two weeks and five movie-slash-dinner dates later with little more than tender kisses I hesitated to give and with Morgana wondering why, she invited me to Sunday dinner with the family. But first, Saturday. We went shopping for what Morgana called the all important casual wardrobe, one acceptable to her father for at least three minutes before he found reason to throw me out. Literally, her words not mine. She picked the place: an exclusive men's shop in an exclusive mall bleeding pseudo charm and inflated prices. She also picked the clothes, with a few extra just in case: white jeans and shorts, one plaid and two polo shirts, and leather sandals. That was it, no boat shoes, no socks, no way.

"What about briefs?" I asked. To any other girl, I would've added: I'll show you mine if you show me yours.

"Maybe next time," Morgana said. "Depending on how well tomorrow works out."

While she ran her fingers through a rack of fall merchandise, I followed our prince of a sales clerk to the register. This guy belonged on the front cover of the mall's glossy catalogue, his image oozing such phony perfection I'd almost mistaken him for one of the shop's mannequins. The plastered hair never moved, the mouth, only enough to quote the purchase price as he, my equal in height, managed to look down his friggin' nose at me, and say, "That'll be three hundred seventy-four dollars and sixty-three cents."

"What, no please?" I shot back for his ears only. Had sales boy been that much better than me, he wouldn't have been pedaling jeans for a living.

Morgana's antennas must've popped up, sensed possible trouble, because she hurried to my side and whipped out the plastic, prepared to fork it over to his outstretched palm until I stopped her with a phrase I'd practiced for days. "I pay my own freight or I stay home."

She didn't argue as I counted out the bills and exact change, earning an almost sincere thank you from sales boy when he turned over a designer shopping bag containing my designer clothing.

Same story at the hair salon, Morgana took charge. I learned the difference between a cut and a style—one hundred bucks for Kim Henri the stylist to yin yang with Morgana over how much hair to remove from my head without compromising the dark and strong elements controlling a complex personality I had yet to figure out. I gazed into the mirror until they finally agreed on one and a half inches, enough to cover the ears and barely skim the shoulders. Kim Henri picked up his scissors and Morgana stepped back six feet or so, determined to observe every snip and clip. That is, until Kim Henri objected, claiming her very presence stifled his artistic juices to which she called him nothing more than a glorified barber. He banned her to the waiting room to calm herself with herbal tea and what he called cookies-to-die-for. Two of which she saved for me, stuffing them in my shirt pocket after Kim Henri invited her back to applaud his latest creation while I modeled from the electric chair.

"You like?" he asked her, not me.

"It's absolute genius," she replied, kissing him in the same harmless way I'd been kissing her.

I paid, again with cash, and left the tip Kim Henri deserved, no bigger than I'd have given for a regular haircut anywhere else. All in all money well spent if it brought me closer to a goal now making me queasy.

Back in the parking lot, Morgana and I climbed into her Miata, both of us smiling over the new, improved me.

"I don't suppose we have time for the orthodontist today," I said, still stinging over her comment during our first encounter.

"Tabled for now, along with the briefs."

Briefs … brief … encounter, I came back with, "Did you ever see *Brief Encounter*, the Di Nero/Streep version.

"If you mean doomed romance, stop right there, Daddy hates tearjerkers and so do I."

A doomed romance if it didn't work out between Morgana and me. On the plus side a new beginning for me. Already I stuck myself with a tougher load than expected. Morgana the Ingénue, I'd given her a minor role in my play, no more than a clog in the wheel rolling toward my destiny, connecting with my sperm provider. Now she was messing with my original script; messing with certain feelings I couldn't share with her. Morgana the Fairy, half-sister to Arthur of Camelot; Morgana of Compton, half-sister to Danner of Nowhere—maybe yes, maybe no, either way I smelled a possible screw-up, big time. Not my first and with any luck not my worst.

Chapter 38

Morgana told me her parents had christened the family estate Mira by the Sea, Mira being a portmanteau of their names, Mitch and Rachelle. Not wanting to be outdone, I told her about another Mira, brightest star in the constellation when it decided to shows its face. What I didn't say was their Mira by the Sea bordered on portmanteau hokey even though it made sense for the twentieth-century newly rich copying the nineteenth-century rich. On the other hand, my family's estate was known as JED Farm so maybe a hokey connection wasn't too far off course. That said, I came up with my own private version of the Compton digs—M by the C.

On Sunday with my SUV still shining from its recent ultra car wash and wax, I exited the beach highway onto a private road paved with crushed seashells. I followed a line of palm trees and shrubs concealing the estate from gawking drive-bys, myself included until that day, having gone from *wannabe* to *in-your-face*. I rewarded myself by rolling down the windows and breathed in a combo of flowering shrubs and salty air. A lawn greener than artificial turf, flowers guaranteed to make Delores ooh and aah, and stone pathways snaking through the gardens all spelled high maintenance, probably from an underpaid groundskeeper, maybe illegal like Lark's Hector. Once I knew for sure, maybe reporting the lawn boy to immigration would create a job opportunity for me. Nah, I'd come too far to work my way up from the bottom. What's more, I didn't want trouble for Mitch unless he turned against me too soon. But first things first: me getting to know him, him getting to know me.

The seashell road drifted into one of concrete and then a circular driveway, stretching around to this super modern house, white as the sandy beach and framed with swaying palm trees rising to the second floor. Celebrity quality, without a doubt, and money to spare for what Lark called extra goodies. I parked at the entrance, grabbed two packages from the front seat, and stepped onto the pavement. As if on cue Morgana hurried out the double-door entry, and greeted me with a lay of hands on my shoulders, a brush of lips to my cheek. An okay kiss, between friends or possible siblings, either way harmless in case her father happened to be watching from behind one of those taller-than-tall windows with special glass designed to reduce Florida's sunrays.

"You do clean up nice," she said, slipping her arm through mine. "The shorts are a huge improvement over those embarrassing jorts."

My cut-offs? They were part of me, the extra layer of skin covering my awesome boys.

Inside the tiled entryway, I half expected to find Mitch playing the concerned parent. Instead, I got Morgana's brothers, bare feet spread and arms folded across their skinny chests. Searching their faces for some memory of a younger me, I found nothing more than a smattering of freckles. After Morgana hurried through an introduction, each boy allowed me to shake his hand, one that went from wet noodle to jaws of steel, with me playing the loser, but only as a courtesy.

"Morgana said there might be gifts," Chad the Younger said, releasing his grip.

Evan the Older whacked him alongside the head with the heel of his palm. "Show some manners?"

Manners—get real. Before I could present my peace offerings, they yanked them from my hands. After checking the name tags, they groaned and traded each other for the right gift.

"Boys," was all Morgana said while they ripped off the colorful wrappings.

"Legos," Chad yelled. "How'd you know?"

"Hey, it's a miracle, a DVD I haven't seen yet," said Evan. "Morgana told you, I know she did. Thanks, Sis. You too … uh, what is your name?"

I doubt the kid heard my response since he was more interested in the Lego set meant for Chad. Just then a familiar voice boomed from a remote intercom. "Morgana to the kitchen, ASAP if not sooner, please."

"Coming, Daddy." She excused herself, leaving me alone with the brothers she adored. Whatever Morgana might've felt for me had not rubbed off on them because as soon as she disappeared, Evan hauled off and punched me in the gut. I doubled over but held my footing until Chad came from behind and plowed into the bend of my knees, sending me to the floor for a close-up of the sand-colored tiles. Cute kids, I could've taken them both out but instead decided to play along with this: "Damn, what the shit was that about."

"Oh, oh, two bad words," Chad said. "I'm telling Morgana."

"And ruin her only chance for happiness," Evan chimed in. "Watch out, butthead."

"But what about the house rules on profanity?"

"Only if we actually hear it, that's what Morgana said." Evan poked me in the ribs with his bare foot. "Five bucks each says we didn't hear a damn thing."

They each offered me a hand and pulled me to my feet at which point Morgana returned, all bubbly and apologetic. "Sorry about that, Daddy couldn't find his special apron." Her eyes wandered from me to the brothers and back to me before she spoke. "What's going on? Is everything all right?"

"No problem," Evan said. "We had this bet with your friend and he lost. Right, uh, uh … sorry, I forgot your name."

"Danner," I repeated, pulling out my money roll. I peeled off two fives, handed one to Evan and the other to Chad.

"All squared away?" Morgana asked.

"You bet," the three of us replied as one.

"Good. I hope you're hungry because Daddy just fired up the steaks."

The brothers elbowed each other as they took off down the windowed hallway leading outside, all the while Morgana apologizing for their rowdiness.

"Hey, it's guy stuff, a rite of passage," I told her. "We connected, that's what counts."

"Good attitude, an absolute must where Daddy is concerned."

"I can't get much better than this so bring him on. I'm either in or I'm not."

"Not so fast. Before I inflict him on you, there's one more person you simply must meet."

Of course, the faithful employee who worked for peanuts, every rich family had one. I followed Morgana to the kitchen of stainless steel appliances and floor-to-ceiling windows calling me outdoors to white waves splashing into the bluer-than-blue sky. We stood in the doorway, not wanting to disturb this amazon bent over the sink, dreadlocks falling forward as she wielded a knife capable of serious damage to the pile of gigantic yams. She wore a knee-length dress with big, bold flowers and had ropey arms with biceps tighter than mine. The woman must've known we were there but didn't turn around until Morgana spoke her name. Another intro followed, this time to Juanita, a woman of uncertain age and race, a mix of interesting features and skin lighter than I remembered Butterscotch's had been. Butterscotch, I hadn't thought of her for days.

The utility knife never left Juanita's hand as she slid her eyes over my face. The look on hers revealed nothing but blew my mind because I hated staring back at her. I wanted to say something to make her like me but couldn't think of a single thing that wouldn't brand me as the phony she'd already figured me to be. Too bad I couldn't have dittoed the same for her.

"Without this wonderful lady the Compton family would fall apart," Morgana said, planting a kiss the woman had sense enough to ignore. "Juanita is our chief cook, housekeeper, and laundry expert. She originated from Aruba but she's been with us forever."

"Your forever, not mine," Juanita said in a droll voice. "And please: don' make me out as more than I am. I don' do windows and I don' drive. Nor do I keep secrets so don' tell me any of yours."

Morgana laughed. "Now, Juanita, you know I have no secrets. What about you, Danner?"

"None worth talking about." As if. Who was I kidding, for sure not Juanita.

"In that case you best leave me to my work," Juanita said.

I felt her eyes piercing the back of my head as Morgana led me outside. We wound up on a terraced patio overlooking an Olympic-size swimming pool and beyond the pool Gulf waves lazily rolling into sand whiter than coke, not that I ever sampled the stuff. As for the mansion's backside: windows, windows everywhere—all with a clear view of the water, just in case its live-ins forgot where they were. Or, how privileged they were. Speaking of … the Brothers Terrible were taking turns jackknifing off the diving board, each one trying to outdo the other while the cigar-puffing Mitch was managing five bacon-wrapped filets sizzling on a grill loaded with more bells and whistles than most pro chefs needed. An equally professional apron covered Mitch's tropical shirt and swim trunks. His sandals were on the order of mine. Good choice, Morgana. He stretched out his hand and shook mine as if meeting me for the first time. If he recalled the incident with me pushing the overloaded wheelbarrow, he didn't let on, nor was I about to jog his memory. When he spoke, it was through a belch of smoke I sidestepped to avoid.

"Morgana, your friend needs a drink."

"Daddy, my friend has a name." She handed me the longneck I'd been thinking about all day.

"Danner, isn't that what you said? Surely, there's more to it."

I met his gaze, much easier than with Juanita, and spoke with the balls I thought I'd lost. "Yes sir, John Edward Danner the Second."

"The Second, you don't say, that's quite a mouthful. I'll just call you Number Two."

"No, you won't Daddy. It's too confusing for the boys."

"An excellent point," Mitch told Morgana without his eyes leaving mine. "Okay then, Danner it is."

Time out, I took my first swallow of beer as soon as Mitch turned back to his steaks. He flipped them with a one-eighty, creating perfect grill marks.

"Congratulations," Morgana whispered. "You made it to first base."

"I did? Was it good for you?"

"Silly, I meant you passed the all-important introduction phase."

"Which means I'm staying for dinner?"

"Not necessarily, none of my dates ever got this far before. Just don't say anything to annoy Daddy."

"Better yet, I'll keep my mouth shut."

"No, no, and no. Your silence would indicate possible fear and anyone showing fear, Daddy regards as less than insignificant. You know, vermin he devours and spits out like—"

"Speak up, Morgana," Mitch yelled from his smoke-filled station. "I can't hear you."

"Sorry, Daddy, I wasn't talking to you."

"True, but you were talking about me. I could tell by the twist of your mouth, most unbecoming on a lovely creature such as yourself." Using tongs, he turned one of the filets onto its side. Fat dripped onto the ashen briquettes below, sending up flames that seared a crisp edge on the bacon. "Need I remind you of our Compton Creed, the sanctity of Sunday dinner? Our mutual breaking of bread is neither the time nor the place for releasing one's pent-up frustrations."

Danner to the rescue, I jumped in feet first. "My apologies, Mr. Compton, I shouldn't have distracted Morgana from your family hour."

"Nonsense, my daughter doesn't need you running interference on her behalf. She's quite capable of defending herself."

An in-bred trait I shared with her, I could hardly wait until Mitch was better acquainted with me and my know-how.

"Danner's never given me reason to defend myself," Morgana said, a statement both Mitch and I ignored.

One by one, Mitch finished off the other steaks, creating a smoky combo of fat and wood chips that smelled like apples, luring me into a meal I didn't want to miss regardless of the outcome. At last he squinted through the smoke and elevated me to the next level.

"You may call me Mitch, unless I change my mind and tell you otherwise. Morgana, these steaks are one minute away from perfection. How about giving Juanita a hand in the kitchen?"

"Sure, Daddy, but I expect Danner to still be where when I come back."

She didn't wait for his assurance and left me alone with him.

"You were making fun of me," he said.

"No, sir, nor would I risk offending Morgana by making a fool of myself," I said with all sincerity. "I'm here to enjoy a good meal in the company of interesting people."

"Where have I heard that schmaltz before?" Mitch cocked his head, viewed me through narrowed lids. "And don't lie to me."

"There's no reason to lie. I work for your construction company as a laborer; and no, I'm not interested in a promotion."

"You don't want to get ahead?"

"Not until I finish school, sir. My education comes first."

Saved by the bell—better yet the high-pitched voice of Juanita singing a Caribbean song while balancing a tray of dishes on her head. Morgana came next, a wooded bowl filled with salad cradled in her arms. Intending to help, I started to get up but changed my mind when Mitch shook his head and made some reference to women's work. Okay, it worked for me. After more to and from the kitchen and arranging the buffet table, Juanita announced she was through for the day and promptly left. Good riddance, I didn't need her brain lasering mine, this day or any other.

The rest of us helped ourselves to a spread on a par with anything I'd seen in Vegas, except on a smaller scale. One-by-one we sat around a glass-top table. The brothers' table manners reflected a proper upbringing—please and thank you and no talking with a full mouth. I did the same, thanks to the standards Delores had set for me, not Jed. As for Morgana, she played the naughty princess, smiling at Daddy while rubbing her bare foot up and down my bare leg while I kept up a running dialogue with him about baseball.

"Who's going to win the series," he asked.

"The Cardinals, hands down."

"Good choice, I was born in St. Louis and lived there off and on but I've replanted my roots here in Florida. And you?"

"Born in Southern Illinois," I said, "on a farm not far from Carbondale." Good enough for now, the rest I'd dish out on an as-needed basis.

"Hmm, which explains the bit of twang I detected. So, John Danner the Second, what brings you to Florida?"

"Opportunities, I want to see the country before settling down."

"Take your time, son."

No way, too many incredible ops staring me in the face.

After dinner I insisted on helping Morgana clean up, which relieved her brothers and may've earned me some points with them. So what if they were brats; I needed them on my side. I couldn't help but feel Comptonish, more so on my exit when Morgana kissed my cheek like a sister would've.

"I don't think Daddy hates you," she whispered, "not yet."

"It's a start. I'll try not to disappoint you."

"What about your evening schedule. Is Tuesday okay?"

"Whatever works for you."

"Not me, silly, the orthodontist. Call me on your break tomorrow and I'll give you the time."

"I can make my own appointment, you know."

"And wait three months, I don't think so. Now go, Daddy and I have a movie to watch."

Without me I wanted to ask but Morgana was too busy pushing me toward the SUV.

That evening I dreamed about her, in ways I shouldn't have. Had she been sleeping in next room, I might've jumped her bones. After convincing her it was the right thing to do. Realty check, I took a cold shower instead.

***

The next morning I'd hardly worked up a sweat when the general foreman called me into his cramped office.

"You've been promoted to my assistant," Bucky said. "A glorified gofer, if you will. No raise involved, but a chance to move up if you play your cards right."

"Thanks for the opportunity."

He snorted. "Yeah, yeah, just don't make me sorry."

"No goof-ups, I promise."

The promotion relieved me of some heavy lifting but didn't set too well with the laborers who enjoyed bitching about the heat. About them, I didn't care. Getting what I wanted didn't involve a popularity contest. Morgana was another story. Although we saw each other several times during the week, she didn't mention another Sunday at M by the C, nor did I ask. Plenty of time, I thought, to settle in before the holidays rolled around. But, after the third consecutive weekend with no invite, I asked Morgana if Mitch had crossed me off his okay list.

"Oh, didn't I tell you. Daddy's waiting on the final report."

"On what?"

"Your background, silly, it's not as if you have anything to hide." She kissed my cheek. "You don't, do you?"

Chapter 39

Thanksgiving, what a disaster with me eating alone in the kitchen and Delores in the bedroom, spoon feeding Jed who could've fed himself if only he'd set his mind to it. On the plus side her spoiling him gave me the chance to play Super Mario whenever and wherever I wanted as long as my chores were done in what Delores called a timely fashion. I really didn't bother much with Jed, more like avoided him. The old man had grown a full, white beard, which Delores said would be easier to groom than all that shaving. Jed's social worker arranged for a nurse who came every day and for a therapist who came twice a week, but when the social worker suggested a nursing home for Jed, Delores called her a busybody before showing her the door.

If it hadn't been for Rowena and our time in the janitor's closet, I probably would've hitchhiked back to St. Louis and explained what happened between Jed and me. But I didn't, big mistake. Instead I endured a miserable Christmas and every day thereafter. Always trying to avoid Jed's eyes that blamed me for the accident, always waiting for the time to make things right.

That time came on a cold day in January. After the visiting nurse gave Jed his bath and changed the bed sheets, she hurried on to her next patient. With more snow in the forecast Delores decided she needed groceries. We both knew what she really needed: an excuse to get away from Jed for a while. She kissed him goodbye and promised me another video. I stood at the window, watching her truck creep down the driveway. A field of snow covered the entire farm, creating a geometric effect of buildings and trees silhouetted against the gray sky and white landscape. It would've made a great picture. Too bad I hadn't asked Delores to buy me a camera, maybe next time. She pretty much gave in to whatever I asked for, unlike Jed who'd always made me beg like some dog wanting his bone.

Old age had crept further into the house, its only sound coming from the creaking and popping that told me how alone I really was. Except for Jed, that is, but he didn't count anymore. I went into his room, sat down on the chair Delores always used, the one next to the hospital bed that had enough room for him but not for her. I leaned my feet to the side rail and fired up Super Mario. He came forward, ready for action. Leaning over, I showed the screen to Jed and tried to explain the game. Even if Jed wanted to smile, which I doubt, the pig in his head wouldn't let him. But the eyes said what his mouth couldn't so I gave up trying to entertain him.

One thing was for sure: the old man had not been pulling his weight for some time. I left the room and came back with the shotgun loaded. I held it up for Jed to see. Then I leveled with him.

"It's your call, Jed. I don't care one way or the other, but Delores is wearing herself out. At night I can't sleep because she makes so much noise with her crying. She feels guilty watching her soaps and that's not fair. You know what I mean. And, she's worried about the insurance money, how much the nurses cost, things like that. So maybe it's time you gave her a break."

Not wanting to rush him, I leaned the gun against the wall where he could see it. His eyes forgot the hate for me. Instead they grew desperate for my understanding. "I guess you want to think about this," I said. "Maybe pray or something, confess your sins."

I went into the kitchen, popped a soda can, and ate some apple pie with ice cream. Vanilla, the only kind Delores ever bought even though she knew I preferred cookie dough. Nothing decent was on TV and I didn't want to get Mario involved in family matters so I went back to the bedroom. Jed may've shed a few tears, maybe not. I couldn't tell for sure. Maybe it was a case of eyestrain, from watching me too much.

"So, whadaya think, Jed. Give me a sign: how about one blink for yes, two for no."

Jed blinked once. His hand flopped against the blanket, as if to say 'whatever.'

"Good choice. You wanna take charge, right?" I stepped back and cocked the gun, just like he'd showed me. Once was all it took for a quick learner such as myself. I put the barrel in Jed's left hand, the tip in Jed's mouth, and wrapped Jed's finger around the trigger. Make no mistake, this was all about Jed. I was only there to do his bidding. "Okay, whenever you're ready."

After stepping back, I stuck my fingers in my ears, squeezed my eyes and waited. Not for long, all things considered. The noise blasted through my ears. It forced my eyes wide open. Cripes, this whole deal turned out worse than I ever imagined. Jed had lost his face and most of his head. Blood and other stuff had splattered all over me, the pillows and sheets, even the wedding picture on the wall. I started gagging and couldn't stop. After puking in the nearest container—Jed's bedpan—I walked away from the disgusting mess he'd created. A sudden urge to piss sent me to the bathroom. One look in the mirror made me puke again, this time into the toilet I hadn't bothered to flush earlier. I scrubbed the gook from my face until it burned like crazy, stuffed my dirty tee into the hamper, and got a clean one from my bedroom.

Back in the living room I plopped down on the couch, and reached for Game Boy. By the time Delores came home, I had advanced Mario into the third world. She hadn't bothered with the groceries, probably expected me to help with them later. On her way to the bedroom, she asked the usual, "How's Jed?"

"Doing a whole lot better than when you left." Not a lie in my opinion.

Her first scream lifted me off the cushion, I'm not kidding. Mario fell off the screen so I pulled up Luigi while Delores screamed some more. She came running out, as wild-eyed as Jed had been that day in the barn loft.

"Why, Johnny, why?"

"Jed needed help," I said with a shrug, "same as Rusty."

"Oh ... my ... god." She leaned over and whopped me across the face, a first for her and one that knocked me for a loop. "You stupid, stupid idiotic shit, we should never have taken you in."

"Did I ask to come here? No." I wanted to take away the sting of her fingers with mine but needed them to advance Mario.

Delores didn't care. She grabbed Game Boy out of my hands and threw it at the TV, smashing the screen. Sparks flew like a Fourth of July fireworks. Great, there went my programs and hers. Okay, I got it. She loved the old fart, even if he couldn't love her back. I said the first thing that popped in my mind. "Since you don't want me anymore maybe Lark will take me back."

Her face was wet with tears. She jerked me to my feet, shook my shoulders until my head rattled. "Forget about Emily. She doesn't want you. Not now, not ever."

"In that case, can we still go to Silver Dollar City, just the two of us, you and me?"

First Delores wobbled. Then she crumpled onto the sofa, pulling me down too. I patted her arm, anything to calm her down.

"Come on, Delores, don't cry anymore."

She wouldn't look at me, not that I blame her. I said what I thought she wanted to hear. "Give me a break, will you. I promise not to cause any more trouble."

Chapter 40

Three long weeks since my Sunday at M by the C, damn. On top of that Morgana hadn't returned my last two phone calls which really ticked me off. No way, no how would I have groveled by leaving a crapload of messages she wouldn't dream of answering. As far as I was concerned, we'd had a nice run that ended with me getting one foot in the door, my number one motive from the gitgo. Moving to the next level would involve a kick-ass plan, one I had yet to devise.

As for my job at Compton Construction, the company had never employed a more efficient gofer than yours truly, on that I would've bet my studly balls. When Friday rolled around, Bucky forked over my paycheck along with a summons for me to report to Mitch's office, a trailer twice as big as my studio apartment and equipped with the air conditioning mine lacked.

"Don't bother knocking before you go in," Bucky said as I turned to leave. "Mitch is expecting you."

He was expecting me all right. As soon as I walked into the office, his fist connected with the tender spot between my eyes. A blow like that could've killed some guys. Instead, I fell backwards, my ass skidding across the linoleum floor until it slammed into a file cabinet. Two drawer pulls jabbed my upper and lower back, inflicting more pain than Mitch's less-than-friendly howdy. My head bobbled. Out-of-control tears blurred my vision. Was that one or two hands reaching down to me?

"Get up, crybaby," Mitch said. He latched onto my forearm, yanked me to my feet.

I could've taken him out with my right hand, one karate chop to the neck. Bam! Now or later, either way I wanted to kill him. Instead I took the high road with, "This had better be good."

My remark almost drew a snicker from Mitch. Halleluiah, maybe he did have a sense of humor, however warped. Let the fun begin, I thought. He shoved me into a chair, took his place behind the desk, and fired up a fresh cigar.

Too much puff-puff further irritated the damage already inflicted on my sinuses. I spoke through a clogged nose, the words distant to my ears. "Either the cigar goes or I go."

"My, oh my, the boy does have a matching set of balls. I was beginning to wonder." He tapped the cigar tip onto an ashtray, leaving a slight smolder I managed to tolerate. "So, you killed your own grandfather—an act of parricide, revolting yet somehow intriguing. The old man must've twisted your balls into quite a knot."

Ah-h, the background check, I should've known. "It's not what you think. I was a kid, trying to make things right."

"And now you're a full-fledged parasite, trying to worm your way into my family."

"My family too … unless our DNA proves otherwise, in which case I can continue my pursuit of Morgana, innocent now but capable of heating up in the event we're not blood-related. Either way, it's a win-win for me."

Bingo. I'd rubbed his Achilles heel raw, right down to the bone. He jumped up, leaned across the desk and into my face. "Why you no-good, ass-kicking bastard—using my daughter to ingratiate yourself with me, you're worse than despicable."

"No more despicable than you deserting a pregnant woman."

"Sonofabitch!"

"You got that right, which tells me you did know … uh—Emily, Charity, Desiree, or Lark. Take your pick, four in one."

"Smart ass." He opened his desk drawer, pulled out a bottle of Jack Daniels, and to my surprise poured two glasses and passed one to me. No 'here's-looking-at-you,' but I did give him the respect of going first. He downed Jack in one gulp while I took a single sip from mine. He leaned back in his swivel chair, mulling over god-knows-what. His studly days, I guess.

"She was something else," he said in a far-off voice. "I can still picture her, this beautiful creature few guys could resist. Pardon my brutal honesty: free as a bird with a brain to match."

"That would be Lark."

He straightened up, took a defensive position. "She went to my old man instead of me. He paid her off and sent me back to Florida."

"To the wife you left behind, what a stand-up guy."

"Look who's talking, grandpa killer. Hell, I didn't even know Lark was in trouble, not that we had an exclusive relationship. How many others paid her off is anybody's guess."

"Please, it's not like Lark and I lived high on the gourmet hog, more like Mickey D's and Taco Bell."

"So I surmised. You don't come across as top-of-the-line. Whatever happened to her modeling career?"

"Waitressing paid better. But enough with the history lesson, let's talk biology. As in the guy who knocked up dear old mom. Sure, she's an airhead but one with balls. What Lark lacks in common sense she makes up for in math. Diaries, journals—the woman kept perfect score, then and now."

Okay, so I'd stretched the truth about her recordkeeping, whatever it took to hold his interest before the A.D.D. kicked in, his which I recognized from my own.

He tapped four impatient fingers onto the polished desk. "Make your point. I don't have all evening."

"After some coaxing, I convinced Lark to give up the names, three potential sperm donors. The first two didn't pan out so I'm counting on you."

"And my money, don't take me for a fool. Just out of curiosity, who failed the criteria?"

"Sammy Lawford, a stand-up guy but unfortunately not a match. He practically died in my arms."

"Sammy dead?" Mitch shook his head, poured himself another drink, and passed over mine. "How'd it happen?"

"He was losing his battle with the Big C but that's not what took him. Call it a reaction to too much action … you know, as in the sack."

"What more could any man ask for." He lifted his glass; I lifted mine higher. We drank to Bish's memory. "So long, Sammy," Mitch said. "What about the other?"

"An actor, Blake Turner."

He nodded. "Why am I not surprised. Mr. Hollywood always preening, he considered himself quite the stud."

"One who shot blanks, according to the woman who's either his black widow or his grifter wife; I'm not for sure which."

"How much did they take you for?"

"Enough to hurt but not enough to waste my time recovering."

"Which leaves me, at least for now, how convenient."

"You do fit the timeline."

"Daddy Warbucks with deep pockets and you want a piece of the family biz. Take it from one who knows: money's not everything."

"It is when you don't have any."

"Well said." He poured another drink while I still nursed my first. Another minute passed before he spoke. "All right, John Danner the Second, as of now no kin of mine, this is how I see it. You have reached a fork in the road leading to ambition. Choose wrong and you travel alone. Choose wisely and maybe, just maybe, you can travel with me."

"Where are we going?"

"Not so fast, this is my parable. Ever hear this one: feed a man a fish, he eats for the day. Teach a man to fish, he eats for a lifetime. You could be that fisherman."

"Well now, that depends on what I'm fishing for."

"Good pay and interesting assignments. The right to refuse work unpalatable to your conscience with no questions asked. Trust me: for this position I consider you more than qualified."

Chapter 41

Another weekend without an invite to M by the C, but I expected that to change in the near future. Talk to Juanita, Mitch had told me, she'll supply the particulars. Code words for the nasty *who, what, when, and why*—give me a break. One thousand bucks, Mitch promised, just for listening to Juanita's spiel; add nine more should I agree to the shit-ass job, another yet-to-be-determined amount upon its completion. My soul traded for quality time in the Compton family loop, time for Mitch to decide if and for how long he wanted me hanging around. At this point I didn't have anything else to lose.

On Monday morning the sun forgot to show its face, which didn't mean rain but another muggy day with me fighting for every breath while working off my brown-nose ass. I'd been gofering a good hour when Bucky called me into his office.

"What's with the shades?" He meant the wrap-around sunglasses planted on my face. "Too much weekend fire water?"

"Close enough." My souvenir from Mitch: two raccoon eyes, not my first but most definitely the worst.

An important errand, Bucky explained in all seriousness. And get this: of all places to the Compton Estate. Imagine that. The guy had no clue as to my involvement with the family nor did I let on when he gave me the specific directions.

"The pick-up may not be ready when you arrive. However long it takes, it takes, so don't worry. I can manage here without you. One more thing more important than it seems: in case you're invited into the house, don't forget to wipe your feet on the doormat. Otherwise, wait outside and no poking around. Understand?"

Yeah, yeah, if only he knew.

Nothing about M by the C had changed since my last visit. Other than two south-of-the-border guys doing yard work, the golf-course green outdoors appeared deserted. I parked in the same spot as before but this time no Morgana ran out to greet me, no sisterly peck to the cheek, only Juanita guarding the doorway, her greeting a single nod of dreadlocks. At least she hadn't armed herself with the dreadful knife.

She motioned me to follow, neither of us speaking on the way to her kitchen domain. A Coke would've been nice but I didn't have the guts to ask. Maybe later, if and when I established myself a more comfortable position. Hers, I had no intentions of ever disrupting.

"Not here," she said. "We go to my quarters."

Her quarters were above the attached garage and way nicer than anything I'd ever occupied. Bright colors and long strings of glass beads oozed with an attitude that spelled Caribbean.

"Not here," she said again, this time leading me into another room, her private chapel where one whiff of incense cleared my clogged sinuses faster than any over-the-counter nose spray. A crucified Jesus hung on the wall; a bust of Jesus weeping rested on a sideboard alongside an alabaster replica of the Blessed Mother holding her dead Son. Okay I got the picture: Juanita treasured her faith. Motioning to a painted table in front of the window, she ordered me to sit on one of two rattan chairs, which gave me with a terrific view of the Gulf. If this paternity thing didn't work out, maybe I could land a job at M by the C. Butler, companion, whatever, I was trainable, according to members of the juvy board when they returned me to the civilized.

Juanita sat across from me, opened up a three-ring binder, and shoved it in my direction. One of her long finger nails tapped on this black and white glossy of an older guy, late fifties early sixties. His dark, slicked-back hair and pencil-slim mustache reminded me of a character actor from the forties, most definitely the loathsome villain. As in Blake Turner, a part he could easily have played.

"Memorize this man's face," she said. "He must go, do you understand?"

"Not exactly, maybe you'd better explain."

"He has defiled young children, boys and girls, forced them to do the unspeakable. See for yourself."

A series of photos, him and other degenerates with zombie-like kids who should've been playing in the park instead of doing what they were doing, I wanted to puke. More photos involved him butchering household pets. Nothing was off-limits—pit bulls and poodles, beagles and mutts, Siamese and Angoras and greeting-card kittens. Clearly the man was a certifiable perverted nutcase but when I spoke, my voice didn't reflect the disgust I felt. "The police need to see these."

"They already have, not here but elsewhere. He is an American who takes his pleasure in one of the remote Caribbean islands where respectable tourists do not venture. Two of his child victims are dead, another crazy with fear because the man killed her mother. I have all the documentation." She turned to another section of the binder. "Right here, look."

While I scanned the reports, Juanita poured me a glass of iced tea, sweetened with honey, just the way I like it. Even so, I couldn't handle more than one sip. Somehow it didn't seem right, what with the gallery of horror spread before me.

"The man is too clever, too evil. He must be stopped," she said after I finished reading the details. "Fallen angels and all the damnations of Hell await him."

"So what does that make me, the UPS man? Sorry, I'm sticking with my gofer job."

"Do not underestimate your capabilities. First time we met I looked beyond those tell-nothing eyes and delved deep into your soul. Such pain I observed in one so young. But pain is not always a bad thing. With pain comes compassion. And with compassion comes the need to react, to right that which is wrong. Not everyone can do what is now being asked of you."

Enough, she could put a curse on me, whatever. I wanted out, now. I stood, held up my hands, and showed her the palms. "Whoa! There's been a huge misunderstanding, Juanita. And you're propositioning the wrong guy. I don't work for Satan."

"Of course not, you work for Mitchell Compton, a righteous man who aligns himself with Almighty God when the justice system fails. Good against evil, the very foundation of our existence, do you not agree?" Juanita didn't wait for me to answer, as if I had much choice. "Then you must help. Show him you are worthy."

"Of what: a place at his table, in his company?"

"That, John Danner Number Two, is between you and that which created you."

"As in Almighty God or the almighty Mitch Compton?"

"Don't ask what you already know. I'm just the messenger."

She yanked off my shades, pressed my face between her man-sized hands, and lasered her eyes into mine for what felt longer than my daily jack-off. I don't remember saying yes to anything but I must've said something relevant because I left Juanita's pad with the promised thousand in my pocket and all the pervert's essentials burned into my brain. And no paper trail whatsoever.

Chapter 42

Jed's dying turned out ten times worse than the stroke that started this whole thing. Especially for Delores, which made me think maybe I should've waited until she wanted him dead more than she wanted him alive. Too late now, one of these days she'll thank me, in her head if not in her heart. She had been right about the weather though. Snowflakes were dropping faster than last month's leaves when the police cars came plowing up the driveway, three of them with lights spinning red, just like they did in St. Louis. Cops spilled from their cars and onto the porch, stomping snow from their feet. Just as Delores would've expected had she been standing at the door. Instead it was me who let them in—the sheriff, three deputies, and some guy carrying a camera and other stuff. It was me who showed them the bedroom but didn't go in. No thank you. Not with the terrible mess Jed had left. I couldn't imagine Delores cleaning it up, or me helping her.

I sat down on the sofa with Mario, my fingers so out of sorts I couldn't make them work. Pretty soon Sheriff Yates and one deputy came out, both white-faced and shaking their heads. While they tried to quiet Delores, the coroner walked in. Him I recognized from his reelect-me ad in the newspaper. Then the ambulance drivers showed up, same ones as before and telling me how sorry they were. As soon as Sheriff Yates gave his okay, they put a blanket over Jed and carried him out for the last time. I stood by the door, touched the blanket as he rolled past me. "So long, Jed, it's been a blast. If you get into heaven, tell Rusty I said, 'Hey.'"

This really upset Delores, causing her to cry even harder. So hard she wouldn't or couldn't talk to me, or anyone else. Good thing, otherwise the cops might not have understood her leaving Jed and me on our own while she went shopping for things we could've done without. Since she was pretty much out of it, Sheriff Yates motioned me into the kitchen. As soon as we sat down, he wanted to know exactly what happened.

"Jed asked for his shotgun." Okay, I sort of lied. But he would've asked if he could've. "And whatever Jed wants, he gets. Or used to. That's how it's been ever since I came here."

"And how long ago was that, son?"

"June of this year," I told Sheriff Yates. He'd called me son. Something no man had ever done before. Well, maybe Jed, I couldn't say for sure, but he didn't count, leastways not anymore. "I was supposed to go back to St. Louis when school started but …."

I stopped, tried for the right words so this wouldn't look any worse than it already did. Good ol' Mario, I fired him up, anything to buy me some time. Except Sheriff Yates had other ideas; he slipped one hand over mine and took Mario with his other.

"Later," he said. "I understand about Game Boy. My son loves his Game Boy too."

"How old is he?"

"Just turned eleven, and you?"

"What difference does it make?"

"None but it does make me wonder what else you might consider hiding from me."

He leaned back, started tapping his fingers on the table. Tippity-tap, tippity-tap, just like the driver waiting for me to get off his bus—that day Lark dumped me. Forget Jed's stroke. If she hadn't sent me away, none of this would've happened.

"Okay, if you must know, twelve." I almost said going on thirteen but changed my mind. Instead, I sunk down, tried to make myself smaller.

"Look, son, I know how hard this is for you so bear with me. Now, why are you still in Illinois and not St. Louis?"

"It worked out better, me staying here with Jed and Delores."

"You mean your grandparents."

"Yes sir. I call them Jed and Delores. They call me Johnny, even though Lark calls me Free."

This made him sit up. "Who's Lark?"

"My mom, has anybody called her?"

"One of my deputies will. What's her telephone number?"

"Delores wouldn't give me the new number. She didn't want me bothering Lark."

"Tough break, kid."

"Yeah, tell me about it." Forget the son part; he'd demoted me to kid.

We went on like this for a long time, every so often Sheriff Yates taking me back to Jed and the shotgun and why didn't I just say no.

"Jed always said it was his way or the door," I told him, although I'm not for sure those were Jed's exact words. "If you don't believe me, ask Delores."

"Later, your Grandma's too upset right now."

But not too upset to give Lark's telephone number to one of the cops. He walked outside to make the call so I couldn't hear him give Lark the bad news. Oh well, I figured I'd being seeing her within the next day or so. Finally, and she'd have to take me back. She wouldn't have much choice, unless Delores decided to stop crying and pull herself together.

Chapter 43

When Lark stepped off the bus in Carbondale, I made sure to see her before she saw me. There she was, wearing last year's boots, fur-lined with three-inch heels that made her wobble on the snow mixed with melting ice. She made sure nothing splashed onto the tan trench coat that Greg or Jeff, I can't remember which, bought her the year before last. Was I worried, you bet. I figured St. Louis had a skimpy Christmas season, what with people buying gifts instead of eating out or eating out and not leaving fat tips. Not good for Lark meant not good for me. Or the bus driver Lark didn't tip when he pulled her suitcase out of the bin.

She looked around, as if to say what now, so I walked up to her, and said, "Hey, long time, no see."

She stepped back, wobbled on the boots again. "Free, is that you? You scared the shit out of me."

"Sorry, I didn't mean to."

"Come here, you. Give me some sugar."

She squeezed me harder than a six-pack of soft toilet paper. I let her kiss me.

"My, oh my, how you've grown, no wonder I didn't recognize you right off."

"Yeah, I have to eat whatever's on the table."

"Uh-huh, been there, done that. Be a sweetheart and grab my suitcase, actually it's on rollers. That's right, just let the thing drag behind you. So, where's the car?"

"More like a truck, it's with Delores."

"Delores, Ma lets you call her Delores?"

"She calls me Johnny."

"Ugh! So, where is she?"

"At the funeral home, we're supposed to meet her there."

"Okay, but first I need to refuel. Where's McDonald's?"

On the way there she told me about working a double shift to earn extra money for just the right outfit, a basic black that would take her anywhere. We didn't talk about the funeral or Jed's dying, leastways not then. It was my first McDonald's since we split and set her back seven dollars, money I knew she didn't have to throw away. We hung out there for thirty minutes before she checked her watch and said we could leave; something about her figuring Ma should be finished with those horrid arrangements.

We were ten feet away from the funeral home when Delores came walking out the front door. Her face had ballooned from so much crying I don't think Lark knew her right off.

"You're late," Delores said. "I could use a hug."

Lark gave her best but I could tell it wasn't enough because Delores squeezed harder. It'd been years since they last hugged, well over ten, what with Lark working St. Louis, Delores and Jed working the farm. One thing I knew for sure: with Jed gone, Delores and Lark would not be working together.

"Sorry about the delay," Lark said with a straight face. "Wouldn't you know: my bus broke down." Delores never would've bought the urge for burgers and fries.

The three of us walked to the parking lot with no back and forth about Lark's reason for coming. Actually we didn't talk at all before stopping at the truck. The look on Lark's face spelled disgust with a capital D. Delores sniffled, wiped her nose with a grubby tissue, and said with a crabby voice, "Johnny, put your mother's suitcase in the back."

"Johnny?" Lark's eyebrows shot up. "Free allows you to call him Johnny."

Delores' rosy face turned white. "Later, Emily, we'll talk about the boy later."

"No one's called me Emily since you and Pa."

Oops, Lark shouldn't have gone there because Delores turned on the faucets and tears shot out. Lark waited a while before giving her a hug, slowly at first and then like she meant it. After they pulled apart, Lark asked, "What really happened? The police were kind of vague."

Not Delores. She practically vomited the straight and skinny of Jed's passing, every detail of how she'd found him, shotgun in hand, brains decorating the wall. Between all the crying, that is, and while Lark weaved back and forth, not saying a word. That is, until she accused me of being way too proud and smacked the pride right off my face. Afterwards, she shook her fingers as if they'd been set on fire. My cheek burned too but I didn't let on. I expected tears, apologies. But what did she give me: a smack across the other cheek, harder than the first.

"You stupid fuck!" she yelled, shaking her fingers again. "What were you thinking?"

"About trying to help, which is more than you ever did. Oh right, you were always working, making out in St. Louis while Jed in his bed kept Delores hopping."

"The nerve of you … you simple-minded cheeky bastard, you ruined everything!"

Lark turned into a wildcat, just like the one that killed Rusty. She came at me with her teeth ready to chomp and nails ready to scratch. I held my arms over my face until she knocked them away and clawed at my face. Then I fought back, something I'd never done with Lark before, giving as good as I got while Delores pitched another one of her fits. Not as bad as the night Jed died but bad enough that it brought the funeral guy running. Good thing he broke up the fight before me and Lark killed each other. Blood dripped off my face, Lark's was smeared with snot and matted hair. Dirty snow had messed up her precious raincoat which made me feel better about the whole throw-down.

Just when I thought things couldn't get any worse, they did. Sheriff Yates showed up in his squad car. He stuck his nose in what Delores referred to as Danner business. Lark mumbled something about wanting to know which nosey neighbor had sicced him onto us. And may the do-gooder bitch rot in hell. When the sheriff threatened to call Social Services, Lark went into her positively mortified routine and begged him to reconsider. Delores dropped to her knees, lifted her arms to Heaven, and asked Sweet Jesus for help, not a pretty sight. With that, Sheriff Yates ordered us into his car and off we went to the Emergency Room of Carbondale's only hospital where the doctors calmed Delores down with a shot and told Lark to shut her mouth. All this before we put Jed in the ground.

On the plus side, leastways for Delores and Lark, some good did come of what Lark called a situation totally off the charts. It brought them closer than they'd been in years. And the one thing they did agree on: with Jed out of the picture neither of them could handle me. The boy had to go, no two ways about it. Most definitely, the boy had to go.

Chapter 44

The Perv had a name, one I decided to disregard because I didn't want to think about the life he led growing up, of the people he cared about and those who cared about him, the before he went haywire and descended so far into Hell there was little chance of his ever getting out. Like a once lovable dog now gone mad with pain or disease, there was nothing left but to put him down. This I already knew firsthand, thanks to Jed. Stick to business I told myself, whatever it would take to keep the deal moving to a satisfactory conclusion and with no unexpected snags along with way.

I'd been following Perv for almost a week, hiding behind various disguises adapting the posture of Jonesy and the B & B gang, all the while learning Perv's evening routine, which mainly consisted of cheap dining with a variety of low-lives every bit as sleazy as he was, followed by a round of in-your-face girlie shows and porno movie houses. Boring with a capital B, you'd think he would've picked reality over fantasy. Good thing Perv didn't shit where he ate. To my knowledge he left the Florida kids alone, the dogs too, although I know this for sure during the day since my gofer duties came first. As for Mitch I hadn't been alone with him since the getting-to-know-you moment that left me nursing two black eyes. Nor had Mitch ever acknowledged my meeting with the go-between Juanita.

Big Shit Perv employed an honest-to-god chauffeur, I don't mean the uniformed variety but one who wore tropical shirts, Bermuda shorts, and open-toed sandals. The chauffeur drove his perverted boss everywhere and then cooled his heels behind the wheel of this black Lincoln, reading paperbacks or talking on his cell until the next drive-to. Not once did I see said chauffeur grab a burger, or snort coke, or pop a beer. He did, however, drink from a thermos—what I don't know—and when the need arose, he trotted off to the nearest john. But as soon as boss man reappeared, the chauffeur hopped out of the Lincoln and opened its backdoor, like a scene in the movies although I didn't figure him for a gun-toting bodyguard but instead a law-abider who adhered to the speed limit and kept the Lincoln free of fingerprints. Somehow this didn't seem right, catering to evil but maybe the job paid well enough for the flunky to overlook his boss's creepy perversions. Money, it was all about money, and when I really thought about *it*, the chauffeur was no different from me. No better or worse, just older. My guess: a good forty years, maybe more, a retiree trying to survive on social security, not that I cared. I'd been surviving on scraps my whole life.

If it hadn't been for the money and my sense of justice, I would never have agreed to this one-time deal. I guess I agreed, although I don't remember the exact moment, just Juanita fingers pressing into my temples, maybe a cop-out on my part.

On evening five at a joint reeking of stale smoke and love-handled hookers wearing clingy dresses, I hunched over the bar top, fingering my fake but pricey beard and listening to Perv discuss the dog races with a bartender so patriotic he had the American flag tattooed on both arms. Perv told him he planned on going to Ebro Track the following evening. What a coincidence, so did I.

Later during my drive home, the cell phone I'd jammed in my jeans pockets started vibrating like crazy. Digging it out forced me to straddle the pavement and from there the roadside gravel. The SUV skidded, and pebbles dinged its fenders. Bish used to hate when that happened, as if the whole thing was my fault and wouldn't have happened if he'd been driving. I wondered how he would've felt about my current project, considering what he'd asked of me regarding Jonesy. Maybe he'd seen in me what Juanita and Mitch saw. The phone which I never answered the first time rang again, its tone shrill and annoying. Nobody ever called me except Morgana and we hadn't communicated in weeks. When I finally answered, hers was the voice that came back at me.

"You gave up too soon," she said. "I can't decide if I'm disappointed or just curious as to why."

"I figured you weren't interested. When it comes to rejection, a guy can only take so much."

"Some girls like being pursued."

"Thanks, that's all I needed to hear. How about Saturday night, a real date."

She paused before answering. "Hmm, tomorrow night would work better."

Duty first, I'd made the races my top priority. "No can do."

She sighed, big time. "You're seeing someone else."

"Not exactly."

"Look, either you are or you aren't. And tomorrow night you will be or you won't."

"Depends on whether dogs at the track count as someone, or something or two or ten." Perv didn't count and Morgana didn't need to know who was pushing my buttons.

She did, however, insist on tagging along, after assuring me the monster brothers would be over-nighting with friends and not hanging with us. Tomorrow evening I'd make strictly surveillance, more of getting to know my subject without him knowing I even existed. No disguises this time, just Morgana.

***

Friday night. Another non-date, I couldn't risk picking up Morgana at M by the C given the nature of my assignment and her daddy having instigated it. Morgana didn't argue the pick-up point and insisted on driving to my place. Arriving ten minutes early, she parked on the street, clueless to my eyes following her from inside my studio's only window. I made a quick exit, all smiley-faced as I turned and locked the door as soon as her feet hit the thirty-six-inch concrete patch known as a porch.

"What's the hurry." Her breath warmed my neck while I yanked out the key. "I expected a grand tour of the bachelor pad."

"Uh, it's such a mess. Haven't had time to straighten up, what with work and all."

"That is so sweet." She kissed my neck, all but sending me into orbit. "I never figured you for a neat freak, maybe next time."

"And have your dad run me out of town, I don't think so."

"Daddy, Daddy, it's all about Daddy. What a chicken-baby wuss your mama raised."

I put my hand on her shoulder, steered her toward the driveway. "Sorry, I can't help myself."

"I know. That's what I find so intriguing. Shall we take the convertible?"

"No, I'll drive my vehicle." Tonight belonged to me; I was calling the shots.

Mixing business and pleasure, maybe I should've rethought it before letting Morgana tag along. And yes, I should've let her drive so I could do my thing—mentally prepping for the upcoming dog races of which I knew jack shit. Instead, I was dealing with Morgana's ho-hum chatter clashing with my idiotic responses. The heat didn't help either. Ninety-two degrees at six in the evening made no sense whatsoever, even for Florida and air conditioning. I thought about the dry heat of Vegas but only until exiting Route 98A.

We continued onto the Route 79 corridor, where a forest preserve filled with tall pines sent Morgana into quiet mode and relieved me of the dull blade sawing on my raw nerves. Why the edginess, I didn't know. It wasn't as if this night was slated to be *the* night. Bloody retribution or forbidden sex or family ties, I'd put them all on hold.

With nothing to observe but a few houses mixed with countrified shops, I fought with my head, trying to keep my chin from rubbing my chest. Morgana to the rescue, she pointed out this gigantic billboard advertising Ebro Park and its entrance up ahead. After pulling into the half-full parking lot, I cruised up and down every aisle searching for Perv's Lincoln. Not a sign of it, which could've meant he'd changed his mind, was still on the road, or already dead. Whatever, as long as I secured my place in the Compton family loop.

"Just pick a spot, any spot," Morgana said. "Near or far, any one of them will do. It's not like we can't walk the few extra feet."

I parked at the next available slot and we both exited my SUV at the same time. As if on cue, a choir of greyhounds from the nearby kennels started barking. "Their way of welcoming us," Morgana explained.

"They do that for everybody?"

"Only those they want to win."

Right, she had such a way with words. Relax just relax, and suck in the air too thick for breathing and ignore the birds circling overhead like hungry vultures or the swarm of pesky gnats surrounding us as we walked toward the bright lights hovering over Ebro's track.

"Don't bother getting tickets," Morgana said. "I have season passes to the Clubhouse."

"You've been here before?"

"Of course, silly, Daddy sits on the racing board."

"But does he know you're using the passes tonight and with me?"

"No, no, and no."

"I only asked two questions. What's the third 'no' for?"

"I haven't eaten dinner yet. And yes, I'm positively famished. The dining room is air conditioned and even Daddy considers the food acceptable. We can eat while we watch the races."

Not what I had in mind but then Perv showed up ten minutes after we were seated and wound up two window tables away, alone and with his back facing me. Perfect. I could watch him and the races below, all the while listening to Morgana who by now had switched to another topic, this time from her monster brothers to an in-depth explanation of the greyhounds and track betting—The Quinella, The Trifecta, The Super Trifecta. Okay, she'd overloaded my brain with enough info to see me through a few bets.

The waitress taking Perv's order finished with him and then stopped by our table. She nodded with a smile, obviously recognizing Morgana who took it upon herself to order for both of us.

"Two salads with blue cheese dressing, twice-baked potatoes, and strip steaks—medium rare," Morgana said. "Iced tea for me, a Coors Light for my friend, right away please."

My friend—here's looking at you, kid. If only you knew, maybe more than a friend, maybe not. Either way I had nothing to lose.

Down on the field track, lights flashed on the tote board. A twenty-foot cylinder of water sprayed non-stop from an adjacent fountain. Pampas grass rose high alongside low-growing shrubs, I figured to entice the nearest greyhound, poised and ready. A statue made of bronze, too bad; otherwise, he would've lifted his leg and done a number on the greenery. Alongside the track general admission folding chairs were filling up fast—die-hard smokers and almost dead retirees, parents hoping to entertain their young kids, and anybody else wanting a close-up of the action. Anybody for a soda, beer, or hot dog, yeah me. I'd eaten zilch since noon.

A bugle blared, announcing the first-race parade. Eight greyhounds, leashed and dragging a personal escort, guys and girls dressed in red shirts and khaki shorts, all young and clean-cut, they appeared to enjoy the show as much as the hounds. Maybe I could get on here if things didn't work out with Mitch. Nah, dog sitting was not my style. After Rusty, I'd grown detached from canines and any other pets dependent on my time and affection.

Morgana was really into the whole scene, quietly observing the dogs while working out various betting combos on her program. "Okay, we'll go with number four." She slid two dollars in my direction. "And number two and number eight, in that order for a trifecta."

A first for me, I checked the tote board on the field and with a crap shoot of confidence, said, "You sure about that? The odds say you picked all long shots."

She touched two fingers to her lips. "Long shots are my specialty. I picked you, didn't I?"

Not really but this wasn't the time or place to go there.

As usual, she didn't wait for my comeback. "You'll have to place my bet."

"You're not twenty-one?" Damn, how'd I slip up on that?

"Not for another month. These track officials are so paranoid about the legalities of betting. God forbid, I should embarrass Daddy."

No, we wouldn't want to embarrass the fine, upstanding Mitch Compton, the by-proxy avenger of evil who'd hired me to do his dirty work. I walked over to the Clubhouse betting area and lined up at a window, not coincidentally behind Perv, and listened as he selected two, eight, and one. Moving away, he didn't even glance in my direction. I bet his numbers as mine plus Morgana's for her and again for me. By the time I returned to the table, our waitress had delivered the salads, along with warm rolls and real butter. Not bad, I ate like there was no tomorrow while Morgana played around with her next picks.

Below at the starting gate the eight dogs in eight separate stalls began to bark when their escorts rode off in a single golf cart. More barking welcomed this guy riding a roller-equipped tractor to remove all traces of dog and human footprints from the track. Then all the lights around the track went out except for those at the finish stretch. The barking had gone beyond amusing and reached a level so annoying I was ready to shoot me some dogs, if only I had … if only … saved by the bell, in this case the announcer.

"Here comes the bunny!" he yelled, referring to this fake rabbit riding the extended tip of a motorized cart. The cart moved from the far right end of the track and when it circled around in front of the gate, eight chutes opened up. Out came the dogs, determined to catch their impossible prey. Once around the track ended the race, over before it hardly began. The lights came on again.

"How'd we do?" I asked.

Morgana smiled. "Watch the tote board."

Four, two, and eight—Morgana squealed. "We win, we win!" She leaned over and kissed me, not a sisterly peck but on the mouth, a feel-good I should've ignored but instead savored.

"About this one," I said, showing her my other bet—two, eight, and one.

"Idiot!" She grabbed the ticket from my hand, shredded it between her fingers.

Okay, the betting thing finally sank into my brain. Two dogs winning in either order made a Quinella; a three-dog win in the exact order, a Trifecta; a four-dog win in the exact order, a Super Trifecta.

Morgana's luck, and mine, lasted through four more races and made us eighty bucks richer. By then dinner was history, except for Morgana's key lime pie. Perv, who hadn't cashed in a single ticket, stopped betting after the third race and had resorted to yakking on the cell.

"I should talk to Daddy about adopting." Morgana pushed her dessert in my direction. "It's been a dream of mine forever."

I dug my fork into her pie, relished the first bite before my brain digested her last comment. "A baby, you've got to be kidding."

"Silly, not a baby, I mean a greyhound. Those dogs only run for so many years. The owners used to put them down. Thank god, euthanasia's no longer the case. Now they're available for adoption."

Perv, I pictured him adopting a greyhound, stringing it up like a dead antelope about to be butchered. Only his greyhound wouldn't be dead. Perv liked working on animals while they were alive. His kicks came from the pain he inflicted on others. Humans or animals, they brought the deranged bastard a shitload of joy.

"How long does adoption take?" I asked Morgana.

"I'm not sure but Daddy would know. Are you interested?"

"For now, just call me curious." Mostly about Perv who'd finished paying his bill and was heading toward the poker tables, which meant Morgana and I would stick around for a while. No way would I have left before he did.

Perv belonged to me now. Fulfilling my end of the deal, his destiny and mine, had become my number one priority—before Morgana or any other family obligations.

Chapter 45

Fire and brimstone, I'd been thinking. Not the kind where if you miss Mass on Sunday and die on Monday, BAM! You're headed straight to hell with no stopover in purgatory. But more like the sulfuric garbage I imagined spewing from a coach's fiery halftime speech at the Rose Bowl. "Boys, we suck worse than titty babies. We're fucking up this, we're fucking up that, and if we don't change in the second half, we will get our asses handed to us, big time. Do I make myself clear?"

Yes, a little more fire and brimstone, that's what I needed to stay awake through the ten o'clock at St. Francis of Assisi, parishioners sitting shoulder to shoulder with me wedged between the oh-so-hot Morgana and her adoring father. And next to Mitch, Blake the Younger who'd insisted on the aisle seat because his brother wasn't there to take it. Instead of playing Mister Nice Guy, I should've shoved Monster Brat into the pew and let Morgana go next.

During Mass in my life before this one, I often revisited my most shameful sins or those I dreamed of some day committing, if only given the chance. Or, maybe I'd imagine a pretty girl kneeling in the pew in front of me instead of the juvy inmate who should've been born the girl he loved imitating, poor confused bastard. Straight guys like me, we'd put our thoughts on carnal pilot while suffering through rhetoric that left us clueless to its true meaning. Readings and gospels repeated a dozen times over, homilies no more than impassioned pleas of well-meaning priests, challenging us to live honorable lives. Well-spoken pleas, but nonetheless passive—give me a break. Pro-active, that's what should count. Take a stand or sit down and shut up.

Oh, yeah. I'd already taken one stand and where did it get me? Six years in Juvenile Detention, and then some. Years of prostrating myself before God and all that's holy, years of begging forgiveness, years of watching my back, of sticking it to the worst of the worst before they stuck it to me. And for what—doing what I believed was the right thing to do. Delores had me to thank for getting her out from under. But when my time came, did she stand up for me, no way. Instead she banned me from the farm, disowned me. As if she ever owned me; nobody owns John Danner the Second. Or Free Danner.

And don't get me started on Lark, refusing to take me back after Jed offed himself, as if the whole incident had been my doing and mine alone. O-o-h, she was afraid I might do her great bodily harm. Never mind the damage she'd done to me, her word against mine. Nobody listened to me, an unredeemable parricide according to Delores who first heard it from the psycho psychiatrist.

Nor had I now been listening to Father Josh in Florida's Panhandle. Although I'd been aware of him prancing up and down the aisle in the open-toed sandals of his Franciscan order. He was preaching into this microphone clipped to his brown robe, something about holding out an olive branch to those who done you wrong. As in the butthead who treated you worse than shit on a Popsicle stick. If Father Josh had been hammering us on lust, even thinking about coveting thy neighbor's wife, I might've gotten a free pass that day. Ditto for not dreaming about Rowena or Butterscotch or the countless lays I should've enjoyed if my teen years hadn't taken the unavoidable detour. Instead, I allowed my thoughts to drift into the most private of my comfort zones. I'd hardly entered into that forbidden realm of coveting worse than my neighbor's wife—the unspeakable wanting of what I could never have—when I heard Father Josh shout a name all too familiar.

"Free Danner, wake up. The time has come for you to prove your worth to the Master of us all!"

Was he talking to me, aka John Danner the Second? My head snapped to attention, my eyes fell squarely on the Franciscan. No longer working the aisles, he'd now positioned himself in front of the altar, its towering crucifix serving as a backdrop for phase two of his performance. Standing straight and tall, he extended one arm to reach far beyond its normal length and leveled his forefinger in my direction.

"You, Free Danner, have been living in blissful ignorance, not knowing from whose loins you sprang or why someone as despicable as yourself is allowed to associate with the good people of this earth, to breathe the same air they breathe."

Hello and what the fuck, where had this priest been all my miserable life. He knew jack shit about me. But did that stop him from continuing his tirade, no.

"Your life has been nothing but twenty-two wasted years of eating, drinking, sleeping, occasional fornicating, and chasing pipe dreams just so you could start all over again. Have you no shame?"

Not when it comes to helping the needy, as in those who cannot help themselves.

Father Josh left the sanctuary of his stage and strolled down the long aisle toward me. A man in no hurry while I, his sacrificial lamb, stewed in the pew, looking for an escape route or hoping some other Free Danner was the target of such bull, as if anyone else in the western hemisphere would've been burdened with a name created by a whacked-out, self-centered excuse for a mother. No such luck with the escape, not with Mitch blocking my way. I'd put myself in another shit-out-of-luck position. A clammy film of sweat sprang from my pores. A rush of blood surged through my neck and upward, nearly lifting off the top of my head before sloshing around in a brain overloaded with Juanita jive. What thoughts I tried unscrambling were cut short by the Franciscan now before me, a drop of spit on his lower lip all that remained from the tirade he'd foisted on me. More was forthcoming, that much I knew. He bent over so only those nearest and dearest to me could hear his words.

"Free Danner, you've played long enough and now it's time to do Our Lord's bidding. You will answer whenever you are called. And you will do as you are told. Follow orders, no excuses. Do the deed, and then move on." He leaned in closer and whispered into my ear. "Get your mind right, young man. Fuck up this opportunity and you will go down, just like the rest of those juvy inmates you supposedly left behind. Mark my words: straight to hell with no stopover in purgatory. Do I make myself clear?"

I turned to Morgana, expecting her sympathy and a witty response leveled at the priest. And what did I get instead: more jack shit. She sat mesmerized under the spell of good versus evil, her focus on the looming crucifix, the altar where Father Josh had first started his homily. Ditto for all the holier-than-me parishioners, did no one care about the embarrassing assault on yours truly? No, no, and no. Everyone as mesmerized as Morgana, the same focus on the crucifix weeping blood. Everyone but Chad the Younger, who didn't care about the blood; he was too busy texting some teeny-bopping chick whose daddy made more than his daddy who might also be my daddy. I considered bopping Chad alongside the head but I didn't want to deny Mitch the pleasure when he caught on, if he caught on. Right now he was caught up in altar, his face the picture of saintliness. What a crock.

One more word from the priest was all I needed. One more and I would've taken him out. Not permanently, because the killing of a priest spelled serious sin and one more reason to burn in everlasting hell I didn't need. And then, poof, just like that he was gone. Not just gone, more like he'd never stood before me, never spoken those words to me.

Father Josh had returned to the altar and the crucifix I couldn't compete with, even though the blood had disappeared. Or, maybe it had never been there. The priest was smiling now. He lifted his arms as an invitation to stand, and his entire flock obeyed including a confused but somewhat relieved me for not having made a scene which would've blown my chances with the Compton clan. Still smiling, Father Josh led us into the next prayer, one I knew by heart. A heart that now confirmed what my mind had already accepted.

"We believe in one God, the Father Almighty, maker of heaven and earth, and of all that is seen and unseen."

Chapter 46

Mission accomplished. And life doesn't get any better than this. I'm kicked back on a cushiony lounge next to Mitch, on the upper terrace of his mansion by the sea, the two of us staring in silence at gulf waves thrashing onto the white sand and sea oats swaying with the non-stop breeze. Mitch has been avoiding my eyes, which I interpret as his inability to appreciate the on-going value of my damage control. In other words, he's looking for a way out of the arrangement he first instigated and I now wish to continue. This, of course, comes as no surprise to me. Our silence continues when Juanita makes an appearance, carrying an oversized bucket jammed with beer and soft drinks, enough to quench the entire family. After setting up the beverage station and pouring Mitch a scotch, she leaves without so much as a nod in my direction. Such loyalty confirms my current status as the irrelevant nobody. Mitch clears his throat before sipping the scotch. I reach for a Coors Light and pull the tab.

"Too bad about Jimmy Two Shoes," he says. "According to my sources, several eye witnesses told the police about some night critter, perhaps a weasel or a possum, crossing the highway in front of Jimmy's car. His driver swerved to miss the damn thing and in doing so, crossed the center line and crashed into the side rail. A truck coming from the other direction finished off Jimmy and the driver. Of course, you already know this."

"Yeah, who'd've thought, me one car behind, a witness to the whole bloody scene. One very weird coincidence, all things considered. Too bad about Jimmy's driver but that's life, or death, or whatever falls between the cracks."

Okay, so I gave Mitch an opening, one he can't resist, anything to keep his A.D.D. from kicking in too soon.

He turns to me, the corner of his mouth twitching as he says, "It hardly seems fair."

"Jimmy's dead, isn't he." I take my first drink of the beer, and swish it around like mouthwash before letting it slip down my throat. "You and me, we made a deal."

"On the other hand, my boy ...." Mitch shakes his head, slowly as if pondering what I figure he's already pondered before my arrival. "You did absolutely nothing to earn your money."

"About that other hand: I'm not your boy, unless you care to revisit our relationship."

"No, no, my original claim still stands. And don't ask about a DNA test. We're not clowns in the Maury Povich circus. If anything, you should return the ten thousand I already advanced you."

"Don't go there, Mitch." I clench my hands, again and harder to feel the fingernails dig into my palms. "Don't even think about it."

"Go where, Danner? Are you and Daddy having an argument?"

Another voice in the mix, I shake my hands loose and look up to see Morgana leaning against the door frame. An angel dressed in white shorts and a white tee, who takes my breath to a new level. She's so beautiful, too beautiful to be my sister. Which I now know she isn't, having received the results of her DNA against mine earlier today. She is, however, rich enough to someday be my wife. Morgana Danner, the name flows as naturally as sand through my fingers. I can make *it* happen, if I want her bad enough. I can make anything happen, if I set my mind to it.

"An argument, no way," Mitch says, as if I can't answer for myself. "Danner has become quite the businessman, with a mind of his own and a flair for the entrepreneurial. I was merely trying to convince him to remain in Florida."

"You're thinking of leaving?" Morgana asks as she straightens up. "Just when we were getting to know each other, how could you?

Especially after last night, that horrible accident I'll forever see in my dreams."

Mitch is really looking at me now, oh yeah. Forget the A.D.D. "My daughter was there ... with you?" he asks with hate spewing from his eyes to mine. He crushes the glass in his hand, sending a ripple of scotch and shards onto the stone floor. Had Morgana not been with us, he would've ripped my throat with one of those shards, just like Jonesy offed himself with help from me. How long ago? Months, they felt more like years.

"Hold on, Daddy," Morgana tells him. "None of this was Danner's doing. After Mass on Sunday we got to talking about how much he enjoyed the races at Ebro and that one evening he might try his luck at Mobile's track. Knowing there was a marvelous greyhound going up for adoption there, I insisted on tagging along. Unfortunately, someone already beat me to the greyhound, not that I would've made a deal without first consulting with you. Still, we had a wonderful time in Mobile, the best part driving past Mommy's old house ... the grand dame she loved to visit. We really need to take the boys there. They haven't been back since ... you know."

Morgana is rambling, and I love her for trying to protect me. But business is business and I've made my own deal with Mitch. The slight nod of his angry head tells me I will get paid for a job however well done. But first Morgana needs reassurance. I get off my ass, walk over to her, and hesitate before kissing her tanned cheek. I linger there, wanting to take her in my arms but ... another place, another time.

"Hang tight." I whisper in her ear. "It won't be forever, just until I make something of myself."

She pushes me away, directs her next words to Mitch. "You paid him off, didn't you, Daddy."

Quick, do something, anything to make her want me all the more. I take her left hand and press my lips to the open palm, all the while knowing I'm pissing off Mitch big time. God, what a feeling, I love the virtual smoke curling from his ears. "Nobody pays off John Danner," I tell her, and him. "What money I earn, I earn fair and square, every last dollar. Right, Mitch?"

He grunts, which I take as a yes.

"You want to catch a matinee?" I ask her. "We still have time."

"I can't." Her fingertips touch my cheek, prepping me for what's to come. "I promised the boys tennis at the country club. Do you play?"

"Some games yes; tennis, no."

More like Game Boy, I want to tell this Princess Peach to my Super Mario but I don't think she would make the connection. I feel Morgana slipping away and know I've lost her, at least for now. The trip to Mobile hadn't been exactly what I'd planned. The races—yes; the adoption—yes, although Morgana didn't know the man who beat her to the greyhound was none other than the perv Jimmie Two Shoes. He couldn't take ownership of the dog for another week, a delay I'd arranged for a mere five hundred bucks. But the drive home, the fatal accident—maybe so maybe not. For sure, I'd never have made my move with Morgana in the passenger seat but I did feel Juanita's magic within me, willing the night critter to do what I couldn't, leastways not then.

***

Later while Morgana puts on a country club show with her brothers, Mitch and I close our deal in his trophy den filled with animal heads hanging from the walls and dead snakes curled up in see-through jars. He pays the forty thousand owed me, and another sixty for my promise to stay away for a minimum of two years. Can't say I'll miss Juanita, the go-between mother of vigilante revenge. But here's the killer: no communication whatsoever—no letters or phone calls, no emails, no texting to his daughter or any other member of the family I can no longer think of as possibly mine, which puts me a step ahead of Mitch, unless he lied about his own DNA testing and now considers me just as much a threat as before.

Mitch offers another hundred thousand if I agree to stay away forever. But I decline the offer. Forever is too long for a guy like me who doesn't know where he's headed or what to do when he gets there.

For now, I'm half-way considering another visit to St. Louis and Lark. Who knows, with any luck and a show of money maybe she'll change her mind about taking me back.

Added bonus, an excerpt from

Lethal Play

Newly widowed Francesca Canelli would do anything to help her son Matt. Financially strapped and emotionally devastated, she accepts a sexual proposition from his soccer coach who promises to help Matt secure a coveted scholarship. Their bargain quickly sours when the coach abuses her, demeans Matt, and threatens to renege on the deal. The coach with more enemies than friends soon winds up dead and Francesca becomes a prime suspect.

Chapter 1

The night was too quiet, laboring under a murky sky that offered momentary glimpses of February's moon. It cast a faint light over Missouri's Show Me Soccer Park, deserted except for a St. Louis County Police car cruising through the stark winter landscape of the complex. The vehicle turned onto a narrow service road that ended behind the main field and parked on a large rectangle of asphalt. Two uniformed police officers exited their sedan, strolled over to a nearby SUV, and inspected the vacant interior with their flashlights.

"Rex Meredith again," said Officer Raymer. "He must be around here somewhere, probably designing some amazing new strategy for his team."

"Since when do soccer coaches work in the dark?" asked his sidekick, a probationary officer with barely two weeks under his belt.

"Good point, Baker. I'll switch on the lights and you can check out the field."

While Raymer headed for the utility building, Baker walked the hundred feet or so to where he stood beside the pitch, a field of turf that enthusiasts of youth soccer considered the finest in the Midwest, perhaps the entire country. He waited another minute before the area transformed from a silhouette of geometric forms and eerie shadows to a panorama of bright lights which seemed out of sync with the unnerving calm. He took his time scanning the entire pitch, starting with the south goal and ending at the north, whereupon he did a double take, shifted his stance, and then looked again, allowing the distant scene to finally register within his brain.

"Holy Mother of God," he managed to yell in a voice shaking with disbelief. "We have a huge problem over here."

"Rookies. Dear god, why me." Raymer shook his head but still came running. He stood beside Baker and squinted, trying to adjust his eyes to the glaring lights before addressing the north goal. There, hanging from the crossbar was the figure of a man swaying with the slight breeze. He appeared to be wrapped in mesh, probably stripped from the goal post. White socks covered his feet dangling fifteen inches above the ground, nearby an orange water cooler lay turned on its side.

"What now?" the rookie asked, his voice reduced to a quiver that made Raymer wanted to haul off and stuff some guts down his throat.

"For starters, don't piss your pants," Raymer said. "Instead, get your ass to the car and call for backup. While you're there, grab a roll of yellow tape and meet me at the goal." He hurried onto the field, yelled from over his shoulder. "And make it snappy, Baker."

One look at Rex Meredith told Raymer the man was beyond saving. Raymer figured the rope squeezing Meredith's neck must've been the same one used to anchor the net to the post. His neck was stretched like that of a dead bird, head bent to the side, his face swollen and battered, a deep gash cutting a diagonal across one eyebrow. Blood had oozed from his nostrils and both corners of his mouth. His eyes were wide open, locked into a sightless expression, of what—disbelief, desperation, regret? The stench of feces and urine sent a message to Raymer, urging him to toss his coffee and donuts, an invitation years of discipline had taught him to ignore. Still, observing the aftermath of violent death never came easy, especially with the victim someone he once knew. As did most everyone connected with youth soccer in the St. Louis metropolitan area.

"Baker, dammit where are you," he yelled.

"Right here, sorry."

Where, dammit. He jerked around to see Baker stopped within two feet of the goal, his head leaned back for a better view of the deceased, like some hayseed gawking at a piece of museum artwork. Raymer waited for the anticipated reaction and Baker didn't disappoint him. The rookie doubled over, hands to his mouth and seconds away from tossing his donuts.

"Dammit, Baker, don't even think about contaminating this area," Raymer said. "Take your business elsewhere, and be sure to mark the site after you've finished."

As usual, Baker obeyed. He stumbled over to a patch of frozen grass where he emptied his stomach with four gut-wrenching heaves, and then sectioned off the area with tape. "Sorry 'bout that," he said on his return.

"Quit apologizing and help me tape the crime scene. You did call for backup, didn't you ... never mind."

Raymer already had his answer. The sound of sirens wailing into the night announced the arrival of two more police cars plus an emergency van carrying the paramedic unit. One of the paramedics checked the victim's vital signs, confirming what everyone already knew: Rex Meredith, the illustrious coach of St. Louis's nationally-ranked boys soccer team, was indeed dead. His body continued to hang from the crossbar while a team of crime scene investigators collected evidence, starting with one of them snapping photographs, first an overall view before moving in for medium range shots, and finally, close-ups of the deceased. The investigators tagged every scrap of paper, every bit of fiber, strand of hair, footprint impression, and scruffy dirt pattern before depositing their findings into paper bags and cardboard boxes.

Two CSI worked in respectful silence as they unwound the netting from Meredith's body. After releasing his body from the crossbar and onto a stretcher, they wheeled it over to a woman with arms crossed over her chest and boot-laden feet stomping the frozen ground. Having already observed Rex Meredith from a suspended position, Dr. Hannah Cooper spent a few more minutes studying him from a lateral perspective.

"This must've been some fight," she said through puffs of cold air, "one-sided, judging from the lack of trauma to his hands or knuckles." She leaned in closer. "What's this on his left pec? The tattoo of a winged horse in flight, how befitting for the coach of Pegasi United."

She touched her fingertips to her lips, as if to say goodbye.

"I take it you knew the deceased," said one of the first responders.

"You're standing in my light, Detective."

"Sorry, Doc." He moved three feet to the left.

She slipped on a pair of surgical gloves and began her preliminary examination while the offending detective hovered with no further comment. He waited a good five minutes before opening his mouth again.

"Is it too soon to ask?"

The coroner ripped off her gloves, stuffed them in her coat pocket. "The body's still warm and rigor mortis hasn't started yet. Given the outdoor temperature, I'd set the time of death around ten forty-five, give or take a few minutes."

"Life and death minutes," he said. "Raymer got here around eleven."

"A tough break for Rex."

"So, how well did you know him?"

She lifted one shoulder. "He coached my kid some years ago, but only for one season. According to Rex, our David didn't have what it takes; he'd never meet the standards of an elite soccer team."

"Too bad, it must've been a real downer."

"Nah, we got David on another team right away. He's still playing with the Dynamos and loving every minute. My husband never misses a game. I see as many as my work permits, which puts me in the category of a lackluster soccer mom."

"That's a bad thing?"

"Not in my book. Poor Sunny, she's Rex's wife … widow, the epitome of soccer moms—such unwavering dedication. I don't envy the detectives who have to make that home visit. As for me, I've done all I can, at least for now." Looking around, she raised her voice. "Anybody from CSI?"

A squat woman in her mid-thirties answered the call. "Right here," Fran Abbot said. "Can we bag the hands yet?"

"Be my guest." This time Dr. Cooper patted the shoulder of the deceased. "Dammit, Rex, I hate seeing your life end this way."

"You think he offed himself?" Fran asked while securing a paper sack around Meredith's right hand.

"After the beating he took and all that netting, it seems doubtful," Dr. Cooper replied. "Still, at this stage anything is possible. I'll know more in the autopsy room."

Fran moved to secure the left hand. "Whoa, you said something about the deceased having a wife."

"Yes, there's a problem?"

"No wedding ring on his finger."

"So maybe he didn't wear one," the detective said, holding up his left hand. "I don't."

"So maybe he took it off, leaving a telltale band of white in its place," Fran said. "As is the case with certain husbands inclined to fool around.

Chapter 2

Five weeks earlier on the twenty-ninth of January a single runner jogged through the pre-dawn streets of a sleepy St. Louis suburb. Ben Canelli didn't believe in short-changing himself, especially when it came to maintaining a physique that celebrated its forty-two years with few apologies. He adhered to a strict discipline of running every morning at five-thirty, rain or shine, as long as the temperature registered above twenty degrees and snowshoes were not a prerequisite for navigating through his Richmond Heights neighborhood. Before leaving home on this overcast but unseasonably warm day, he'd consider waking Matt but then decided against inviting him along on such a routine run. Fifteen-year-old boys need plenty of rest because they grow while they sleep; at least that's what Ben's dad used to tell him. And Ben always relied on those pearls of wisdom which would eventually define his dad's legacy. The late Al Canelli had been a respected athlete—a soccer standout into his thirties and later the coach of a topflight St. Louis mens team. To Ben's regret, he hadn't lived up to Al's athletic abilities, not that the old man ever complained. He'd been too much of a gentleman to show any disappointment, one of many admirable traits Ben strived but often failed to emulate.

The light drizzle peppering Ben's face reminded him to pick up the pace since he hadn't thought to bring along his windbreaker. Still, the navy sweat suit and turtleneck underneath should keep him warm until he returned to the brick Tudor on Windsor Lane. He'd left Francesca there, still in bed and purring in the aftermath of wake-up sex. One thing he could count on when he got back was the smell of freshly ground coffee brewing, a pricey gourmet blend she preferred and he tolerated. Sweet Francesca, she loved him almost as much as he loved himself. Besides Matt, she'd given him Ria. What father wouldn't be crazy about an eleven-year-old showering him with kisses and then executing an enthusiastic though less than perfect string of back flips. Matt could turn back flips too, from a crouched position and as smooth as any seasoned gymnast. Those flips made a great show on the soccer pitch, as long as the kid didn't overdo it. No coach likes a grandstander.

Ben nodded to a passing runner he encountered once or twice a week. He wiped a patch of chilling droplets from his brow and pulled up the hood to cover his damp hair. Using long strides, he skimmed over the wet pavement and turned westward, away from the muted rays of the rising sun. Where was he? Oh yeah, about Matt. Fortunately, the kid had inherited his grandfather's genes, those microscopic gems blessing him with the ability to run faster and jump higher than the average teenage athlete. Of course, for Matt to reach his full potential, it would require unlimited nurturing, creative financing, political savvy, and just plain luck.

Too bad the Thunderbirds went belly up. Ben had coached the select team and Matt had played on it since the age of nine. For Matt—and Ben—it meant having to start over, scrambling for acceptance on one of the few teams that had openings for the spring season. They'd pinned their hopes on numero uno. Pegasi United consistently ranked in the top forty of U.S. Youth Soccer and offered the most advantages, as in winning seasons, financial backing, a demanding schedule thriving on prestigious tournaments, and for the best of the best—athletic scholarships to Division 1 universities. Reaching for the moon an unreasonable goal? Hell no, not with Matt standing on his dad's shoulders. About the Pegasi coach, Ben wasn't sure, only because he didn't really know Rex Meredith, although the solid grip of the cocky bastard's handshake did seem sincere, too sincere. In fact, it bordered on unctuous, that slippery hand sliding through Ben's.

As with most mornings Ben had timed this run to perfection. On Clayton Road the wrought iron security gates leading to Hampton Park swung open, allowing him to enter at the precise moment a familiar green 911 Carrera drove through the exit. In keeping with their usual routine, the female driver and Ben acknowledged each other with a simple wave of the hand. More droplets fell onto his eyelids; he blinked them away. Ahead on the asphalt lane towered the massive sanctuaries of the privileged, a state of upper class grace Ben harbored no illusions of ever achieving, unless he somehow maneuvered a takeover of the sporting goods company that recently promoted him to a divisional manager position. Not bad for a guy who struggled through five years of college before graduating. Along the winding route of homes striving to outdo each other, he stopped but once, to jog in place while admiring his favorite estate, a sprawling gray Tudor that reduced his Windsor Lane knock-off to that of a rich kid's playhouse.

Ben checked his watch, only a few more minutes in the land of make believe before he headed home. His mouth watered at the thought of sausages and eggs for breakfast but he'd already committed himself to sensible skim milk over dry cereal, the sugarless kind with a paltry few almonds bottoming out the box. What the hell, maybe this morning he could sweet talk Francesca into making him an egg white omelet swirled with no-fat cream cheese. It couldn't compete with her mother's cholesterol-be-damned-version but, what the hell—he couldn't fault Francesca for making every effort to keep him healthy.

He executed a quick U-turn and picked up his pace another notch since the drizzle was on the verge of escalating into a major downpour. When he arrived at Hampton Park's exit, the gates into the real world were closed so he eased through a narrow opening he'd created in the tangled hedge the previous fall. Back on Clayton Road rush hour for the local overachievers had gotten a jumpstart, with headlights from late model cars beaming their reflections onto the glistening pavement and mesmerizing him into a state of euphoria.

Ben turned right and made his re-entry into the affordable middle class, now under a siege of unrelenting rain. He watched his feet kick up puddles for two blocks before moving toward the middle of the street. He rounded a corner, taking it wide to avoid a car parked where no car belonged. Looking back to check out the make and license plate, he missed seeing the Dodge Caravan that was approaching from the opposite direction.

He did not hear the brakes screech as they ripped rubber from the tire treads. Nor did he feel the impact of the vehicle when it tossed him ten feet into the air. Nor the devastating damage his toned body suffered when it landed on the slick concrete, a good twenty feet from where he the final step of his early morning run.

Chapter 3

Nine days later dusk had settled over the pseudo Tudor on Windsor Lane. A mourning wreath of eucalyptus, protea, lilies, and baby's breath hung on the arched front door Ben Canelli had painted a welcoming red the year before at his wife's insistence. The twelve-over-twelve paned windows surrounding the door projected a muted glow from inside to offset the red that now begged for privacy. At the rear of the house a single light flickered from the family room television as Francesca Canelli shifted on the burnished tan of her leather recliner. She bent one elbow, made a fist on which to rest her head, and cocked it toward the light.

Matt walked into the room. She didn't acknowledge him but she heard the sofa groan from the weight of his one hundred and forty pounds. She heard him speak but whatever words he mumbled must've gone astray before the final transmittal to her brain. She sensed the laser beam of his eyes, willing her to look in his direction, just as Ben's used to do when she couldn't be bothered. But that was before.

How dare Matt intrude on her grief, a mere five days after they'd buried the only man she'd ever loved, the most important being in her life and Matt's. And what about Matt, the piss-poor way he handled his own grief. Teenagers, one minute they're too depressed to crawl out of bed; the next minute they want to know what's for supper. What a crock. One thing was for sure: the loss of his dad hadn't affected Matt's appetite, his never-ending quest for food and more food, whatever was required to fuel the energy needed to perform as a top athlete.

"So, whadaya think, Mom?"

Only that she wanted to be left alone, to lose herself in a rerun of Ben's favorite game show, some idiotic program she'd always detested and refused to watch with him.

"Hel-lo, anybody home?" Matt asked, trying to inject humor when she wanted no part of it.

He'd assumed his most enduring position, leaning forward with arms resting on his knees, puppy dog eyes pleading for attention. His mother the bitch narrowed her eyes to the hint of a cookie duster sprouting from his upper lip.

"You need to shave, again," she said, "which is what you get for picking up a razor when you were barely twelve"

"Twelve and a half, which Dad didn't think was too early to start."

"Neither of you thought about asking me."

"It was a guy thing, Mom."

A milestone for Matt, one of many and particularly bittersweet for Francesca—the first time she hadn't been consulted. Ben had usurped her authority, taken over the role she'd cherished since Matt's birth.

"Don't make me repeat myself," she said. "Get rid of the fuzz."

"I will, I will, but not this very minute. Okay?"

She waved him off. Matt usually kept his word, especially when he wanted something in return. About his cell phone, he knew better than to ask for its return any time soon. She'd confiscated the damn thing after he ran up five hundred dollars in text messages, most of them following Ben's accident and not with some girl since he hadn't reached that stage yet. So much for the miracle of electronics, he could've communicated the old-fashioned way, a one-on-one-in-your-face. With her, except she didn't feel up to chit-chat. Maybe tomorrow, but that's what she thought yesterday.

"Now about Pegasi," he said with a patient voice as opposed to the inside or outside voice she'd taught him ages ago. "I heard two of the players aren't coming back and the coach might cut another two, which means I stand a pretty good chance of making the team."

Using her thumbs and forefingers, she treated her drooping eyelids to an ever-so-gentle massage. "Do we have to talk soccer now, with me enduring the most god-awful headache of my entire life?"

"At this point all I need from you is an okay, nothing more. If it was the other way around, Dad would've … sorry, I didn't mean that the way it sounded."

Of course he did, and Ben would've backed him all the way. "Leave your father out of this. Is Pegasi what you want?"

"More than anything else. Playing for Pegasi was our dream—Dad's and mine."

"In that case, go for it with all your heart." The words came from her mouth but belonged to Ben, a phrase he often used during his mini pep talks.

Matt must've recognized it too, judging from the smile lighting his face. "Thanks, Mom. You won't regret this, I promise."

She couldn't think of anything else to say and was relieved when he got up and headed for the kitchen, probably to raid whatever was left in the fridge once brimming with sympathy food from friends and neighbors. The variety of calorie-laden pies and cakes fighting for space on the kitchen counter had also dwindled to a precious few. With any luck and maybe one more care package Francesca figured she could go another two days without having to open a can of hot tamales or what passed for ravioli. Good thing Matt and Ria weren't picky eaters. Nor was … had Ben been picky, as long as she didn't go overboard with the fats and starches. In fact, he'd often raved about her cooking, even the occasional disasters marking their seventeen years of marriage.

She cranked her head back to the TV—only three more hours until bedtime, and the security of Ben's pillow. She'd changed their bed sheets after the accident but couldn't bring herself to replace his pillowcase. That final morning he'd left his scent behind, just for her, and she had no intentions of losing what little remained of him until she was ready to let go.

Chapter 4

Two days later on a Saturday afternoon so cold it required nothing less than her down-filled jacket and wool knit cap, Francesca drove Matt to the first of three tryouts for Pegasi United. Ria had insisted on tagging along, having refused to spend any more time with young friends who, according to Ria, had their own stupid agendas. No one spoke during the twenty-minute drive from Richmond Heights to Show Me Soccer Park, which suited Francesca fine. But as soon as she pulled Sybil, their faithful SUV, into a parking space, the sound of seatbelts loosening their restrains broke through the silence. Then came the labored effort of sliding doors, perhaps Sybil needed a shot of WD40. Another task of Ben's Francesca would have to assume.

"Are you nervous?" Ria asked Matt as they got out.

"Do I look nervous, Pickle Face?"

"No, but maybe you should. This is the big time. Somebody has to get cut."

"But not me."

Ria, ever cautious but still giving encouragement. Francesca stepped onto the asphalt and locked the doors with her remote. "Don't forget, Matt: I'm leaving early with Ria for her gymnastics class."

"No problem," he said, slinging his bag over one shoulder. "I'll get a ride home."

Along the sidelines of the practice field mother and daughter made themselves invisible as they sat on folding canvas chairs, Francesca hiding behind a pair of dark, oversized sunglasses and Ria turning the pages of a paperback at predictable intervals.

"Another book?" Francesca asked, neither hoping for nor expecting much of an answer.

"My fourth in ten days." Ria never took her eyes off the page. "This one's a dumb story about some girl without a father. My teacher thought it would help."

Right, as if any book could make a difference. "She should've checked with me first."

Ria peered over the top of pink-rimmed eyeglasses. "I told her you wouldn't mind, that you were dealing with your own problems."

"What did I tell you about that?"

"It's okay, Mom. My teacher's pretty cool." She patted Francesca's arm with one hand and with the other hand turned another page.

Grief, in a few short weeks the Canelli survivors had found ways to absorb the aftershock: Matt with his soccer, Ria with her books, and Francesca in a slump, as Ben would've said. Wherever he was—Francesca wasn't sure if she still believed in heaven or in God—but wherever Ben was now, he must be sending his paternal vibes, demanding to know when Ria had become the adult and Francesca, the child. Not that Ria seemed to mind, or perhaps she was marking time, waiting for the right opportunity to express her dismay, which may not come for another twenty or thirty years. At forty-one Francesca was still waiting for that time with her mother.

Ria adjusted her glasses, turned another page. The roots of her hair, blond since the toddler years, were now turning as dark as Francesca's and Matt's. In another year or so her daughter would evolve into a full-fledged brunette. Sooner if Ria made good on her threat to whack off the long ponytail, in spite of a harsh warning Francesca had given the previous year after Ria shaved off her bangs, leaving a hairline of awkward stubbles she succeeded in hiding with a comb-over for several weeks. Keeping Ria's hair down to her waist had been Ben's idea. So had the ear-length bob, designed to swing across Francesca's cheeks whenever she turned her head.

"It fits your personality," Ben had told her, "a kind of sophisticated innocence."

"In other words, an oxymoron," she'd replied.

"Yes, but you're my oxymoron."

Ben always had a way with words, not so with Francesca. Rather than say the wrong thing, she kept her mouth shut.

"Matt's on the pitch," Ria said.

Right—the pitch, not the field, would she ever get that right. Francesca watched him sprint toward the mouth of the goal, along with nine other hopefuls, their sturdy legs encased in the warmth of Under Armour, their heads lifted high against the biting wind of early February. He finished second; good or bad, Francesca didn't know.

"Not bad," Ria said. "Matt ran with the best."

Thank you, my daughter the blond mind reader. From the corner of one eye Francesca caught a glimpse of another blond, her shoulder-length locks bouncing in rhythm with each footstep bringing her closer. Only one soccer mom walked with the assurance of her kid never getting cut from the team—Sunny Meredith, the coach's wife. During the previous soccer seasons when Matt played with Thunderbirds, Francesca had only known Sunny by sight and from a distance, her husband Rex too. She first spoke to the faceless Ken and Barbie couple at Ben's wake and still shuddered at the memory of them hugging her tighter than old friends at a high school reunion. Rex had pumped Matt's hand, all the while encouraging him to still come out for the team, as if Ben's tragedy was nothing more than an inconvenient disruption to the precious pursuit of soccer. This, of course, made perfect sense to everyone outside the immediate Canelli family. Or maybe Francesca was the only oddball. Get over it, Ben would've said. Don't expect the world to stop just because you want to jump off.

Sunny hovered over her. A whiff of musky perfume assaulted Francesca's nose before the pressure of Sunny's pampered hand assaulted hers. What was it with this touchy-feely stuff, not only from Rex and Sunny but every other person who felt the need to connect with a widow before her time. A different vital statistic box had come into play for her to check, she'd gone from single to married to this, having bypassed divorced, which would never have been an option for her and Ben. 'Til death do us part, they had vowed, erroneously believing it meant 'til old age took them within a week of each other.

Sunny squeezed again, this time harder.

"Francesca, so good to see you out and about, even in this dreadful weather. I do wish I could offer some encouragement about Matt but to be perfectly honest, I have no idea what Rex has in mind. You know, in terms of what players he'll need to strengthen the Pegasi roster."

"Yes, of course." Focusing on the pitch, she eased her hand away from Sunny's. The woman needed spread her good cheer elsewhere, around those who would appreciate it.

"You'll have to excuse my mom," Ria said. "She's not herself."

Sunny straightened up. "Don't you have some cartwheels to turn, little—"

"Ria, my name's Ria."

Do something, Francesca, show your mom stuff. She lifted her head to Sunny's amber sunglasses, and spoke to a row of long thick lashes. "We're only staying for a short while; Ria has gymnastics."

Sunny flipped her hair; a smile crossed her perky lips. "Ah, those were the days; gymnastics paid my way through college. But I digress and don't want to keep you, knowing how busy you must be." She knelt, took control of Francesca's hand again, this time patting it. "There is one thing, a rather awkward situation I feel compelled to mention." She leveled a discreet forefinger toward the pitch. "That Hispanic boy over there, the one dribbling the ball—"

"Is Jeff Manuel," Ria said without looking up. "Matt already told us."

"I'm so sorry, Francesca. What with his father driving the van—"

"Please, Sunny. I can't talk about it." Not to you or anybody, Francesca wanted to say. Hector Manuel had already made his guilt-ridden visit to the house, wept as he explained how he'd been delivering the Post Dispatch that fatal morning and hadn't seen Ben until the van actually hit him. Two eyewitnesses to the accident, both outside picking up their newspapers, had corroborated Hector's account to the police. Given the circumstances, any possibility of a financial settlement seemed remote, according to Mort Gellman. Maybe she should talk to another attorney, one who specialized in personal injury. Of course Ben had carried life insurance, which, true to those hard-sell agent pitches, didn't seem nearly enough now when they actually needed it. There'd never be enough ... money. How crass of her, dwelling on the monetary value of her husband's life, as if the sum of it had been reduced to a financial statement, a postscript to his once vital statistics. Still, Ben prided himself on being a practical man. He would've understood.

"About the tryouts," Francesca said to the empty space next to her chair, only then realizing Sunny had taken her good will elsewhere. No sign of Ria either. Francesca scanned the sidelines, her gaze moving to the bleaches where she located Ria behind a cluster of parents, no doubt getting the lowdown on various players. Another Ben trait, except Ben would've been participating in the discussion, ever respectful of Matt's toughest competitors, those who made him a better player.

Francesca turned her attention back to the pitch. She counted twenty-five boys, all gathered around Rex Meredith. The muscular forty-something stood no taller than many of the players, including Matt, who at five foot seven and according to his doctor was due for another growth spurt. Rex stood with a span of ten inches separating his feet. While talking, he balanced a soccer ball on the tip of his fingers and then held the ball between his hands, as if he were holding the athletic destiny of each boy. One by one and without hesitating, Rex divided the boys into two scrimmage teams. Francesca recognized several players from Thunderbolt—Ryan Masters, Eric Stegman, and Jack Salina. Both Eric and Jack exchanged high fives with Matt when they wound up on the same side. From Francesca's limited perspective, the teams appeared evenly divided, at least according to size. As for ability, she was in no position to judge. Two or three excellent players could make the rest of a team look better. Two or three so-so players could make the rest of the team look worse.

"I'm back," Ria said, turning a cartwheel before she sat down.

"Next time, don't leave without telling me."

"I did, but you weren't listening."

"Sorry, kiddo. I'm trying, really I am." Francesca checked her watch. "If we hurry, we can still be on time for your gymnastics. You know how the coach feels about late-comers."

"But, Mom, don't you want to hear about Pegasi?"

Francesca got up, started to fold her chair. "Sure, while we drive to the gym."

"Don't make me go, Mom. Not today."

Another Ria cope-out, but Francesca didn't feel up to arguing, nor the sympathetic gestures she was bound to receive at a second location. She sighed, sat back down. "Okay, bleacher girl, so what did you learn?"

"Well, about those four openings on the team, figure on maybe five or six 'cause not all the guys came back. At least that's what John Aquinas told Clark."

"You know these people?"

"Sort of, Clark's a lawyer and John an orthodontist, pediatrics if we ever need one."

"You're teeth are fine."

"Right, if you say so. But I asked John and he said you should give him a call."

"Ria!"

"Not really, give me some credit. Anyway, Clark is married to the white lady sitting—don't look at the bleachers. They'll know I'm talking about them. Besides, they're pretty cool. Their son is—"

"The team's only biracial goalie, that I figured out on my own."

"See the redhead sliding into Matt, he's Payton Meredith."

"The coach's son, I remember him from when Thunderbolt played against Pegasi." Matt and Paton were battling for the ball that eventually went to another player.

"And the Mexican-looking kid who's dribbling the ball now lives with the Merediths. His name is Angel. You know, An-hil in Spanish, but everybody calls him Angel, as in the opposite of devil. Ian Shepherd—he's the assistant coach's son—just kicked the ball to ... to ... Payton." Ria hopped up. "Oh my gosh! Matt just stole the ball away from Payton. Matt's passing it to Marcus Aquinas. Marcus passes it back to Matt."

Francesca leaned forward. "Move, I can't see."

"Matt's going for a goal. Shi-oot—sorry 'bout the slip, Mom, Grady Greenwood blocked Matt's shot. Did I tell you, Grady's dad sells cars? His mom teaches fourth grade, at some private school in West County. And if you ever need a plumber, call Maurice Elliot for the team discount—if Matt makes the cut, which I think he will. The Eliot kid's a pretty good defender."

Ria's chatter lulled Francesca into a peaceful vacuum. It ended along with the scrimmage when the boys trotted off the pitch. Matt broke away from the pack and headed toward her and Ria. Standing before them, he slapped his hands together in a warming motion. Whatever he might've been thinking didn't register on his face.

"You've still got a better than even chance, right?" Ria said.

"Same as the other guys, Pickle Face." He stopped the hand warming and yanked on her ponytail. "Aren't you supposed to be at gymnastics?"

"Some of us still have issues."

"Knock it off," Francesca said. "Both of you."

"Can we give two guys a ride home, I sort of promised, okay?"

"Do I know them?" How stupid of her to ask. Ben wouldn't have cared who they were. He used to haul kids wherever they needed to go, just as other parents hauled Matt.

He spoke with a touch of irritation. "No, you don't know them but Ian's dad is the assistant coach. He couldn't make it today. These guys live in the same neighborhood, not too far from here."

"Of course I will."

"Yuck!" Ria stuck a finger in her mouth, faking a gag. "In other words I have to sit in the back with the sweat hogs."

"Shut up, Pickle Face. Here they come."

"Well, whoop-de-do," Ria said, lowering her voice. "Get a load of the rich boys."

Ria did have an eye for sportswear, from the low end to the high. Judging from their confident stride to their designer clothes and gym bags, Francesca figured these kids were out of Matt's league, at least from a financial standpoint. But on the soccer field, where it really counted, talent would reign supreme, at least that's what Ben often said, and what she wanted to believe.

"Just watch your mouth, Pickle Face."

Matt wrapped his arm around Ria's neck, locked her in a mock stranglehold. She stuck out her tongue, pretending to strangle.

"Enough, already," Francesca said.

To which Ria replied in a Donald Duck voice. "Hey, I'm the one forced to suck up their sweat."

"Not in this weather." Matt shoved her aside and put on his best smile for his new friends. "Mom, meet Ted Logan and Ian Shepherd. They've been playing with Pegasi for five years."

"So sorry about your loss," Ted said, pumping her hand as smoothly as any adult would.

"Ditto, Mrs. Canelli." Ian applied the same sincerity with his handshake.

What was it with teen-age athletes, her son being no exception. Somehow they managed to project an aura of young immortals, even when they needed a shower. At least these two displayed some manners, which money didn't necessarily guarantee. Perhaps they'd taken their sympathy cues from Rex Meredith.

Not-to-be-overlooked Ria nudged Matt with her elbow.

"Oh, and this is Pic …" Matt hesitated with a grin, "I mean Ria."

His potential teammates exchanged the usual "Hi" with Ria, who for the moment had lost her ability to say another word.

With hands jammed deep into her jacket pockets, Francesca led her charges to the parking lot and Sybil. On the way they passed within twenty feet of Rex Meredith loading soccer equipment into his SUV. On seeing her, he stopped and crooked his finger, expecting her to join him as if she were one of the Pegasi hopefuls. Had he not been the almighty, all-powerful coach, she would've ignored the arrogant gesture. But Matt needed her, needed this opportunity. She opened Sybil's door via remote, and told the gang she'd catch up with them in a few minutes. She approached Rex with cautious optimism. Perhaps he would single out Matt as having considerable potential. On the other hand—

"We need to talk but not here," he said, rubbing the cleft in his chin. "I wouldn't want anyone getting the wrong idea, you know, about the coach showing favoritism to some and not others."

He spoke with words barely squeezing through his tight lips. What little she saw of his face registered a ruddy complexion flushed from the cold. A pair of dark aviator sunglasses obscured any expression from his eyes. Talking to him would be like talking to a yackety-yak. She couldn't recall any of his pertinent features, having barely looked at him during Ben's wake.

"Well, I'm pretty busy," she tried to explain, "what with running Ria here and there, plus wrapping up—"

The lips stayed tight when he replied. "Hey, not a problem, I'm just concerned about your boy. As of now, he's teetering on the cusp of making the team or getting cut. Naturally, I want to give Ben Canelli's kid every chance to prove himself."

Matt teetering, no way, and to bring up Ben, as if doing the Canellis a favor—who did Rex Meredith think he was. Soccer be damned. She refused to acknowledge the tears welling in her eyes, to blink them away, unthinkable. She used Ben's ploy of counting to ten before speaking. "I don't understand. Ben always said Matt played a mean left foot. He scored most of the goals with Thunderbolt. His teammates voted him captain two years in a row."

Rex loosened his lips and expelled a patronizing chuckle. "Not to put Thunderbolt down, but that team was in deep do-do before it slid into extinction. Pegasi, on the other hand, has led our mid-west division for three consecutive years. We're ranked—"

Blah, blah, blah, blah, blah, tell me something I don't already know. After Thunderbolt folded, Ben and Matt had talked of nothing else. Now through accidental default and on Matt's behalf, she'd been tapped to play her own game, the delicate politics of select soccer. She forced a crooked smile. "Why not call me later this evening, at your convenience."

Rex concentrated on his Nikes, digging one toe into ground that refused to yield. He raised his head, focused the sunglasses on her eyes, still stinging from his earlier remark. "I'd prefer you call me around ten tonight. My cell number's listed on the Pegasi information sheet."

"No problem." She turned and walked away. Whatever you say, Mr. Meredith, whatever you say, Fuckface, whatever it takes to insure Matt's acceptance.

Back in the parking lot Francesca climbed into an SUV of overripe warriors who had exceeded Ria's earlier prediction. She cracked her window, the back ones too. After easing Sybil out of the parking space, she glanced over to the passenger seat where Matt had assumed a trancelike position, chin lowered to his upper chest. She adjusted the rearview mirror to see Ria heaving a deep sigh. To Ria's right Ian and Ted were crunched down, heads resting to opposite sides on their shoulders. After exiting the complex, she cleared her throat and spoke to their reflected images. "Where to, boys?"

Ian straightened up. "Sorry, Mrs. Canelli, I guess I dozed off. Turn right at the second stoplight and go about a quarter mile. We live within a block of each other but you can let us both off at my house since Ted's spending the night."

"Right, my parents are vacationing," Ted said, "a second honeymoon in Cancun."

"How lovely," Francesca said because his comment deserved a response. She and Ben had honeymooned in Acapulco, the only vacation they'd taken as a couple. After Matt got involved in soccer, every trip corresponded with one of his tournaments. They'd dragged Ria along too. She'd only complained once, when the motel didn't have a swimming pool, an irreparable error on the part of the tournament organizer.

Ian directed Francesca through a neighborhood of affordable houses and when she pulled up in front of his brick ranch, she loosened her grip on the steering wheel. In spite of the expensive sportswear these kids didn't have anything on Matt. Still, she couldn't resist posing the one question most St. Louisans were compelled to ask one another, either in the present or the past tense. "So, where do you boys go to high school?"

"Parkway South, both of us," Ian said. He started to follow Ted out of the vehicle but paused as a matter of courtesy. "How 'bout you, Matt?"

"Bishop Dubourg," he said.

Middle-class public versus middle-class parochial, kids on a similar tract but in Francesca's opinion Matt had the advantage of a Catholic education, a necessity which may become a luxury without soccer providing a hefty collegiate scholarship. Not just any university but a Division I, Ben would've said.

That evening on Windsor Lane Francesca faced a dreaded inevitable: the funeral food had dried up, forcing her to go through the motions of grilling gooey cheese sandwiches and opening a can of chicken noodle soup. For dessert she squeezed a plastic container of chocolate sauce over two scoops of vanilla ice cream. Neither child voiced displeasure with the menu; perhaps they were concerning about upsetting her. Mourning did have its advantages. After Matt muffled a satisfying burp, he tossed back his vitamins with a single gulp of milk.

"Did you get enough to eat?" she asked, more out of habit than out of concern.

"I couldn't handle another bite, really." He didn't get up but wiped his upper lip with the back of his hand.

"Aren't we supposed to have three or more veggies every day?" Ria said as she swirled her spoon through the moat of dark syrup surrounding her ice cream. "Does popcorn count?"

"Shut up, Pickle Face. Can't you see Mom's not feeling well?"

"Enough with the name calling." Francesca willed her fingertips to rub circles into her pounding temples while issuing a half-hearted command. "No TV for either of you until the homework is finished."

Matt pushed his chair back, scraping it across the floor tile to mimic chalk grating against a blackboard. "Great, by then, it'll be time to crash."

"Not for me. I finished my homework before I ever left school." Ria looked at Francesca, waiting for a sign of approval. Getting none, she carried her plate to the sink and returned for the remaining dishes. Working as fluidly as two underpaid grunts, she and Matt loaded the dishwasher while Francesca remained at the table, directing their efforts with an occasional wave of the hand.

After the kids had returned her kitchen to a reasonable semblance of order, they scattered in opposite directions, leaving her to stare out the window, waiting for the end of another day. To make it more palatable, she got up, poured a glass of wine, and later poured another.

By ten o'clock a cloak of darkness shrouded the Canelli household. Upstairs in the master bedroom, Francesca had retired for the night. She punched her pillow for the tenth time. She checked her digital clock, only thirty minutes had passed since she first crawled into bed. She rolled over to Ben's side and cuddled his pillow. Sleep would come when it damn well pleased, or maybe not at all. Either way, she prayed to a higher being that tomorrow would bring her enough strength to muddle through another day. Her eyes were fluttering with drowsiness when the telephone rang. She fumbled with the receiver before muttering a laconic hello, only to hear a sudden click from the other end. Someone must've dialed her number by mistake and didn't have the courtesy to apologize. Oh well, back to her little piece of Ben.

End of Excerpt

**To find out where LETHAL PLAY is available,
visit Loretta Giacoletto's website:
www.lorettagiacoletto.com**

ABOUT THE AUTHOR

Loretta Giacoletto divides her time between the St. Louis Metropolitan area and Missouri's Lake of the Ozarks where she writes fiction, essays, and her blog, Loretta on Life while her husband Dominic cruises the waters for bass and crappie. An avid traveler, Loretta has written several Italian/American sagas inspired by her frequent visits to the Piedmont region of Italy, a chick lit mystery centered around Italy's Cinque Terre on the Mediterranean Sea and a soccer mystery that takes place in St. Louis. Her short fiction has appeared in numerous publications including *Literary Mama, which nominated her story "Tom" for Dzanc's 2010 Best of the Web.*

Connect with Loretta Online

www.lorettagiacoletto.com
Facebook: Loretta Giacoletto Author
Or e-mail: loretta@lorettagiacoletto.com

Made in the USA
Columbia, SC
17 November 2018